AWAIS KHAN
IN THE
COMPANY
OF
STRANGERS

hera

First published in the United Kingdom in 2022 by

Hera Books
Unit 9 (Canelo), 5th Floor
Cargo Works, 1–2 Hatfields
London, SE1 9PG
United Kingdom

Print ISBN 978 1 80436 011 8
Ebook ISBN 978 1 80436 903 6

Look for more great books at www.herabooks.com

Printed and bound in Great Britain by Clays Ltd, Elcograf S.p.A.

For Senator Gulzar Ahmed Khan (Bade Abu Jaan)

"Be who you are and say what you feel, because those who mind don't matter, and those who matter don't mind."

Bernard M. Baruch

Prologue

The early morning scent of damp earth and mown grass greeted him as the doors of the overcrowded bus were thrown open. A child, having lost control of his bowels, had caused the driver to make an unscheduled stop. The old bus groaned, its pistons emitting loud whistles as it ground against the curb, the people scrambling out in droves, some muttering, others hurling curses at the child who sat cowering in the soiled seat, his red knickers stained brown. His mother sat beside him, fanning her face with her *malmal dupatta*, a disapproving frown etched between unplucked eyebrows.

The bus conductor simply slid the dusty windows open in an attempt to lure a breeze, ignoring the mess on the seat.

While something like that would usually drive him crazy, it didn't affect Ismail today. He was grateful to step out sooner than planned; it gave him more time to revel in the glory he was bringing his family – his entire village.

Wrapping his shawl around him, he whistled a familiar tune from an Indian film, the one where the actress struck up all manner of provocative poses, causing the movie halls to erupt with hooting.

The tune did nothing for him, but appearing inconspicuous was paramount. Sliding his hand along the rusted bars lining the sidewalk, he strolled toward the great den of activity – the Chowk. In the absence of the thick layer of smog that usually pervaded the city, the Chowk looked almost beautiful in the embrace of sunny blue skies. The fruit vendors shouted out tempting prices from their carts as they scratched their armpits, cars attempted to make their way through the gathering mess. The traffic wardens were absent, the dysfunctional traffic signal watching over everything like a silent ghost. A tangy smell emanated from the public park beyond, where a group of gardeners were busy with antiquated lawn mowers, bits of grass flying in the air like dust. The blueness of the sky reflected off puddles of water on the pavement, the crisp March breeze stirred his hair. It was exactly the kind of day those foreigner *Goras* called 'beautiful'.

Perfect, he thought, smiling to himself.

Luck proved to be on his side all the way through. The Chowk was packed, and in the midst of the hundreds of people commuting to work or selling their wares, he was as good as invisible. Walking alongside a donkey cart loaded with cheap furniture, he peeped into the residential colony guarded by barricades. The quaintness of the area was a glaring antithesis to the loud, swarming mess of the Chowk. His nose drew him toward the aroma of manure where a pair of black buffaloes idled in an open field littered with garbage.

For a moment, he froze.

Disgusting, but the stench bore the unmistakable stamp of home, of mud walls and open drains, and it was with reluctance that he pulled himself away, shaking his head at the familiar sight of steaming dung, round cakes of which had been plastered on the walls lining the field.

Focusing on the task at hand, he edged closer to the enclosed colony, his eyes searching for the policeman responsible for the morning shift. The policeman in question seemed to be in significant distress, the way his head swivelled in every direction, and his fists clenched and unclenched. Ismail sent up a silent prayer of thanks as he caught him abandoning his post at the most opportune moment, presumably huddling off for a leak with one hand firmly clutched around his genitals. Who would have imagined that a full bladder would be a catalyst to such destruction?

Don't presume anything. Don't allow overconfidence to swamp you! The words rang clear in his head. *Everything is God's will.* Wasn't this what he had been learning for years now? *Let this be a lesson for the murderers, those traitors who have ravaged the country, uprooted families, destroyed legacies. Let this be a solid punch in the CIA's gut.*

He navigated his way past the concrete barricades like a silent shadow, his muscles taut in case he had to break into a run. Adrenaline coursed through his veins, his empty stomach groaned, but he maintained a clear head, and strolled past the checkpoint without inviting any suspicious eyes in his direction.

He arrived at the junction between the tranquil streets without incident, but even though he had memorised the route, for a moment everything looked the same to him: idyllic streets with concrete and brick houses rising in both directions. This part of the city held none of the rustic allure of his village. Its overreliance on concrete depressed him, made him think of prisons and subservience.

He took a deep breath, and closed his eyes, allowing his mind to guide him in the proper direction. As his breathing calmed, the map of the area lit up like a bulb in the darkness, and he recalled the directions that had been given: *First right, and the third left from there.*

Another ten minutes of suspense, but it seemed that he had at last arrived at the desired place. The dented black gate stood out like an anomaly, quite unlike its shiny counterparts that lined the entire street. It did, however, serve its purpose of shielding the short one-storey building from view. To the ordinary person, it would look like an abandoned place with the white paint peeling off the walls, revealing ugly graffiti.

A clever ruse.

He stepped closer, visualising how the end would be, and a plethora of confusing notions assaulted his mind. How would it feel? Would it hurt? Would he feel the head splicing off his body, and rolling across the floor? Would he even feel a hint of the savage triumph he had been promised?

The voice of their Leader rang in his head again like a drumbeat. 'It will be painless for you, *jihadi*, but the pain of those *kaafirs*, those non-believers, will be unimaginable. Remember, they are not humans; they do not feel. They do not love. You shall be rewarded for this noble deed, my boy, you will go to heaven. Kill those kaafirs!'

Kill those kaafirs. He recited it like a mantra in an attempt to ward off other, more disturbing thoughts. The cocoon of indifference he had created around himself threatened to burst, and reveal something ugly, something forbidden... something that smelled like fear. He felt an urgent need to tear away the shawl, and fling the jacket into the rubbish, leaving the button intact, and

4

the world unchanged. Was this what going to heaven was like, through so much pain, through such cruelty? Did he have to stoop as low as those Goras to exact revenge?

Coward!

These were the workings of *Shaitan*, the Satan. Their Leader had warned him about this. Shaitan will tempt him; try to deter him from the virtuous path to that of sin and cowardice.

He must fight this.

He trudged toward the ancient gate, the breeze drying beads of sweat that had erupted across his forehead. His hand slipped inside the shawl.

Kill those kaafirs.

An ice-cream van approached. The gate to a house on his left opened. A woman emerged, carrying a small child in her arms as the ice-cream van blared the familiar tune that heralded happiness, lighting up the faces of children everywhere.

He paused, waiting for the child to receive his ice cream. He thought the child deserved that much. Ismail watched him as he slurped it down, resting his head on the woman's shoulder. *Possibly her son*, he thought.

Not so long ago, he had done the same – rested his head on his mother's shoulder as his father came back from a hard day's work, smelling of sunshine and well-earned sweat. Not so long ago, he had been innocent too, oblivious to everything happening around him, running alongside the ditches with his siblings, relishing the potent possibility of falling into the black muck. So filthy, and yet so exciting.

Until they had bombed his village.

Killed his entire family while he brought back fried fish for dinner.

Everything lost in a second.

He remembered the polythene bag speckled with condensation falling to the floor with a wet smack, the crusted fish sliding out on the floor. Slick with congealing blood, the floor wore the red colour of shame, the shame of being branded terrorists in their own land. Steam issued from his family's still-warm bodies, dissolving in the cold air, the head of his infant brother lay in the ditch; his eyes wide open in fear or question, he couldn't tell.

That was it; he couldn't take it anymore.

He flicked open the plastic casing that protected the button, and closed his eyes as his thumb punched it hard.

Chapter One

Mona

In the bathroom, Mona closed her eyes, but the gruesome images kept playing in her head. The news channels had had a field day. 'The children… the suicide bomber didn't even spare the children!' the newscasters had all yelled in unison. The whole street had worn a scene of helplessness: dead bodies covered in white sheets being carried away on stretchers toward the ambulances; every house on the street standing bereft of its windowpanes, multicoloured curtains billowing out in the crisp March wind like a scene from a horror movie; shocked and dishevelled men pointing at a disintegrated mass of concrete and steel, which had just hours ago been the hidden office of some clandestine agency's headquarters.

Reports coming in from the hospitals were also far from encouraging. The terrorists might never stop, they said. Not until they've destroyed Pakistan.

Mona sighed as she opened her eyes. Pakistan was under attack, and all the people in this house were concerned about was what to wear tomorrow. Rolling a wad of tissue paper over her index finger, she leaned toward the mirror, and tried to wipe the mascara that seemed to have leaked from around her eyes, but looking closely, she noticed that the blotches were actually dark circles. A solitary tear escaped her left eye and slid down her cheek, staining her pink chiffon *kameez*.

She had been crying a lot these past few months; each bomb blast shook her in a physical way, deepening her fear that the world was falling apart just like her marriage.

Opening her Chanel handbag, she rummaged inside for her Touche Éclat to hide the tear tracks. She had left her friends in the drawing room with their favourite Belgian chocolate and Brazil-imported coffee. It was imperative that she should join them soon, lest they started questioning her whole existence.

Inside the bag, her hand brushed against her iPhone. She hesitated before fishing it out.

No messages or missed calls.

For the tenth time that day, she dialled the same number. The line rang and rang. Mona tapped her foot on the hard stone floor. Suicide bombs and an absent husband… How had it all come to this? Reciting an Ayat from the Holy Quran, she took a deep breath, and blew it across the bathroom in an attempt to ward off evil.

Bilal picked up at the last ring. 'What?' he asked irritably.

Gripping the marble slab supporting the wash basin, she took a deep breath. 'Where have you been?'

'Work.'

Mona took another deep breath. 'Why haven't you called me back?'

'What part of the word "work" didn't you get?'

'Typical, Bilal. Do you have any idea how terrified I've been?' Her voice rose as she pronounced each syllable with force, something she knew Bilal hated. 'Your secretary wouldn't tell me anything! Do you realise a

bomb just detonated in the city? And in our neighbour-
hood!'

Bilal tutted. 'Saira is sitting right in front of me, and it's
not her fault. I've been busy, Mona, and for God's sake,
don't make a fuss. You know how important this deal with
the investors from Dubai is for me. I hardly ever check my
phone these days.'

Mona lowered her voice knowing that it carried out of
mobile phones, and that Saira would be trying to listen in,
ever hungry for a stray crumb of gossip. That bitch. 'But
the bomb blast,' she said quietly. 'Surely you must have
heard—'

Bilal cut her off. 'Of course I heard, but I simply
presumed that you were safe at home since I called Amma,
and honestly the work here has been so hectic lately, I
just...' His voice tapered off as he realised his mistake.
'Listen I—'

Mona forgot about Saira. 'You called your *mother*, and
didn't even bother to check on me? What kind of a person
are you? Do you even care about me? The country blows
up, and that still doesn't make me any more worthy of
Bilal *Sahab's* attention? I mean, I left you ten calls. Ten!
And you didn't see fit to reply to any of them. Oh, but
you had time to call your dear *Amma*.'

Bilal was silent. The sound of his deep breathing and
the occasional rustle of papers in the background was the
only indication that he was still on the line. After what
seemed like ages, he replied, 'Don't tell me that all of a
sudden you care, Mona.'

The line went dead.

Blood rushed to her face, her fingers still gripping the
cold marble slab. Her hand had turned blue from the
pressure, the white knuckles protruding out like giant

hills while the rest of her body shook as if in extreme pain. Chucking the phone into her bag, she wiped her clammy hands on one of the imported towels she had had flown in from Dubai. *What a waste*, she thought now. She threw it in the rubbish. Before a rogue sob could escape her mouth, she unlocked the door, and went off to the drawing room.

–

'Oh yes, oh yes, yes, yes!' Kulsoom squealed, jumping up from the divan in excitement. Her generous bosom heaved as she danced about. Wrapping the expensive *shahtoosh* shawl around her shoulders, she did a little twirl around the drawing room. 'Look at this, Mona! Isn't it a rare beauty?'

Mona looked around in surprise. Moments ago, before she had left for the bathroom, the drawing room had been a picture of solemnness, with each of her three friends – Kulsoom, Shabeena and Alia – distraught at the injustice of sixteen people losing their lives, not to mention the dozens that were still fighting for theirs in hospitals. Kulsoom had even made a bold claim to visit the public wards of hospitals to commiserate with her fellow Lahoris.

But now, the maroon velvet curtains had been thrown back from all the windows in a bid to invite a steady stream of sunshine. A steaming pot of aromatic coffee complete with a porcelain china set had been laid out on the coffee table, and the disturbing announcements from the television had been muted. For a moment, Mona simply stood there, inhaling the scent. Whatever they said about coffee was absolutely true: there was something about it that soothed the mind.

Shugufta, one of her maidservants, scurried in bearing a tray laden with sandwiches and pastries from the exclusive bakery near Hussain Chowk. Mona knew that because, like always, the blundering woman had forgotten to remove the food from its paper boxes. With the lids thrown back and the food ensconced inside, it looked like something a middle-class family would serve. She rolled her eyes (what had happened to the crystal serving dishes?), but before she could chastise the maid, her eyes caught a pair of smiling Pathan salesmen leaning against the giant wooden fireplace, starched turbans standing upright on their heads and smart Peshawari *chappal* so polished that they shone. The younger of the two had his arms stretched wide, and balanced on top of them were the most colourful and expensive shahtoosh shawls she had ever seen. Shugufta laid out the food on the table. Her fearful eyes darted toward Mona, and then back at the packed food on the tray. She clapped a hand to her mouth, and hastily retreated to the kitchen, her plastic flipflops making a distinct and unpleasant sound.

Shabeena and Alia also stood gawking at the shawls, their eyes round with wonder. Alia had her hand pressed against her chest, though it was difficult to tell whether this was in appreciation of the shawls or a desperate bid to flaunt the huge rock on her finger. Mona winced at the light reflecting off the diamond. Her eyes swivelled toward the shawls once more. They really were handsome. Each shawl cost a whopping one million rupees, much more expensive than the average Chanel or Louis Vuitton stole. Even in her despondent state, Mona felt a prick of desire for them.

'Made from the finest fur of the chiru, *Bibi*,' the older Pathan whose hands were free announced. 'The best in the entire country. End of season sale.' He nodded at Mona, the new arrival. 'Specially brought to you from Kashmir.'

Mona's eye caught a light beige-coloured one with heavy embroidery of gold, red and green thread. It was gorgeous, but her earlier disappointment at Bilal's behaviour still stood stark in her mind, and ignoring the Pathan, she sank into the armchair without a word.

Gazing out in the vast gardens of her mansion, she sighed. People would laugh at her if she told them that despite everything, her home felt like a prison to her.

Holding her scarf in place over her head, Shabeena leaned forward. At forty-eight, Shabeena believed that she had seen everything there was to see, and done everything there was to do. Her main priority now was her dedication to Islam and its teachings. Or so she liked people to believe. Raising a cup of coffee to her lips, she arched a plucked eyebrow. 'Kulsoom thought it would be a good idea to break the dreadful monotony of listening to people getting killed. You were in the bathroom so she decided to take matters into her own hands, and asked for these gentlemen to present themselves here.' She gestured at the Pathans behind her.

The older Pathan spat a gob of chewed paan on the floor. He had been aiming for the dustbin in the corner, but instead the bits of betel leaf, stained red with spices and *supari* landed on the white marble. This time, another maid – Mona had forgotten her name – ran inside holding a wet rag.

Alia grimaced. 'Gentlemen, indeed!'

Shabeena shot her a dirty look before pursing her chapped lips, and busying herself with her coffee. Not wearing any lipstick was her way of making a religious statement.

Mona felt a nudge from Alia. 'Shabeena got herself the new limited-edition Estée Lauder fragrance,' she whispered, raising her eyebrows. 'Can you smell it? It smells like tuberoses.' Chuckling, she added, 'Looks like someone's dying to make an impression at the party...'

Shabeena seemed to have heard her. She tucked a stray lock of hair beneath the scarf, and fixed Alia with a solemn stare. 'I doubt that I'll go. The event seems a bit decadent for my taste.'

Alia scowled. 'Oh please, Shabeena, this statement doesn't suit you. This is what the ones not invited to the party are saying. You know better than that.'

'Oh Meera's party, you mean? Oh *haan*!' Mona cried, just remembering the thing they had been discussing for weeks. In the midst of the bomb blast and Shugufta's blunders, she had forgotten it.

Meera Siddiqui, her long-lost friend who had left Lahore right after they had graduated from college. Now twenty-odd years later, she had returned. Thrice divorced at the age of forty-one, and now the proud owner of a successful modelling agency, she had purchased a sprawling property in Cantt, and had decided to throw a huge housewarming bash. Also poised to be her inaugural fashion show in Lahore, it had the temperature soaring in the Lahori society circuit for days. People had even cut short their holidays abroad, just to be at the party.

'Oh yes, about the party,' Alia continued, biting into a pineapple-glazed pastry. 'She's invited all the politicians too! Imagine the nerve. She barely arrives, and everyone here is clamouring to meet her. And they blame us for giving Lahore a bad name. Fine, we like to party, but we're not as crazy as to host modelling shows. In our own homes! Who wants that kind of bad publicity? I mean, I caught Fahad trying on his Walima tuxedo the other day. For Meera's party! Paunch and all.' She threw her head back and laughed. Mona liked it when she did that; it made her look a decade younger. Crossing her legs, and settling her hands around them, Alia exclaimed, 'I bet you every scrawny ass will be there, and probably most of the fat ones too. Thank God Kulsoom wasn't invited or she'd have driven us crazy by now.'

Busy with the Pathans, Kulsoom was oblivious to the whole conversation.

Mona's stomach clenched. Twenty years. She couldn't believe it had been that long since they had last met. She thought of those moments when, depending on the season, they would share a hot cup of chai or a cone of watery vanilla ice cream in Liberty market. Young men would gawk at them as they tossed their dyed golden-brown hair from side to side, and sometimes, Meera would make deliberate eye contact with them to which they would respond with expressions of alarm and outrage.

'If they can stare so openly, then why can't we?' Meera used to say. On occasion, she would also show a guy the finger. Back then a girl showing you a finger was considered a *taxi*. 'That's the name for a woman of bad character,' Meera informed her, when Mona had expressed her confusion. There would always be a knowing gleam in her eyes, a sense of superiority regarding such matters. 'A taxi accepts anyone who is willing to pay for its services just like a woman from Heera Mandi is ready to sleep with anyone who throws her money. These women are adept at showing guys the finger as sometimes they don't cough up the money after they've had their fun.' She winked at her, and being young and carefree, they fell into fits of laughter.

Good times, Mona thought. She could hardly remember her youth anymore; perhaps, meeting Meera wouldn't be such a bad idea. Even with the curtains pushed back to expose the lovely March weather, she felt claustrophobia in the overheated drawing room. With the air conditioners undergoing maintenance, the room seemed to have heated up like a stove. She looked down and her eyes caught the light, barely discernible blemishes on the backs of her hands. And to think that she had never cooked or cleaned in her entire life.

The claustrophobia gave way to helplessness as she thought of her futile attempts at fighting aging. All those lotions, the ground-breaking crèmes that came with the promise of eternal youth, they were all useless. There was no escape from the sharp, twisted tangles of time as they continued to scratch and devour you.

Kulsoom was laughing away, trying shawl after shawl, while posing and blowing kisses in the air like some glorified model. The Pathan salesmen's smiles widened with each passing minute.

'I'll have that one, that one, and this one!' Kulsoom cried, pointing at three shawls, each being in the same shade of the colour brown. 'Are you sure they're pure shahtoosh?'

The older Pathan held a hand over his heart in mock horror.

'Why, Bibi! Upon my word, this is pure shahtoosh. Pass it through that diamond ring on your finger. I'll cut off my head if it gets stuck in it!'

The Pathan formed a circle with his thumb and forefinger and passed his forefinger from the other hand through it.

'Well, that's a fancy way of showing it,' Alia mumbled, and before Mona could stop to think, the two of them broke into gales of laughter. She blushed at Alia's childish implication to sex, but that was partly the reason why she loved her friends; they would burst out laughing at one thing or another, and suddenly every former grievance was forgiven and forgotten – not that she had any with them at the moment. Even tightly wound Shabeena let out an uptight giggle, her scarf falling off to reveal golden-streaked hair.

Kulsoom stood looking confused and embarrassed.

'Oh Kulsoom!' Alia exclaimed. 'You're just like that donkey in the zoo that never gets the joke.'

That elicited even more laughter from everyone, and poor flushing Kulsoom covered her face and ran out of the room with the Pathans close at her heels. 'I'm never going to forgive you girls for this!' she wailed from the doorway.

'Oh, she'll come around,' Shabeena said, wiping the black *kaajal* that had smudged around her wet eyes. 'Where would Kulsoom be without the drama in her life?'

The sound of Shugufta's rubber flipflops sounded in the hall once again, and Mona looked up to see her maid wearing the grim expression she reserved for special occasions. 'Bilal Sahab has arrived, Baji,' she announced. 'He's asked for you in the study.'

Mona sat stunned for a moment. So, he had finally arrived. He must have taken the lounge entrance into the house. The fact that he hadn't stepped in to greet the ladies meant that he was still seething from their earlier conversation.

'We'll show ourselves out, shall we?' Alia spoke up, rising from her seat.

Chapter Two

Ali

Ali took a deep breath as he regarded the huge crowd of people in front of him, all of them clamouring to get inside the Emergency section of the hospital. News reporters hovered over the crowd with cameras held over their heads, filming footage of the chaos. Mothers screamed to be taken to their kids, while others howled as stretchers bearing dead bodies were brought in by the ambulances. The air was so full of the stench of sweat and blood that a bitter metallic taste hung in his mouth. Even the mild March weather felt oppressive with so many people packed together in one place.

As soon as he stepped into the crowd, a mean push from somewhere slammed him into a news reporter. The entire camera set came crashing to the ground, breaking into a dozen pieces. Ali gaped open-mouthed as the reporter resorted to beating a frail, weeping woman, mistaking her for the perpetrator of the incident. The poor woman tried to shield herself from the blows, and before Ali could step in to help, he heard the sickening crunch of bone breaking bone. Seconds later, the woman passed out in the arms of a younger woman – presumably her daughter – while the reporter, realising the gravity of what he had done, silently fled from the scene. Ali tried to catch him by the collar but a wave of people carried him away, dumping him at the back of the crowd once more.

His legs began to shake, and a sense of disquiet spread through him. Even as a young man of twenty-seven, it was impossible for him to tackle this malevolent force of nature; he shuddered to imagine how his poor mother had managed it. Nausea clawed at his throat as he thought of the frantic message she had left him on the phone. 'Hussain gravely injured. Not an accident. Can't call. Going to G. Hospital.'

At first he couldn't imagine why anybody would want to hurt his thirteen-year-old brother, and for a moment, he immersed himself back into his routine of assessing bank accounts. It wasn't until a few seconds later that the message sank in, and then snatching up his mobile he had called his mother.

Her phone cut straight to voicemail.

Steeling his heart, Ali summoned the courage to look up the latest news on his office desktop. What he saw almost made him pass out.

Hussain had been in the bomb blast. That must be what his mother was talking about. He might be dead.

But his mother had said injured; he might still be alive. Immediately he had latched on to that thought, and abandoning everything he had rushed to the hospital.

Picturing his brother's face in his mind now, he pushed himself into the first gap he spotted with as much force as he could muster. The impact sent at least three people flying. After witnessing that, the other people just jumped out of his way like scalded cats, so that in less than ten seconds, he was right in front of the main aluminium double doors. Ali was breathing hard, but he had made it.

'It's my brother,' he shouted to the nearest officer in the awful din. 'Hussain-ud-Din. He's thirteen years old. Only a boy.' *Only a boy.* Tears threatened to spill as he explained his brother's physical appearance to the portly security guard. 'Is he? Is he…?' He couldn't bear to articulate what he was thinking.

The guard shook his head. 'Trauma cases have been taken directly to the OT. We have no other information,' he shouted. He nodded at his fellow security men. 'Let the boy through.'

Ali could only nod at him, his throat too thick for him to make out words. He squeezed through with some other woebegone relatives of bomb victims, and together, they stumbled into the emergency hall.

He was immediately assaulted by the smells of anti-septic and urine. He crossed the well-trodden marble floor toward the reception desk. Compared to the ruckus outside, the crowd was more subdued here, with many people whispering to each other so as not to disturb the dozen women who sat in front of the operating theatres, beating their chests and weeping. Their dupattas lay forgotten on the floor.

He scanned the room for his mother, but there was no sign of her. The reception desk teemed with people demanding the whereabouts of their loved ones as porters in white *shalwar kameez* tried to usher them to the empty benches and waiting rooms. Harried nurses jotted down details into huge leather-bound registers, while at the same time pointing out directions to people. In the wall behind the desk, Ali spotted a half-open door beyond which stood a male and female nurse. They were both smiling, oblivious to the bedlam outside. The man ran his hand down the woman's bottom, and squeezed it gently. Blushing, the woman smacked his hand away, but still allowed herself to be guided deeper into the room.

An open display of such raw intimacy turned his stomach. Did these people have no respect for what was going on around them? Were they so heartless?

But then, as he surveyed the gruesome scene, he realised that these incidents were a daily chore for them, a never-ending cycle of blood and screams. A respite from such a nightmare would be welcome anytime.

Pools of maroon blood had congealed on the floor leading to the operating theatre, but instead of cleaning it up, the porters simply skirted the wet areas, their blood-shot eyes vacant, and mops lying idle in buckets of brown water. Ali turned in a full circle, but there was still no sign of his mother.

A sense of panic began to claw at his chest. Each second without information on Hussain made his throat clench tighter. He had to repeat his brother's name twice before the nurse at the reception understood him, and even then she just waved her hand toward the operating theatres.

'All bomb blast cases are being dealt with in the OT,' she snapped. 'There is no mention of a Hassan-ud-Din here, but it is possible that he escaped our notice.' She was a middle-aged woman with a mass of oily black hair wrapped in a bun, and though her answer was rehearsed, Ali detected an edge of contempt in her tone. She gestured around the hall. 'As you can see, things have been kind of busy.'

Ali took a deep breath. Now was not the time to delve into the inefficiencies of hospitals. In a level voice, he asked, 'Where does that leave me? How will I even know my brother is out of the operating theatre when there is no record of him?'

The nurse slammed the register shut. 'What do you want from me, Sir? I just told you we don't have any record of your brother ever being admitted here.'

Ali blinked at her, cowed into silence; he could feel the cloud of rage building inside him, but before it could gain any traction, someone touched his shoulder. He whirled round, and briefly saw the tear-stained face of his mother before she crashed into him, sobbing on his shoulder. 'Oh Ali, where were you?' she cried. 'I've been all alone this entire time. The doctors wouldn't tell me anything at first, and I was just so scared—'

He looked back and saw the nurse raising an eyebrow at him, and in that moment, he wanted to bash her face into the marble desk. Instead, he reined in his anger, and steered his mother away to an isolated corner by the porter's cupboard.

'Is he alive?' For the first time tonight, his voice cracked.

His mother's cries which had assumed the sounds of an animal in pain, tapered down as she broke away from him. She nodded once before breaking down into renewed sobs.

His heart stopped for a second before beginning to beat faster. *Thank God*, he thought. *He's alive*. Putting his hands on his mother's shoulders, he peered at her. 'Tell me. What is it? If he's alive, why are you crying? Speak, please.'

'He is alive,' his mother gulped, 'but... Oh Ali, they cut off his leg!'

'Oh.' Ali stared at his mother, his arms falling to his sides, his back straightening of its own accord. His little brother had lost his leg. Always so quick on his feet, deft in his movements, football captain for his school team… he had lost the use of his leg. He would never be able to run down the road now to buy hot *naans* for lunch. That thought alone pained Ali more than anything. His brother had lost his independence.

However, with sorrow came a peculiar sense of relief. He was alive! It could have been worse.

'I booked a private room for him for after he comes out of the recovery room. God help us if he had ended up in the public ward. It's horrible over there. The smell of the place alone…' His mother's voice was calm now. She ran her fingers through her dishevelled hair before adjusting the dupatta back on her head. That was the one thing he admired most about her – the ability to stay pragmatic even in the most desperate circumstances. He was relieved that she had had the presence of mind to book a private room for Hussain.

'When can we see him?' he asked, wiping his cheeks with the back of his hand. 'Has he woken up yet?'

His mother bit her lip. Taking his hand, she led him to where half a dozen cheap plastic chairs had been thrown about. She sank into one of them. 'We won't be able to see him for a few more hours, but Ali, there is a more pressing concern.' She paused. 'Money. We don't have any. Your father, God bless his soul, had left me some, but I'm afraid that over the years we've all but consumed it. We will need money if we want to keep him in a private room.' She looked up at him. Ali was surprised at how old she looked. Premature wrinkles had ravaged her face, giving it a haggard look. The pink hue with which her skin used to shine was gone, replaced by a sheen of unhealthy yellow, and her beautiful oval face that had once captivated his father enough to marry her had lost its shape, the skin sagging around the edges of her mouth and all the way down her neck. Only her ocean-blue eyes shone with life.

His mother wrapped her arms around herself. A tear leaked out of her eye. 'I am not throwing him to the horrors of the ward, Ali. We need money.'

Ali ran their finances over his mind. His salary from the job at the bank combined with his father's pension amounted to only 50,000 rupees, all of which was spent on their monthly expenses. Over the years, they had burned through his father's savings, and now nothing remained in their bank account.

Perhaps, if they could have spent less in the past year, enrolled Hussain in a public school instead of a private one; if he had not bought those cheap second-hand suits, and set aside a little money for emergencies...

Ali shook his head. The truth was that ever since he had quit modelling, they had fallen into poverty. Every month, a maelstrom of expenses descended upon him, most of them so basic that sometimes, to his mother's chagrin, he ended up in fits of laughter. His inability to make enough money for the family had reached ludicrous heights.

He sank into a chair next to his mother, and covered his face with his hands, trying to block out his mother's description of the public wards. He had seen those wards: three patients to one bed, hundreds of visitors swarming all over the place, the stench of excrement and vomit everywhere. He pulled out his mobile phone. The screen lit up with a bright, cheerful close-up of Hussain.

He thought of calling his boss at the bank to ask for an advance, an overdraft – something! It would be of no use. His boss hated him, hated his guts for keeping his customers waiting, and yet still winning them over. 'How on earth does he get away with it?' he had once heard him say to another colleague.

He scrolled down the list of messages, pulling out and reading ones he hadn't bothered to open before. There was one from Majeed, an old friend that he had fallen out of touch with. He frowned. This was the third time in one week that Majeed had messaged him, but Ali hadn't paid any attention.

His thumb hovered over the *Open Message* button. He was surprised to discover that he felt no trepidation, just an odd sense of resignation as he looked at the familiar number. Wiping the sweat on his face with the back of his shirtsleeve, he opened the message.

Chapter Three

Mona

The security guards stamped their right feet on the ground, and raised their hands in a salute as Bilal and Mona's car passed through.

The black wrought-iron gates creaked.

'Oil them,' Bilal shouted at them without lowering the window pane. Mona waved at the head of security's five-year-old son. He looked like a little soldier with his upright body and perfect salute.

'Bastards,' Bilal said under his breath as they drove into the night.

Mona ignored him.

She loved Lahore at night. During the day, a battle of endurance raged through the city. From the people in luxury cars to those in donkey carts, there pulsed an incessant need to survive, to overtake fate and transform it into something desirable. Street vendors shouted out lunch specials, beggars paraded posh avenues, while busy executives sped down boulevards in their swanky cars, leaving the sweaty, grim-faced, middle-income people to board buses and minivans. Everyone jostled to get the most done in the least amount of time. In the punishing sun, clouds of dust, and smell of sweat and rot, every day was a bitter fight.

At night, however, everything fell into place. The smoke and dust of the day settled, the *tonga wallahs* and street vendors returned home, and the beggars abandoned their usual haunts to retreat into the shadows, their rags trailing behind them like the tails of lost dogs. Everything assumed a rhythmic cadence. As night fell, Lahore seemed to rise again from the ashes, pulsing with the same sensuality that had once lured the Mughals into making it their capital city. A city fit for kings. Lahore was like a capricious woman that vacillated between happiness and sorrow, order and disorder, putting up a brave face as bombs rained down on it. Most importantly though, no matter how hard the city fell to its knees, it always managed to stand up again. Life went on. Perhaps that was the reason she had never thought of moving away from Lahore. The city had conquered her heart.

Bilal was silent as they drove. His broad hands drummed against the steering wheel as he skirted the infamous potholes, pregnant with yesterday's rainwater. Turning a corner, they arrived at Gulberg's Main Boulevard, the mighty eight-lane artery that cut across the heart of one of the oldest and most affluent residential areas of Lahore. The city's finest shopping malls shone with fairy lights that hung all the way from the roofs to where people milled about the entrances. It seemed that everyone had already forgotten about the bomb blast. The newspapers and channels had been the first to jump ship, latching onto a new political scandal of corruption and power outages that had just erupted.

Mona held up the end of her shawl against her nose briefly as they crossed a large open drain near a college. Heaps of rotting rubbish lined the banks of the drain, the inky black water thick with refuse, rushing to its destination somewhere in the River Ravi.

Bilal frowned at the smell, a network of deep wrinkles erupting across his broad face. He ran a hand through his thick salt-and-pepper hair, but said nothing.

The silence was intolerable.

Mona coughed.

No response.

She coughed again, but all it did was deepen Bilal's frown.

When she was about to break the silence with words, Bilal finally asked, 'What?'

'I know what this silent treatment is for, but if you're expecting an apology for yesterday, that's not going to happen.'

Bilal sighed. 'I'm driving, Mona.'

'You're doing it again.'

'Doing what?'

'Pushing me away.' She crossed her arms. 'I don't understand what I've done to deserve this from you. I mean, if anything, it should be you apologising to me. Do you know how much it hurt realising how little you care for me?'

'You didn't come to bed last night, and neither did you come to the study, even when I called.'

'What?'

'I said that I – didn't – see – you – last – night – at – all.' He enunciated each word with his lips pulled back from his teeth, a habit that usually drove her crazy.

Today, however, she flushed. He was right. She had spent the entire night alone with a glass of whiskey in the guest room adjacent to their bedroom – several glasses of whiskey if she were to judge by the half-empty bottle and that massive hangover in the morning. She cleared her throat. 'I was trying to calm my nerves.'

Bilal snorted. 'With what? A drink?'

Mona's eyes widened. 'How did you…?'

'Oh please, Mona. Do you really think you can hide these petty little things from me? I know all about that secret drawer in the glass cabinet. Just because I don't say anything doesn't mean I don't know.'

More than the words, the tone stung. It was dismissive, like he was addressing a servant. He didn't care. Angry tears broke out in Mona's eyes. She struggled to speak. 'You take pride in spying on me? You know, as deranged as that sounds, it doesn't really surprise me. What pains me is how little you have understood me over the years.'

Staring at the expression on his face, she tilted her head sideways. 'You really don't care, do you?'

Bilal slapped a hand across his forehead. 'Oh please, don't tell me it's still about that bomb blast. How many times do I have to tell you, I was busy!'

Mona laughed – a watery, mirthless sound. 'Oh Bilal, that's nothing compared to the torture you inflict on me every day. You say that I drink. Fine, I do! But did you ever stop to think why? Did you ever wonder what could make me so unhappy as to take up drinking?'

It was Bilal's turn to laugh. The deep, husky sound of it resonated throughout the whole car. 'Pray tell me, what's ailing you now, my dear wife? Is it another one of those solitaire diamond rings?'

'Oh, get lost, Bilal. You're disgusting.'

He laughed again, swerving the car to the right, and down the road through which they exited Gulberg and entered Main Cantt. 'No, no seriously, tell me, darling. What's the matter?'

One look at his sneer, and she knew that he was only going to mock her further. She dug her nails in the soft leather of her black clutch. 'I'm meeting Meera after ages. Please don't ruin it for me. Not now.'

Bilal shrugged. 'Have it your way. Sulk all you want, but honestly, you know I'm getting a bit tired of this hurt wife act. How old are you? Do you know how childish it looks, making a fuss out of every little thing?'

'It's the little things that have grown into these walls between us today. I try, Bilal, honestly I do, but when you don't even call me for days on end, and stay away on your so-called business trips, what should I believe? Do you take me for an imbecile to believe that those trips are purely business?'

'You're welcome to accompany me, my love. If only you could spare a minute away from those horrible hags you invite over to our house every day.'

'Oh for God's sake!'

Bilal scoffed. 'You're forty-one years old, goddammit. Grow the hell up, woman! Are you even listening to what you're saying? You're paranoid.'

Mona turned away from him and faced the window. Her heart ached with humiliation. 'Yes, it's always my fault, isn't it?' she murmured.

'Whatever Mona! What a great way to ruin a perfectly good evening. Uff!' He hit the steering wheel hard with one hand. The car seemed to shake in terror.

Mona pursed her lips, gazing unseeing at the towering 100-year-old trees flashing by. She wondered why she even bothered to reason with him. Let alone the desire, he didn't even have the decency anymore to sit down and talk to her. Her life had become a series of intolerable lunches with his beloved mother, an endless expanse of long nights spent tossing and turning in bed. It had been years since they had even exchanged a friendly peck on the lips. Now, it was just the occasional night of hurried groping of rough hands in the dark that left the soft skin of her upper arms scratched and her breasts bruised. Tender emotions had given way to bitter struggles, and sexual fulfilment had become a mirage. A vast emptiness crept up on her when Bilal slid off, and no matter how hard she tried to stop them; tears always flowed. She was alone, bereft of companionship, like an empty shell. But this was her burden to bear; she thanked God that Farhan and Aimen were in Canada; thousands of miles away from witnessing their mother's descent into a solitary abyss.

The rest of the journey passed in silence; Mona ignored Bilal by wiping away the foggy window with a piece of tissue and peering out of it. Bilal passed the time by listening to the local news on the radio; it was running the news of the same bomb blast that had rocked Lahore yesterday. The severed, mutilated head of a young man, allegedly the suicide bomber, had been recovered, and the government had ordered an investigation into determining its identity. *Nothing new there*, Mona thought. This had become the norm. Bomb. Head. Investigation. Case closed.

They breezed through the Sherpao Bridge that curved into the Cantt area, and Mona leaned forward to look at the railway lines below, the shantytowns encroaching on either side.

Tonight, the heaps of rubbish and grimy houses stood plunged in darkness, and the slum almost looked picturesque. The power outages seemed particularly harsh in this part of town. Other than a couple of donkeys braying in the distance, the slum was quiet. Even the young children who could always be found playing along the railway lines were absent, either put to bed early for a change, or loitering in some other part of the city.

Mona thought of the project she had taken up with Meera as a college student. Their task had been to personally visit the slums of the city, and draw an accurate picture of life there. She could still remember the smell of burning logs and weak tea, the smoke interspersed with the stench of buffalo excrement that was shaped as pancakes and stuck on the walls to dry.

Contrary to popular belief, the people in the slums were quite affable; seeing two well-to-do girls researching their area, they had invited them to their houses with heads bowed and arms spread wide, offering them rich delicacies that they couldn't possibly have been able to afford. Even the poorest of them wouldn't let them leave without shoving a cold bottle of Pepsi in their hands, their eyes shining with happiness as they asked, 'Will we appear on TV?' Mona hadn't felt an ounce of fear. In the end, the college project hadn't been the success she had wanted it to be, but it had nevertheless gained her an insight into the world of the underprivileged – the truth about Pakistan that glared them in the face every day, and yet got dismissed with a casual shrug. Meera, however, had always shown a proclivity for comfort and money. Even during the project, Meera's mind used to be elsewhere. Her idea of an ideal life was a quick succession of elegant parties and sordid romances, peppered with trips to Paris.

Now that Mona thought about it, in most ways Meera *had* lived exactly as she had wanted to, jetting off to some exotic locale with whomever she wanted. Mona's own life, on the other hand, had been nothing but a series of disappointments. Her eyes stung. She blinked them furiously. She wouldn't allow Bilal the satisfaction of seeing her cry, and moreover, this evening had to be a success.

For Meera.

After years of acrimony over that ill-fated event, Meera had finally extended an olive branch. It felt peculiar that after all this time of hearing from the gossip mill about her escapades, she was going to meet her old friend in person. Her manager had especially called Mona.

She knew why Meera hadn't called her herself. Meera was afraid of rejection. More than two decades had passed since they had last met. Mona may not have forgiven Meera for what she had done then, but looking back now, she couldn't help but realise how young they had been, that there was no possible way Meera could have foreseen the danger into which she had lured them that night. Mona had never told anyone about that incident, least of all Bilal, but as they turned into a bright street toward Meera's glittering mansion, she knew that it was now time to stop reflecting on the past, and look toward the future. Fairy lights draped the gates, and beyond them, she glimpsed the staggering size of Meera's mansion, decked up like a bride on her wedding day.

For the first time in years, Mona felt her heart pound against her ribcage in excitement; a feeling she had forgotten existed. A small smile crept up at the edges of her mouth, slowly curving them upwards.

Chapter Four

Ali

'Fifty rupees,' the rickshaw driver demanded, as Ali climbed out of the sputtering vehicle onto solid ground. Whoever had said 'practice makes perfect' was a fool. He had been taking the rickshaw for years, but had yet to overcome the nausea. He staggered on the cracked pavement and took deep breaths. Sweat oozed out of every pore of his body. He looked back to where the three-wheeled monster stood spouting exhaust fumes, and covered his nose with his hand.

'Fifty rupees!' the rickshaw driver called out again, drumming his foot against the cheap aluminium floor of his vehicle, impatience etched on his face. '*Jaldi karo!*'

As soon as Ali had paid, the rickshaw gave a deafening bang, and hiccoughed down the road.

'Despicable things,' Ali muttered, as he turned to the towering iron gates. Beyond these, his modelling open call awaited. He sent up a silent prayer for success as he approached the security guards flanking the gates. After a chat with someone inside regarding his itinerary, a guard patted him down, checked his mobile phone, patted him down again for good measure before opening a smaller door embedded in the larger gate, unnoticeable on first sight.

Ali emerged on the other side, and was immediately hit by the full impact of the place. The mansion was huge. He was dazzled by the sheer enormity of the place. A faint smell of wet paint and lacquered furniture hung in the air, which Ali welcomed after spending that excruciating hour inhaling the smell of gasoline in the rickshaw.

The house was an attractive structure of brick and glass, encompassing a delightful blend of both Mughal and French architecture. Except for a few vans bearing the flamboyant logos of an event management company, the porch had been left empty for the guests. Watching the lithe drivers bound from one car to the next, Ali thought of Hussain back at the hospital nursing his stump of a leg. His brother had woken doped up with painkillers, but nothing could have shielded him from the shock of that stump glaring back at him. His mother had smothered him against her chest as he moaned, thick tears falling down his cheeks, the pitiful stump moving up and down as if it could brandish a new leg for itself by doing that.

'The phantom limb pain will begin soon,' the doctor had said. 'You need to be prepared to guide him through this time of confusion and anger. Losing a leg at such a tender age...' The doctor had shaken his head, stroking his enormous white moustache.

Ali aimed a kick at a stand of chrysanthemums. The yellowish-green buds flew high in the air, landing some-where in the distance. He wanted to swear at the top of his voice, but he bit down on his lip hard, tasting blood.

'Oye!'

Ali flinched at the sound. Damn, he'd been spotted.

'Yo Ali! Over here, man!'

The sound was coming from up ahead. Relief washed over him as he looked up to see Majeed jogging toward him. He pulled Ali into a giant hug. 'Long time, man… long time.' His jet-black hair was gelled and combed back, the normally fierce eyes shining with warmth.

'Yes it has been,' Ali muttered, touched by the gesture. He had always considered Majeed a dependable acquaintance, not really a friend, but considering everything now, it seemed to him that Majeed was perhaps one of his only true friends. Feeling bad about ignoring his calls and messages, Ali thumped him on the back. 'How've you been?'

'Ah, the usual, *yaar*,' Majeed said as they broke apart. He ran his fingers through his hair, unsettling the gel. 'I've been doing modelling assignments all this time, mostly in Lahore, sometimes in Karachi. But the work's been bad with the recession and these bloody bomb blasts. And we artists have always been under fire not just from the terrorist elements in the country but also from these damn conservatives.' He shrugged. 'It's sad, but it's life.' He motioned to the house behind him. 'This here, though, is a gold mine, my friend. But, how's your brother? When you told me about him on the phone, I couldn't believe my ears. Your baby brother, man! I remember him so well. Watching the news is one thing, but having this stuff happen to someone you know… Damn.'

Ali's jaw clenched, and for a moment he was unable to speak. He swallowed the lump that had sprung up in his throat. 'Still in the hospital. He's in a lot of pain.'

Majeed patted him on the shoulder. 'Aw, man! That sucks! It really does. Such a nice boy. Give him my best, won't you? Tell you what, I'll come visit him tomorrow, how's that sound?' He tapped his chin. 'Perhaps, I'll even get him a little something.'

Ali smiled. 'He'd like that.'

'These bomb blasts have really screwed us over. God damn these terrorists.'

Ali raised a finger to his lips, and pointed at the guards flanking the main entrance.

'Ah, screw them! I bet they yell shit like that all the time. What will they do? Kick me out? Well, we are screwed anyway. Screw them too!'

They burst into laughter.

'Screw you,' Majeed said to them, louder this time, and Ali laughed harder.

When they had calmed down, Majeed turned and led the way toward the house. Ali walked faster, and fell in step with him.

'Work's really that bad?'

Majeed's hands balled up into fists. 'Just don't ask! Nobody wants to throw a bash anymore, and the designers are all chickening out from showcasing their collections. Female models are one thing, but there is such a dearth of good work for male models. It's as if we don't even exist. Good thing you left when you did.'

Ali looked at his upturned hands. 'I didn't leave because of that.' The memory came up like vomit, but he pushed it down.

'What was that?'

Ali glanced up, and smiled. 'Nothing.' He gestured around. 'So is there any place in this palace where a pair of friends can have a cup of tea? And what about that open call you told me about?'

Majeed smirked. 'Talk about a cuppa Starbucks.' Laughing at the bemused look on Ali's face, he continued, 'The event manager told me that the chick hosting this event got Starbucks flown in from Dubai.' He lowered his voice. 'It turns out that they sorely underestimated the number of models they needed. This chick's been running the open call all day. Auditions have trickled down to a few people now, and she still needs more models for the show. So, let's see if you can impress her with that great body of yours. Come on, two friends reuniting, good weather, and the promise of a cup of Starbucks! What could be better?' With a wink, Majeed guided Ali to a side door that led into the kitchens.

Chapter Five

Mona

There was a long queue of vehicles in front of the gates, most of which were being checked. The security guards took one look at their approaching Mercedes Benz, and without a word, ushered them inside.

The entire place was packed just like the road outside: rows and rows of cars parked in a haphazard fashion, one car taking up the space of two. The chauffeurs and valets were nowhere to be seen.

After taking two turns around the overflowing parking area, Bilal finally managed to stick the Mercedes into a tight space between a Bentley and an Audi. As soon as he shifted the gear to park, Mona unlocked her door, pushed it open, and swung her feet to the ground. The wet grass flattened under her heels.

Bilal called after her. 'Hey, wait up, will you? At least let me turn off the thing.'

Without looking back, Mona slammed the door. Her heart rose. Though there would be hell to pay later, she revelled in this rare act of defiance. The way he had been treating her, he deserved it.

On her way to the main doors, she paused to brush the heels of her shoes against the rugged stone floor. Grass caked with mud fell on the floor. Her eye caught a group of policemen crowded around a police van. They seemed to be guarding a lone Rolls Royce parked nearby. The orange glow of their cigarettes was barely discernible in the blazing light. They watched her with an unreserved stare, their eyes shining like a hungry dog's. One of them, a grotesque-looking man with a curly moustache and a sagging belly that strained the buttons of his police shirt, licked his lips at her. Goosebumps sprung across her skin; she threw the shawl over her bare arms, and quickened her pace. She regretted leaving Bilal behind. It wasn't the first time she had encountered this kind of behaviour; Lahori policemen were notorious for it. If nothing else, Bilal's giant form always acted as a buffer against these lecherous wretches.

At the doorway leading into the house proper, she looked back, and caught Bilal giving directions to a white-uniformed valet. He met her gaze with a glare. Mona sighed, and entered the house, her mood a mixture of trepidation, resentment and vague regret.

It was dark inside. She blinked several times, as her eyes tried to adjust to the soft lighting. Gradually, the large, imposing foyer swam into view. Twin staircases with elegant wooden banisters towered to the first-floor landing, the white marble floor veined with dull grey lines.

Nothing in the world is perfect.

The epiphany hit her with force. If nothing in the world was perfect, why did Bilal expect her to be so? It had been more than two decades, and she had come no closer to guessing the true nature of the person she shared her bed with. Maybe she never would.

Before Bilal could sneak up on her, Mona dashed to the set of double doors leading into – judging by the booming sounds of laughter and footfalls – the drawing room. A tall guard dressed in black shalwar kameez and a matching waistcoat nodded at her, as he pulled open the giant oak door.

For a moment, Mona just stared. There were even more people here than she had imagined. *A thousand?* The crowd was like an undulating wave of black suits and multi-coloured dresses.

Together, they teemed around an enormous stage and runway. She realised why Meera had chosen her home for this event – the size of the drawing room was as colossal as any banqueting hall in the city.

The guard cleared his throat, and with a jolt Mona realised that she was still standing at the entrance. She scanned the hall for a few more seconds, but when she didn't spot any acquaintances, she decided to head for the area where the concentration of people was the thickest. Doubtless, she would find Meera there.

Her mobile phone vibrated.

It was a message from Alia.

> Bloody Fahad fell down the stairs.
> Sprained ankle. Have to cancel :(Alia.

Great. Now what was she supposed to do? She dug her heels into the plush red runner, and contemplated her options. With Alia cancelling at the last minute and Shabeena being a no show, she feared that she'd end up sitting with Bilal. She wasn't sure she could suffer through the entire event with him by her side. They would bite each other's heads off. Her gaze meandered toward the bar in the corner, and her mouth watered. What wouldn't she give for a drink right now...

Rows with Bilal always made her feel like she needed to rally her strength, and lately these fights had begun to tire her to the extent that she felt a crushing burden on her shoulders. She was desperate for a change, gasping for a little magic in her life.

'The lady of the hour,' a cold voice whispered in her ear. 'Late as usual.'

Mona's heart sank as she placed the voice. It was Shahida Elahi, the insufferable wife of the steel industry billionaire, and a regular face at society parties. Incidentally, and much to the chagrin of Mona, Bilal also purchased the steel for his construction company from Elahi Steel. Mona tried to avoid Shahida at ladies' committee parties, but she hadn't expected to bump into her here. *But of course*, she thought. *The entire city is here.*

Although she was well into her sixties, Shahida's cunning hadn't wavered with age. Mona remained cordial with her at Bilal's insistence, but something about her calculating eyes unsettled her.

With a sigh, she turned to greet her, kissing each dry, wrinkled cheek in turn. 'Shahida,' she said.

Tonight, Shahida was shrouded in a purple *banarsi* sari, the bones in her thin body standing out beneath the richly tapered fabric. She looked like a starved vulture. She fixed Mona with her beady stare, and surveyed her from head to toe. Her thin lips curled into a smile, the tip of her bright pink tongue held between razor sharp teeth as she watched her. Having satisfied herself, she jerked her head in the direction of the ramp. 'That crazy girl, Meera, has been looking all over for you. Mona this, Mona that. You two were friends in the past, I presume? Because otherwise, I wouldn't expect Meera to give you the time of the day. But then, who knows? You women of today are

41

so frantic. Tsk tsk. The ladies of our generation, now they had substance! They had poise. You girls are just a bunch of bleating sheep without a shepherd – utterly lost.'

'It's great to see you too, Shahida,' Mona replied.

Shahida wrinkled her nose, made a 'Hmph' sound of acknowledgement somewhere in her throat before delving into the problems of today's women with renewed vigour. *You girls this, you girls that…*

After what seemed like an eternity of disparaging, she paused to point at someone over Mona's shoulder. 'And here she comes now. Thank God. Someone to take you off my hands.'

It took Mona a few seconds to sift through the barrage of insults to realise what Shahida had said. Her heart began to pound in her throat. Plastering a big smile on her face, she spun around. Her eyes recognised Meera at once.

It was her!

Meera's languid gaze found hers. She cocked her head to one side, and the full force of those amber eyes hit Mona. She even grinned in the same mischievous way she used to back in college. The other women around her faded into the background like a bunch of pallid vegetables. Memories of decades past rushed through her like a flood, destroying her carefully constructed dams of indifference, obliterating any semblance of the present. It was *Meera*. After all these years, they had finally come face to face again. Two friends torn apart and put together again. She thought back to the strolls through Liberty market, the late nights of Amitabh Bachchan movies. She remembered the intense arguments over the good-looking guys in college, followed by hushed confessions of what they'd like to do to them. Even now, the memory of those lurid tales caused a blush to creep up her neck.

42

Each recollection hit her in a physical way. She almost staggered from the impact of the final memory – their quarrel. It had always cast a grim shadow on the happy ones, but today, she was surprised to find that she didn't care. Looking at Meera now, it ceased to hold its dominance over Mona, and she realised that she had forgiven her long ago.

So much time had passed, and yet it seemed as if they had met just yesterday. Meera still retained overwhelmingly youthful looks, and her smile today was still like that of the lively girl of nineteen Mona had known. The women surrounding Meera in a semi-circle looked haggard, their tired and wrinkled faces lending a more pronounced resplendence to Meera.

She wore a sequined midnight blue wrap dress, one tanned leg exposed by a slit that reached her thigh. Raising her eyebrows at Mona, she smiled again, revealing rows of brilliant white teeth. She extended her hands toward Mona, and Mona saw that her eyes were shining.

'After all these years... Mona.' Even her voice held the same vitality she remembered so well. 'Oh, I've missed you.'

Mona was struck dumb; she didn't know what to say. Blood rushed through her ears, making her dizzy, and she was afraid she might cry. It had been so long since they had done this, since she had seen her. Still, she only returned the pressure of Meera's hands and smiled; afraid to say anything that may sound too sentimental. She wasn't sure how Meera would react.

'Meera,' was all she said.

'Ladies,' Meera said to the ladies around them. 'You know Mona, right? She's married to Bilal Ahmed. Ahmed Constructions? The biggest builders in Lahore.'

A few women nodded in approval. Meera smiled as she let go of Mona's hands. It was somewhat gratifying to discover the extent of Meera's knowledge about her, although she didn't like how she was known by who her husband was. She never had. Meera must have kept track of her over the years, the same way Mona had been keeping track of her, with subtle enquiries into the life of her friend, enough to give her an idea of her whereabouts, but not enough to instil suspicion in anyone's mind. Except for Bilal and her friends, nobody knew she had ever known Meera – until now.

Meera was beaming at the women. 'Did you know we used to be best friends, Mona and me?' She turned to Mona. 'Gosh, how many years has it been since we met, Mona? Eighteen?'

'More than twenty,' Mona replied.

'Gosh,' Meera repeated.

Shahida took the opportunity to butt in. 'Excuse me, Meera, but we've been waiting so long for your friend here that I'm afraid I've lost my appetite for the show. Letting the guests wait for one person… that is not done.'

Meera gazed at her unfazed. 'And you are?'

Shahida's eyes flashed. 'You don't know me? You invited me! I'm Shahida Elahi. The wife of Hussain Elahi… I even introduced myself to you when I arrived, don't you remember?'

Meera feigned surprise. 'Ah yes, Shahida *Ji*. I'm sorry. With the whole show and the party, I've been having a bit of trouble remembering new people.'

'Pah, I can hardly be called *new*. I am a solid pillar of Lahori society.'

'Regardless,' Meera continued. 'My apologies for having kept you waiting, and I'd totally understand if you would want to leave at this moment. I really hope you don't as the show is going to be phenomenal.'

Shahida was stunned. 'Well, I – uh – of course, if you say so, but I think not...'

Meera smiled her most gracious smile. 'Perfect. I didn't think you'd like to leave just yet. And look,' – she lifted a finger to point at the ramp behind Shahida – 'the event organisers are just dimming the lights. It's almost time for the show to begin. So, why don't you take these fine ladies with you, and go find your seats while we girls here catch up?'

Shahida was livid. She sniffed the air, and surveyed the sycophants Meera had brought along before proceeding to leave. 'Come ladies!'

The baffled ladies scampered after Shahida like a pack of reprimanded dogs with their tails between their legs.

Mona felt an odd weight lift from her heart. Realising that she had been breathing tightly all through the conversation, she exhaled deeply It was liberating.

Beside her, Meera made a face. 'What an old bore. Always churning out that Elahi Steel crap. Bitch.'

'You knew her, then?'

Meera's teeth glinted in the dim lighting as she laughed. 'Of course, I did. But I wasn't about to give her that satisfaction. I bet that Elahi wishes he could throw the old bat in one of the steaming furnaces of his mills and finally be done with her.'

'She won't let this insult slide, you know. She'll harp about it 'til the end of her days.'

Meera waved a hand. 'Let her. Like I care. Did you know her husband is dating an eighteen-year-old? Bloody eighteen! And there's debate on whether it's a girl or a boy. Apparently, our Elahi is diverse in his tastes. No surprise though considering how vile this wretch is. I guess Elahi wants his girls or boys,' she added with a wink, 'as young and innocent as possible to balance the time spent with the bat.' Lost in thought for a moment, she tapped her forefinger on her chin. 'Sort of thrills you though, doesn't it? The idea of dating someone so young... You think it's all worth it in the end?'

Meera raised her eyebrows at her, and for the first time that evening, Mona laughed – out loud. 'I can only expect *you* to say something so preposterous.'

Meera threw her head back, and laughed. The large diamond choker on her necklace glittered as the light flickered off it. 'I think that only I ever had the guts to talk to you like this. Our other friends back in college were so scared of you.'

Mona nodded. 'Well, we were best friends.'

'We are, Mona. In spite of everything, I hope we still are.' In the dim light, Meera looked even younger, her face as mesmerising as ever. Mona touched her own face, and with her thumb and index finger, traced the deep laugh lines. She tried not to feel discomfited.

'So Mona! How's life? How are the kids? Kids! You have children now! Oh my God, I still can't believe how much time has passed.'

'They're not children anymore,' Mona replied. 'They're both in college.'

Meera's eyes went as round as dinner plates. 'College! Weren't we in college the last time I checked? What the hell! You have to tell me all about them right now!'

'What would you like to know?'

'Everything!'

'Oh, I wouldn't know where to start.'

'Then start from the beginning.'

Blissful and unaware of the crowds of people milling around them, they caught up on the years gone by. It was surprising how easy it was to discuss the mundane routine of life as long as nothing sensitive came up. It was like eating a bowl of cereal – pleasant and far from being any trouble.

Most of the people had amassed around the ramp, and were waiting to be seated by the event managers. Mona saw Meera's gaze flicker toward the ramp, but she didn't interrupt as Mona described her daily routine which comprised of nothing more than brief phone calls with her children in Canada, meals with Bilal and his family, kitty parties, and the occasional fundraiser.

'And that's about it,' Mona said. She had left out a glaring part of the bitterness with her husband from the monologue. She shrugged. 'I'm your next-door house-wife, I'm afraid… nothing really interesting happens in my life. Call me an open book.'

'You're certainly not like the next-door housewives, believe me.' Meera looked thoughtful as she stood with her arms folded across her chest. 'You know, I actually like your life,' she said. 'So serene and tranquil… almost like a dream.'

'You never had… kids?' Mona hated the hesitation in her voice; somehow it brought the question into starker light.

Meera's smile eroded for a brief moment before she hitched it back up. 'Oh you know, with all the husbands I've been juggling, I never got the chance. Besides, I didn't want one man's child to be raised by another. You know me! Can I really stay with one man for so long?'

'You could still try.' The words were out of her mouth before she could stop them. She clamped her hand over

47

her mouth, blocking any further traitorous words that might escape her.

Meera was amused. She didn't seem to mind. 'You clearly haven't met my latest boyfriend yet. His children are married. The last thing he would want is to raise another one, especially with the woman of a questionable character. And besides, I'm not sure it's even possible to have babies at this age.' Waving off Mona's protests, she added, 'Don't worry. My body is still functioning fine. It's just the idea of having babies after forty.'

The lights mounted over the iron stands brightened, lighting up Meera's face. *So young!* Mona found herself thinking again. She could have easily have been mistaken for a thirty-year-old with an entire decade of fertility brimming ahead of her.

Before she could articulate the thought, Meera held up her hand. 'I know you'd like to know more about my life, but that will have to wait. I'm sorry, but right now we have to run! I'm delivering the opening speech, and introducing the show's concept to everyone. The designers paid me shitloads of money for this very purpose. I do hope I make an impact.' She paused for a while, her eyes clouding over, and in that moment, Mona thought she caught a hint of uncertainty flicker in those large eyes as they gazed at the ramp. But the spell ended, and all of a sudden, Meera was bright and cheerful as before. 'Come on now. I saved us some front-row seats. We'll catch up later, I promise.'

Mona had a sudden thought. 'Is Bilal seated next to me?' She bit her tongue at the apprehensive tone, but too late, the words were out of her mouth.

Meera's eyebrows shot up for just a moment before she assumed a neutral expression. 'No darling, I'm going be seated next to you. I've had cards placed on the chairs, you'll see.' She interlinked her fingers with Mona's, and together they walked toward the middle of the hall where the ramp was set. Meera's warm and dry hand held her cold and clammy one, and it seemed to Mona that this alone would be enough for Meera to judge how nervous she was this evening.

As if reading her thoughts, Meera pointed to the group of seats on the opposite side of the stage. 'Your husband will be seated there, in the men's section. Just don't get me started on the ruckus these Lahori women make on being seated next to men. God! Do they even look at themselves in the mirror? What man in his right mind would even think of doing something immodest to them? Not to mention that first, he'd have to sift through the folds of fat to find something that doesn't resemble blubber. Anyhow, I have Ambreen, that Minister's wife sitting next to you as well. I thought you could use some social interaction.'

Mona cursed herself inwardly. She was certain Meera had caught the gist that all wasn't right in her life. She had allowed herself to let her guard down – something she still hadn't done with her other friends. There had always existed a peculiar chemistry between Meera and her, and even if they wanted to, they had never been able to keep anything secret from each other. Perhaps this brutal honesty with one another was the biggest reason they had fallen out.

She shook her head.

It was pointless putting up the charade with Meera. Her situation with Bilal was the ugly truth, and if she were going to allow Meera back into her life, she would have to open up. There was no other way with her.

'I know you're thinking it, but no, I did not get a face lift, or any Botox,' Meera whispered as they approached the podium. Winking at her, she guided her to the front row where there was a white card bearing the name 'Mona Bilal' lying face up on the velvet upholstered chair. 'There were several opportunities, but I'm a fan of turning old gracefully.'

Mona burst out. 'But we're the same age! How do you manage to look so young?'

Meera removed a stray hair from her face. 'Oh, Mona! I learned long ago that it is much healthier to inflict stress on others than oneself. I guess it must have worked…'

Chapter Six

Ali

Backstage was in complete disarray. The female models had hogged all the mirrors, and their screeching jarred his ears. Ali felt the beginnings of a migraine as his vision grew foggy, and a dull ache settled in his forehead. The show hadn't even started yet. His entire body seemed to repel this profession with as much energy as it possessed, and yet, here he was, dressed in a garish two-piece red shalwar kameez with a parrot-green waistcoat. A slit in the kameez cut all the way from his chest to his navel, rendering the whole concept of having a shirt on redundant. He could have just pranced on the ramp naked from the waist up, and probably looked half-decent.

Cool air blasted through the makeshift air conditioners, but it was still sweltering in the room. The smell of sweat mixed with perfume and exotic lotions hung heavy in the air.

The models wore uniform looks of heavy make-up with smoky eyes, and ironed hair. Some Ali recognised from torrid one-night stands and drunk after-parties, but most were unknown to him. He detected the transition the Pakistani fashion industry had made toward plus-sized models. The credit went to Meera's modelling agency for embracing them, and Ali was surprised to see that these models weren't as frantic as some of the pros he saw running around, screaming at assistants. These newer models had an air of restraint, a voluptuous femininity that made them desirable. Meera had trained them well. They were the perfect treat for the repulsive old men out there.

He had peeked out of the makeshift door and recoiled at the sheer number of people in the hall. Soon they would be sweating oil and alcohol and the stench would be excruciating. Some would begin groping their way around each other, a few intrepid ones even making their way toward the models. Both male and female models were equally at risk.

The raw silk shirt lacked any soft lining inside. Large pink patches now covered his chest and stomach area where he had scratched away at his skin. What wouldn't he give just to tear everything off, and run outside in the fresh air? But he held his ground. He had to do this for Hussain.

Standing there in the make-up room, his father's words came back to him, from the day Hussain was born. He had placed baby Hussain's tiny hand in Ali's brawny one, and looked him straight in the eye, his black moustache sitting proud on top of his upper lip.

'Do you know who this is?' he asked in a grave voice.

Ali had squirmed. 'A baby?'

'No, this is your brother, your only sibling in this world who your mother has prayed day and night for. You are thirteen years old now, Ali, and it is time that you started taking responsibility.'

Ali remembered feeling no sense of responsibility as his eyes pleaded with his mother, who lay resting on a wooden *charpai*. She raised a finger to her lips, her eyes bulging. A firm, unequivocal NO. His father wasn't of the generic wife-beating type that was so common in their society, but he did command a certain respect, an authority that compelled Ali to lower his eyes whenever he spoke to him.

Ali had wanted so much to go out and terrorise the hens again, deriving the perverse pleasure children his age enjoyed in inflicting injury on defenceless animals. Instead, he stood still, and nodded as his proud father listed the various things he would need to learn to do for Hussain.

'I might not always be around, Ali – no one ever is. You should study hard, *beta*, very hard. Life waits for no one, and before you know it, it slips away from your fingers like sand. Never take the good times in your life for granted. Now kiss your brother's forehead, and promise me you'll do your best.'

With one eye still on the courtyard, Ali had bent down, and grazed his lips against the smooth forehead of his baby brother, inhaling the milky scent babies have, an odd knot forming in his stomach.

He still recalled the way Hussain had opened one bleary eye, and smiled at him, almost as if intending to roll his eyes at their father. God, he loved that smile. Each time he felt depressed or uncertain in life, that lopsided grin rejuvenated him, the two adorable dimples that broke out across his cheeks infusing him with renewed determination.

Hussain never smiled now. When he awoke, he would just wince and look at his stump in amazement until the inevitable groan escaped his throat. He would sob, yell and plead, but never smile. It struck Ali now how much had changed in just one day, how each of their lives would never be the same again. Maybe the smile would come back, but it would always be overshadowed by the pain of having an amputated leg.

A made-up model pushed past him, catching him off guard. He stumbled in the doorway. As he recovered his balance, he felt his mind clearing. His goal was set before him; he would do whatever it took for Hussain, no matter what that entailed.

The model didn't turn around to apologise; she didn't even dignify him with a backward glance or an apologetic flick of the eyes. And why would she? He was just a third-class male model today with nothing and no one to prop him up – a complete nonentity.

'Men are up later,' an event organiser shouted. She gestured to the group of young women, most of them in their mid to late twenties who were smoking and chatting next to the entrance to the main hall. 'You girls, get ready. You start walking as soon as Meera Madam is done with her speech.'

The girls looked like a collection of exotic butterflies with the lawn prints they wore, ready to spread their flower-patterned wings and take off into the sky. Only, they looked bored, making a mess of the cigarette stubs on the floor, their giant heels crunching the lipstick-stained filters on the marble as they rolled their eyes, and fussed with their hair.

'This isn't the first time we're modelling, you know,' an older model called after the event organiser. 'Bloody fool. It's been five hours and no sign of the show starting.'

Another, a younger, fleshier one, spoke up. 'You have to admit though, Iqra… this woman knows her business. Look at the sheer turnout.'

'Hmph,' murmured Iqra, brushing a stray strand of hair from her face. 'I've seen trailer trash throw better events in America. This doesn't come close to what I used to do there. I'm completely wasted in Pakistan.'

'But you have your family with you. It's all worth it if one's close to their family.'

'Hmph.'

Ali folded his arms across his chest and leaned against the doorway again. From the model's words, he knew nothing had changed. This profession was still filled with arrogant, thankless people who would rather be doing a thousand other things instead, but still stood here, readying themselves for another session of being gawked at like animals in a zoo, to be bought and sold like whores on the street. Everyone in this industry had a price. As he witnessed the first round of models leave for the ramp, his heart fell a little for the inexperienced girls who seemed to hover in the air with excitement. They were in for a surprise. They didn't know yet that they had traded in their souls for this profession.

The room got messier as modelled clothes were flung from bodies and fresh ones put on, the designers shouting at the hair and make-up teams to hurry, the sweaty assistants running around the room in a frenzy of fixing up hair, and touching up make-up.

Multiple designers had contracted the same models so that the models didn't have a minute of free time as they were thrust into dress after dress. Ali had only been accepted at the vague recommendation of Meera; the designer was some guy named Khushbaksh, and this was his first show. Ali was grateful for the opportunity. He appreciated how big an event this was – the euphoric faces of returning models told him as much. His meeting with Meera hadn't been much; she had taken one look at him during the open call, asked him to walk around the room, and made him sign the contract. Just like that. 'My assistant will reach you regarding the payment details later,' she had said, with a flick of her pen indicating that he should now leave.

An hour later, the show was well on its way, and the process of models disappearing and reappearing had been repeated several times over when at last, Khushbaksh breezed into the backstage, and clapped his hands.

'Okay guys, this is it. This is the big walk we've all been waiting for.' Here was further proof of his inexperience. Except for Khushbaksh, no one had been 'waiting' for this walk. Some of the female models wore drawn faces as they puffed hard on their cigarettes, their eyes bloodshot, the make-up doing an awful job of covering their dark circles. They twitched in the summery dresses. The male models flexed their muscles, and leaned against chairs or large wardrobes. Their earlier glee at walking for such a large crowd had long since evaporated. Khushbaksh seemed not to notice the restlessness, and continued with his pep talk. 'Remember, you need to captivate the audience too, not just the cameras. Do a little jiggle, add a little skip to your step. Try to remain interesting.'

Ali looked down at his almost bare chest and wondered what sort of jiggle he was supposed to do. The designer had an effeminate air about him as he gestured with his soft manicured hands, the yellow-streaked hair raised about four inches above his forehead, a couple of locks falling out of the thick bunch, giving the impression that he hadn't had any time to get his hair done.

Despite his invigorating pep talk, he seemed tense. He 'tsked' a lot. Placing Ali first among the male models, he later changed his mind, sending him to the third place. He did that a few more times before shifting Ali back in first place. His eyes shone as he regarded Ali, and he whispered, 'I've noticed, you have this raw energy that the ladies outside will find so enticing. I would be a fool not to have you walk first on the ramp, and then perhaps again in a different set of clothes.' He patted his shoulders, and ran his hands down Ali's back, smoothing the fabric. 'I haven't seen you around. What's your name?'

Ali told him, and looked away. He didn't like the way the designer touched him.

Surprisingly, Khushbaksh chuckled. 'A gruff attitude! Yes, you are definitely going first.'

And just like that, their leg of the show began.

The slimmer, more experienced female models went first, holding themselves erect on their gigantic heels, their narrow necks looking peculiar with the knotted vertebrae sticking out from their backs. Although tired, they were still, above all, confident, and it was this perseverance that shone through in the end.

Seeing that, a gnawing sensation clawed at Ali's stomach. Damn Khushbaksh. He wasn't ready to go first. He wiped the sweat off his forehead, and attempted to pull himself together. If it hadn't been for Hussain, he would never have come back to this life.

But wouldn't he?

This was all he had ever known in his working life, and wasn't it true that he had once enjoyed modelling, the adrenaline rush that accompanied walking the ramp, the appreciative, albeit lewd looks he got? It was all part of the game, and he had gone along with it.

Until the inevitable phone calls started.

He loathed how the women had begged for a minute of his attention, and how his firm refusals melted away into acquiescence that in turn transformed into intoxication and desire as he descended into a life of sex and drugs, to the point where he couldn't cope anymore and had to leave the profession altogether. But that had been more than two years ago, and for the most part, the modelling had been an enjoyable and lucrative part of his life, and no reason it couldn't be again today if he just focused on walking the ramp. Meera seemed like a professional woman; surely she wouldn't go handing out his personal details to every woman looking to get laid.

'You're next,' Khushbaksh said, nudging him forward. 'You're up in three, two, one… Start walking!'

Ali paused by the open door leading to the ramp just as another model entered the backstage from the other side. Her face was flushed – the indisputable sign of an adrenaline rush. Ali took a deep breath, pictured Hussain's smile in his mind, and stepped forward.

An event organiser was hiding behind a black cardboard wall, whispering instructions into the microphone. He signalled Ali to move ahead, and gave him a big thumbs-up with a fake smile. Ali accepted it – he needed all the luck he could get.

He stretched himself to his full height, threw his chest forward, and began the slow, determined strut that all male models were taught to do. He needed to appear self-confident, but not pompous, a hint of a smile to go with his features, a controlled swinging of the arms, and a measured spring in the step. It needed to be a walk that appeared carefree and confident.

The hordes of people were the first thing that caught his eye, a sea of heads turned in his direction. It had to be the biggest show he had ever been in. The hall was as big as Pearl Continental's. At that moment the song changed, and in the few seconds of silence, he felt the collective thump of hundreds of hearts, the weight of so many curious eyes fixed upon him. A black shadow descended upon his vision, and for a moment he just gaped, unable to move a muscle. Luckily for him, the last female model was still completing her walk. She raised her eyebrows at him.

He sprang into action, then.

After an erratic step or two, he regained his poise, and suddenly it felt like old times. He had done all this before; he had excelled at it. Had he not left of his own accord, he could have been ruling the modelling world today.

He held his chin high, braving the glare of the search-lights, and the incessant clicking of cameras. Arriving at the end of the ramp, he gave a sideway pose with an accompanying glare. He saw an aunty swoon.

He almost laughed.

Don't go there, a part of his mind chastised him. He had done this before, attracted the attentions of ladies he should have had no business with; the consequences had been anything but pleasant. He had vowed never to fall prey to the grim machinations of the female mind, but, despite himself, he could feel his body reacting to every glance it got from the female admirers. It felt as if he had never left the ramp. His every move used to get him a thundering applause. Would he dare try that again?

He jerked his shoulders in time with the music as he spun away from the lights, raised his hands, and displayed the grotesque creation Khushbaksh was so proud of. The women gave him glowing looks, and clapped harder.

He tried not to make eye contact with the audience, but that excited the ladies even more. He didn't even glance in the direction of the men who he knew must be chewing their tongues. He felt a sweeping sense of exhilaration as he realised that for the first time in years, he was in control again. He was shining; he was wanted; *he* was needed.

Meera sat perched at the edge of her seat in the first row, clapping hard. She was smiling her all-teeth smile at him, when only a few hours ago she had dismissed him with a vague nod. A forgotten model with a newbie designer – so passé. A woman wearing pink was sitting next to her, and during that split-second, their eyes met. She sat watching him, unblinking. The gaze she fixed on him was devoid of emotion, like a chasm of emptiness. It felt as if she was only watching him because she didn't have anything better to do. She looked bored, something Ali had never seen in modelling shows. His heart soared and fell; he couldn't break eye contact.

The light from the ramp illuminated her small face. She was older than him, perhaps Meera's age. He stopped walking to showcase his clothes to the audience again – an unnecessary stunt that allowed him some more time to examine her. Before he knew it, she had blinked and looked away, her hands clasped in her lap as if she hadn't been watching him at all. She was also perhaps the only one who had not clapped. Leaning sideways, she whispered something in Meera's ear, her silky brown hair cascading over her face, concealing those intense eyes from view.

Bursting with curiosity, Ali did the unforgivable thing – he turned back to look while walking the ramp. Although her face was back in view, the woman didn't meet his eye again. Her eyes were set somewhere in the distance, as if lost in memory. Ali shook his head, fixed a smile on his face, and completed the rest of his walk.

He walked into the backstage, and in the midst of a resounding applause from everyone, a big hug from a tear-streaked Khushbaksh, he thought of the strange, beautiful woman no more.

Chapter Seven

Mona

The show was over.

Everyone waited as Meera climbed the steps of the ramp to say some final words. The wife of the Minister, who had remained silent throughout the show, dabbed a tissue at her forehead. It came off slick with foundation. Mona cringed. She pressed her back against the chair to hide the rivulets running down her back. God, it *was* hot.

The show had been intense.

In some ways, Mona thought that it had paid homage to Meera's undeniable sensuality; the female models had reminded her of Meera in her college days, when she used to wear those kinds of clothes. Her actions, looks and body language had caused everyone to ogle at her too.

And the male models… there had been an air of enigma around them. One of them even had the audacity to stare at her straight in the face for far longer than necessary. Usually, male models wore the conventional blank stare, glancing at everyone in a nonchalant way. Some of the moody ones ignored the audience outright, and just glared ahead. The way their jaws were set, you'd think someone had thrust a bunch of stones in their mouths. But this boy, his stare wasn't meant to wound, but rather compliment. He must have been a few years older than her son, Farhan, and Mona couldn't help thinking how well her daughter would look with him. Like Mona, her daughter also had a weakness for men who seemed like they played with fire. Every movie they watched, Aimen would end up rooting for the charismatic villain rather than the hero. It amused Mona since she had seen the same thing in Bilal when his *rishta* had come for her all those years ago. He wasn't quite a villain then, rather the opposite. He used to be a man who made her laugh, sometimes so hard that she'd end up with stomach cramps. And then in bed, he'd have the ability to enthral her in equal measure. She would be flattered by his possessiveness, the way he'd shield her from gawking men in shopping malls. Even at airports. And as her mother had liked to say, 'He's one with money too. The complete package.'

He was the perfect man, Mona thought, not realising until her vision clouded that there were tears in her eyes. She blinked until her vision cleared.

She guessed it was the tittering little designer's idea to make the models stare at the audience like that, and yet… there had been something in this boy's stare that disturbed her. Not the bad kind of disturbance… at her age it was a boon for any man to give her the time of the day (not that she wanted any attention from men) so she wasn't entirely displeased. The more pressing fact was that she was certain Bilal had noticed. Men like him never missed something like that – it suddenly reminded them of their honour. The thought made her queasy. She didn't know how much more of his anger she could stomach. Not for the first time, she found herself wondering whether Bilal would ever revert back to the man he used to be, the man she had fallen in love with.

She still remembered the first time she'd seen him, back when he had come to her house for the *rishta*. His mother, Nighat, had taken control of the entire conversation as usual, making pointed remarks at the décor of the house, the ill-trained staff, the gaudy jewellery Mona wore, but Bilal had watched her with interest, a knowing smile on his face, his eyes crinkling up in amusement when their eyes met and Mona's teacup slipped to shatter on the floor. He had rolled his eyes at his mother's loud exclamation and they had burst into spontaneous laughter. If she didn't know then that Bilal would be her husband, she certainly knew it the next day when a Royal Albert tea set arrived, and Bilal with it.

'A gift for a most lovely if clumsy girl,' he said, producing a single red rose and handing it to her.

She'd laughed. 'I like your honesty.'

'I like you.'

'You hardly know me,' Mona replied, colouring under his intense gaze. She lowered her eyes, fearful that his dark, alluring ones would carry her away. Already she could feel that warm tingling in her stomach, the promise of things to come. After that awful event with Meera, she had given up hope, but here was this handsome man making her go weak in her knees.

'Then it's time we got to know each other,' he replied, and then taking her mother's hand, he said, 'But first, would you do me the honour of having lunch with me?'

Her mother, ravaged by early dementia, had never laughed harder than she did to Bilal's proposition.

That was when Mona knew she would marry this man.

She looked for him in the crowd now, but couldn't spot him. How had he turned from that gallant young man to this monster? Was she to blame, at least for a part of it, she wondered?

One challenge at a time, she told herself, and focused on Meera who had begun speaking.

'I hope the show wasn't too taxing on some of our older patrons,' Meera said, her voice booming from the speakers in every direction. 'Our first-aid team does have a set of blood-thinning pills if you might feel the need. I mean, it was HOT!'

The hall rang with laughter. Even the pox-faced old women renowned for obsessing over their husbands were smiling. *They love her*, Mona realised. Unlike her, Meera had always had the gift of winning people over. One look at her was enough to be captivated.

How ironic, Mona thought, that this endearing quality of Meera should have failed at a time when they had needed it the most. Mona had begged her not to take her there alone, but Meera had insisted. 'Come on, it'll be fun!'

She never allowed herself to think of that incident unprepared, but scenes from that night sometimes came raging back at her, like a sudden gust of wind. She let out a small gasp.

Snap out of it, she told herself.

Meera was still cracking jokes, her voice flowing in cadence with the crowd's guffaws and exclamations. 'Well, I sincerely hope that no one here has any plans of taking any of our models home with them.'

An old toothless man grinned back at Meera, nodding furiously. 'I'd like to take one.'

It was a joke, but the mood in the hall darkened. The men smirked, but an odd silence fell among the ladies.

A flash of concern whipped across Meera's face, and before the chairs could start emptying, she performed an elaborate curtsy, and finished her brief, but effective 'thank you' speech. Mona gave her a thumbs-up when she caught her eye. Jokes aside, the show was a success.

She rose with the crowds of people. The muffled sound of hundreds of chairs scraping, and feet stamping on the carpet sounded like a drum roar. A huge swarm of people engulfed Meera, the sycophants on the forefront. Mona waited with her arms folded until Meera was able to detach herself from her admirers. Beneath the foundation, her cheeks were pink. Embarrassment, or maybe it was the blusher. Or both. When their eyes met, her smile faltered.

'So what did you think? Was it good?'

While waiting, Mona had heard a couple of women muttering about social boundaries being crossed, as well as complaints of too much liquor being served. However, she cast those comments away, and gave Meera a bright smile. 'It was fabulous.'

'I overdid the jokes, didn't I? That creature in the sari looked ready to burn me.' She let out a nervous chuckle. 'I've been in men's company for so long that I'm afraid I've forgotten social conventions entirely.'

'Don't worry about it. We're not as prudish as we look. Beneath this veneer of conservatism, we're practically Westerners.'

'Still, I do hope they didn't take too much offence.'

Mona just shrugged and repeated what she had said before about the show being fabulous. Friendly they may be, but their friendship was still tenuous at best.

'A nightcap?' Meera suggested.

Uncertain, Mona glanced back to where the men were vacating the hall. She didn't see Bilal, but she knew he would be waiting somewhere, ready to pounce on her. She fixed on another bright smile. 'You seem tired. Maybe some other time.'

Meera looked crestfallen. 'Why not now? I really wanted to introduce you to my showstoppers, and let's be honest, you look like you need a stiff drink. For a while you looked kind of frozen during the show. Come on! It's time we shared the juicy details of our lives with one another. It'll be fun!'

She looked so earnest that for a moment, Mona almost agreed before she remembered her fight with Bilal, and that settled it. She didn't want him to see her drink. With a gentle tug, she pulled free of Meera. 'I would love to, but you know Bilal is—'

'I'm what, Mona?'

Mona spun around, and there he was, standing in front of her, a teasing smile playing on his lips. With the hard jaw and sharp eyes, the thick lips looked so out of place, and yet somehow, they fitted his appearance. His smile used to sweep her off her feet, but now, it just seemed calculating. He was holding a half-full glass of neat whiskey in his hand. His eyes were bloodshot. Mona hesitated, and stepped back. 'Meera, I'm not sure if you two have met, but this is my husband, Bilal.' She glanced at Bilal. 'This is—'

'The lovely Meera,' Bilal finished for her. The smile still in place, he extended a hand toward Meera. 'Well, the people don't lie. You are quite a sight for sore eyes. It's a pleasure to finally see you in the flesh.' As their hands met, he added, 'I've heard a lot about you.'

Meera glanced at Mona, her smile floundering. 'Good things, I hope.'

'Of course,' Mona piped in. 'In fact, we were just about to leave, so—'

Bilal wagged a finger in the air. 'One moment. Let me speak.' His grin widened, and he drank deep from his glass, the grin turning into a wince as the whiskey seared his throat. 'The lovely Meera. Who could ever say a bad thing about such a woman? I mean, so hot that... *Damn*.'

Mona gulped, pushing back the bile that threatened to rise to her throat. He was going to embarrass her. She was being punished for her earlier impudence.

'I've heard many good things about you, indeed,' he said with a tilt of an eyebrow, rubbing the back of Meera's palm with his thumb before he dropped her hand. 'Your reputation precedes you.'

Meera clasped her hands together, and Mona caught the fury in her eyes before it was replaced by a look of amusement. Mona felt humiliated beyond comprehension.

'My reputation. I see.'

'I mean, you can't seriously blame a man for admiring you, especially one who has had the misfortune of sleeping in a distant wife's cold, unforgiving bed for far too many years.'

'Indeed.' The smile on Meera's face had vanished.

Mona felt two feet tall.

Bilal laughed. 'I'm surprised Mona hasn't dished out on our private life yet. Perhaps, she's embarrassed about how boring she has become. But, more about that later. I think I just heard someone say nightcap. Best thing anyone could have thought of all night, no? Brilliant! Let's have a drink.'

At least he isn't slurring yet, Mona thought as she prayed for this ordeal to be over.

Meera tilted her head as she watched Bilal, her lips parted. Mona simply stared at her husband and took a tentative step toward him. 'Bilal—'

Meera seemed to jerk into action then. 'Oh my. Where are my manners?' She gripped Bilal's hand again, and shook it with vigour. 'It's an absolute pleasure, and please, I'd be thrilled to offer you something to drink. If you take the door on the far side of the hall, you will find my study. Just give me a few seconds to see off my guests.'

Meera widened her eyes at Mona before scuttling off toward the exit, leaving her alone with her husband.

'By all means.' Bilal said to the empty space. His smile turned to a smirk as he turned to Mona. 'Quite a rack she's got on her. I'm impressed, Mona. And here I thought that all you were capable of was those preachy old tarts that visit you at home.'

'Bilal, please. Just leave. You've said enough.'

'Come to think of it, you're not looking too bad either. It was foolish of me to sell you so short. A lot of men seemed to be staring at you. Well, if it isn't like my wife to fight with her poor husband while ladling all her attention on other men.'

A pair of sari-clad women averted their gaze from them as they passed, wrapping their *pallus* around their shoulders. One of them wrinkled her nose.

That made Bilal smile. 'See the effect I have on women? Priceless!'

'Oh God. This is so embarrassing. Why do you do this to me?' Mona sighed. She wondered how many drinks he'd had. She'd seen him drunk, but this was a new low – even for Bilal.

'But what did I do? You don't want to sleep with me; you don't want to eat with me. Pray tell, what *do* you want, my dear? Don't you want me to talk to your friend here? You never complain when those other friends of yours crowd around me like desperate sluts. That Shabeena's literally asking for it. Maybe one day I'll give it to her. Behind that scarf, that woman is a plethora of possibilities.' He grabbed her hand. 'Come now, don't be such a spoilsport. I assure you I'm not *that* drunk. Only a little.' He finished the drink he was holding and tossed the empty crystal glass on the carpeted floor where it rolled off under a chair, out of sight.

Mona massaged the back of her stiff neck. She felt like she had been carrying a great burden for far too long. She willed herself not to shudder at the sight of him. 'You know what? Let's both leave. I'm not going to have you swearing around Meera like this. You're obviously not in your right mind.' She pushed him toward the exit. 'Just go. I'm coming. I need to say goodbye to Meera.'

Bilal was so inebriated by now that he had even begun slurring, and when she pulled her hand from his, he almost lost his balance. Closing his fingers around a nearby chair for support, he paused to rub his temples. 'Cra-ppp, I am wasted.' He wagged his finger in the air again like some weird ringleader. 'For you, darling. I'll l-leave this one t-t-time for you.'

'Thank you. I'm honoured.'

'That's my girl.' The sarcasm was lost on Bilal, as he leaned forward to steal a kiss, a grotesque smile lining his red face. Mona ducked away. His breath smelled of alcohol and cigar.

In the end, she left without meeting Meera. She waited a while, but knowing Bilal was crazy enough to drive himself off in his wrecked state, she rushed toward the car park.

It seemed like it was going to rain. She hurried across the covered parking area to the grounds where they had left their car. She averted her eyes from the policemen who still stood huddled around the Rolls Royce. Most of the guests had left, so she spotted her Mercedes with ease. It was standing, forlorn, in the middle of the lawn. The headlights were on full beam and blinking. *Oh Bilal!*

The light from the car's headlights illuminated the eastern boundary wall, and Mona caught sight of a crowd of people heading toward the vans parked next to the wall. They were models, Mona noticed as she sized them up with their heights and bodies. A couple of familiar faces confirmed her suspicions.

Away from the spotlight, they seemed like normal human beings in normal clothes, not those ethereal creatures that had scorched the ramp earlier. She could imagine the eyes of the drunken, pot-bellied fools on them, relishing each body part, straining to look past the clothing to catch a glimpse of a curve. Not for the first time that evening, Mona shuddered. She quickened her pace toward the headlights, but she found her gaze returning to the sound of laughter where the models stood chatting.

A bunch of girls seemed to be laughing at a joke one of the guys had told them. Mona felt a stab of envy at those wide smiles and fresh faces. What she wouldn't give to be twenty-five again...

Well apart from the group, a guy stood leaning against a van with his hands in his pockets. He seemed to be waiting for the others to finish talking, and begin hopping into the waiting vans. Even from a distance, she could see he was scowling. Mona stopped dead. He was the guy from the show, the one who had stared at her during his walk down the ramp. He looked so unfamiliar with his clenched jaw, and mane of dishevelled hair that had been so well combed earlier. The fact that she had recognised him even in this state unsettled her.

The car gave an angry honk. She pried her eyes away from the model. What was wrong with her, staring at men half her age? She shook her head, and hurried off toward the Benz.

Sliding into the back seat of the car, she found herself in the midst of drunken cursing. Bilal's head lolled against the side window, as he grunted expletives at the valet, urging him to move it. The poor boy looked terrified. As he reversed the car, the headlights shone on the vans for a last time, and Mona leaned forward to watch the scene again. She may have imagined it, but for a moment she thought the same man was staring in her direction.

Chapter Eight

Ali

The semi-darkness of the room unnerved him. He propped himself against the wooden headboard, and waited. Having already vomited on the pillows, he had flung them out on the terrace, drawing the curtains over the window to hide proof of his actions. He mightn't have bothered since there was no one to question anything going awry in such a place.

Something tickled him under the legs. He thrust his hand inside the bed sheets, and pulled out a gigantic brown cockroach, its numerous legs dangling in alarm. He flicked it on the carpet.

Insects no longer disgusted him.

Humans did.

Without any pillow, the carvings on the headboard dug into his back, and he felt a headache setting in, the pain beginning to pool around his skull, pounding it in sporadic bursts. He wished he had something to drink, or even better, a delicious pill to pop in his mouth, but the only drink in the room was a glass of water sitting on the bedside table with a crummy coaster depicting the Royal Fort covering it. Lipstick marks from previous visitors stained the rim of the glass. He needed something much stronger for what he was about to face; all the alcohol had left his system in the form of vomit and sweat. The scarlet lampshades had bathed the whole room in an eerie glow, similar to that of a photographic dark room.

The bathroom door's lock clicked.

Ali dug his nails into the mattress. Why did he always have to agree to these filthy acts? Why why why, his mind screamed at him. He had posed that question to himself a thousand times, and yet, here he was.

With clammy hands, he reached for the glass of water, and gulped it down in one go. It was tepid like everything else in the room. In spite of the air conditioning, beads of sweat clung to his forehead, droplets running down his back. His boxers were soaked too. The cooler it got, the more he sweated.

The door creaked when it opened, and the rustle of silk and satin filled the room, overpowering the drone of the air-conditioning unit. The curtains were threadbare, but they did their job of shielding the room from prying eyes, and of hiding the evidence of his earlier binge drinking: the stained pillows. He knew she wouldn't appreciate him being drunk at one of their meetings although he wondered if she chose this godforsaken motel each time just to tempt him to binge. The whole place reeked of cheapness. Perhaps that was what got her rocks off…

She approached the bed, the silk gown hanging loose on her body, her face still shrouded in shadow. In a single motion, she shrugged off the gown, and threw it over the footboard.

Ali stared. The sight transfixed him each time.

Ugly stretch marks lined the folds of loose fat around her midriff, and even in the dull glow of the lamps, he saw the cellulite on her legs. Her entire body sagged; perhaps once it had been voluptuous, everything a bit firmer,

God a bit kinder, but now she reminded him of a wilted peach. As if someone had sucked all the juice from her body, leaving only dead flesh behind. Her copious use of perfume compounded his headache; he felt as if someone was driving a red-hot poker into his brain, twisting it with each heartbeat so that the pain reverberated through his entire body. She was wearing that perfume her husband had got her from Germany last month. The awareness of how much he knew about this woman repulsed him. His stomach churned, and his sweating worsened.

'You've been naughty, Ali. Very, very naughty,' she murmured as she drew closer. 'I can smell the alcohol on you from here. And you know what the punishment for drinking is.' Her cruel laugh rang across the room. 'I have just the right punishment planned out for you.'

That was their secret game. He watched transfixed as she stepped out of the shadows.

Ali's eyes snapped open, his heart pounding. In the darkness, he groped for the alarm clock on the nightstand. It was 5.40 a.m. His clothes were soaked, and he shivered as cool air escaped the swaying curtains, and bathed his damp skin.

Someone had left the window open.

His eyes widened in alarm, before he remembered he had done that himself before going to sleep. The dreams always left him feeling disoriented. He rubbed his knuckles against his eyes to banish the remnants of the dream away. It hadn't been a dream though. It had all happened before; he had been reliving the same scene that had occurred two years ago. Her face...

He had thought he'd forgotten her face, just as he was sure he'd forgotten the faces of the dozens of women before her, but no matter how hard he convinced himself, they always came back to haunt him. His heart slowed to its normal rhythm, and his sense of place and time returned but that haggard face still lingered like the taste of vomit in his mouth.

She had been the last one before he had given it all up, and run for the hills. In some ways, he was grateful to her. Something about that evil game of punishment had reminded him of the depths to which he had sunk, and despite the effect of drugs over his mind at that time, he was glad to have had the prudence to return the woman's money before he picked up his clothes, and ran. He remembered the receptionist at the motel desk staring at him with his mouth open as he ran half-dressed out of the double doors, saying goodbye to the most shameful period of his life. Never again, he had vowed to himself. *Never again.*

Ali thrust the blanket off from where it had tangled up around his feet, and crept into the bathroom. It was a sad little place with an age-spotted mirror, and chipping tiles, but it calmed him more than his bedroom.

After a good long shower, he had recovered enough to fling the dream out of his mind in its entirety.

As he fished out wads of blue thousand-rupee notes from his jeans pocket, he felt the familiar dread settling into his heart again. Going downstairs meant meeting Hussain. The powerlessness he felt in the face of Hussain's pain was excruciating. His brother's pain wasn't his own fault; it was Ali's. If he had only made enough money to buy them a car, Hussain wouldn't have had to rely on public transport, and extol the risk of wandering in streets. Hussain's terrified screams in the night didn't make it any easier. They were so loud that they permeated all the way to Ali's room upstairs, and didn't cease until Ali bounded down to his room, and calmed him. 'It's there,' he moaned every night. 'The leg is still there; I can feel it.' Only Ali's measured tone and reassurances helped Hussain doze off into a fitful rest, the tears on his cheeks glistening for a long time afterward.

For a moment, Ali just stood there, drawing a blank gaze over his room. His only consolation was that he now had enough money to ensure that Hussain's initial treatment went on uninterrupted. He shoved the money into the pockets of his black corduroy pants, and throwing on a light jacket over his white vest, he left for downstairs.

To his surprise, his small family was seated at the breakfast table, something that hadn't happened since Hussain had lost his leg. Their house was small, neatly sequestered in one of the quiet streets of the sprawling housing society of Iqbal Town. Having sold off the big *haveli* in the village, this house had been purchased to ensure a more enlightened life for Ali and Hussain. 'I will not tolerate being called a bumpkin,' their father had said.

His mother looked up from the toast she was buttering, and gave him a shy smile. She was never generous with her smiles, and it was a welcome change to see her with an expression that didn't quite involve the quivering of lips. Perhaps the fact that Hussain was silent, and eating something today had perked her up. Ali returned the smile, and hitched up an even wider one for his brother.

'Look who the cat dragged in!'

His brother returned the smile. It was wan, but it was a smile. He was waiting for their mother to finish buttering another piece of toast, and Ali was glad to see that some colour had returned to his brother's chubby little face. Hussain looked at their mother, and they both chuckled.

Chuckled. They never chuckled. He was at once wary and curious. 'What is it?' he asked.

His mother tried to make a sad clucking sound, but failed. Her smile was too broad.

'What is it?' he insisted again.

His brother tossed the *Sunday News* magazine in his direction with a 'There you go!' The effort cost him a wince. Ali leaned forward, and caught the newspaper before it could fall into the bowl of cereal.

He unfolded the document to reveal a picture of himself staring back. It had been taken from the previous night's fashion show, with him wearing the atrocious creation of Khushbaksh's – parrot-green waistcoat, and tattered shalwar kameez. The photo decorated the front page of the news magazine, and the headline went '*Foreign Return Meera Siddiqui steals the show*'.

Below the picture, a small caption read, '*Ali, a prominent ramp model showcases a latest creation by one of the designers at Meera Siddiqui's show.*'

He stared at the words 'prominent model', and felt his body tingle. He was sure his face was flushed as he scraped back a chair from the dining table, and seated himself.

His mother crossed her arms over her thin chest. 'Well? What do you think, Mr Prominent Model?' Hussain sniggered, and then before long, both mother and son had dissolved into a fit of giggles. Ali knew they weren't making fun of him; it had just been ages since they had had something to be pleased about.

He rolled the magazine into a tight tube, and laughed. 'It was just a show,' he said. 'Lots of fun, but in two days no one is going to remember my face.'

His mother passed the buttered toast to Hussain, and folded her arms on the plastic-covered dining table. 'It's still a great opportunity though. We haven't had anything to celebrate for a while now.' Her eyes glistened. 'You have no idea how good it felt to see you in the newspaper. I just feel so content at this moment. Both of my boys sitting with me, eating breakfast. If I could, I would never let this moment pass. I would hold on to it forever.' She sighed before rising from her chair. 'But since it's time for some scrambled eggs, let's allow the moment to pass.'

'Yay!' Hussain exclaimed.

He glanced at Hussain. His brother seemed in good spirits for the first time since his amputation; when he pressed the wad of bank notes into their mother's hand, and announced that a gift was in order for Hussain, he beamed at him.

'Now, now.' His mother waved a cooking spoon at his younger brother, before piling more eggs on top of his half-eaten meal. 'I'll hear no more of gifts until this plate is wiped clean. Look at how weak you've become. All skin and bone.'

'Can I get a pair of skates if I finish my breakfast?' Hussain's face fell as he said the words, but he quickly corrected himself. 'An Xbox would be better though!' He tried to sound cheerful, but Ali could sense the sadness in his voice.

Setting aside his own half-eaten food, he pushed himself out of the chair, and went around the table to wrap his arm around his brother. 'Tell you what buddy, if you finish your breakfast, you can not only have an Xbox, but you can also have a new PS3.'

'Really?' Hassan's eyes went as round as marbles.

'Really. I'll get them from the store today.'

His mobile beeped. He flipped it open to catch his first congratulatory message for the day. It was from none other than Meera herself. *Congrats, you! I knew there was something special about you when I saw you at the auditions. See me at the office on Monday, maybe?*

Ali allowed himself to swell with pride for a moment before reading the message again. Meera's tone was cheerful, but Ali understood the hidden meaning: she wanted to snag him before anyone else could. Though she feigned innocence in everything, it was obvious that Meera hadn't built such an enormous empire just by batting her eyes. That woman was shrewd, and more importantly, she was famous. Ali knew that a big opportunity like this wouldn't knock on his door twice. Edging forward in his seat, he flattened the magazine on the table with his palm, and flicked through Instagram on his phone, searching for the coverage of yesterday's event.

He found another picture of himself with Meera in her midnight-blue dress. Even in the picture, her smile was enchanting, like it could sweep you off your feet. Another picture featured Meera with her arm around another woman. Ali paused. It was the same woman, the one with the bottomless eyes, the one he had stared at. He looked up, and saw that his mother had busied herself in the kitchen again, while Hussain had the *Call of the Wild* opened up on the table. The boy loved books.

Ali looked closely at the picture. She was smiling, her lustrous brown hair shining in the flashlight as she wrapped an arm around Meera. Ali guessed her to be a bit older than Meera, but her arms were taut, and her belly didn't poke out of her fitted chiffon kameez. His gaze travelled to her eyes. They were crinkled up because of her smile, but even in the picture, he detected an elusive sadness about her. Her smile seemed miles away from her eyes. The frown lines between her eyebrows betrayed the many nights that must have been spent in sleeplessness and worry, and even though it was evident that she was trying to be jovial, her smile was nothing like the pert perfection that was Meera's.

He had also seen her leaving the event late last night. Walking alone, she seemed pretty interested in the female models. He had been standing a little far off, so he knew she couldn't have seen him. He remembered her climbing inside the Mercedes, ever the sophisticated lady as she sat down first, pulling her legs into the car afterwards. He had looked in that direction for a long time.

Thinking back to the various flings he'd had, it became clear that the women he had been with had a certain strength about them that prevented them from falling into despair; they would be bored, restless, desperate, starved for love, but none of them were ever as unhappy as this one here looked. It baffled Ali as to how a person could be so rich, and still miserable. He turned to the magazine, and saw more pictures of her. She looked downcast in all of them, and in one where she stood gesticulating with a man – probably her husband – she seemed downright morose.

Bullshit, he thought, suddenly angry as he snapped the magazine shut. How many times had he allowed himself to feel sorry for these women, only to discover he was the one being duped. This was their style – using their looks and emotions to weed their way into a stranger's heart until they owned him. And then they proceeded to rule him, to lord over his every thought. 'Until you learn to respect our patrons, and fulfil their desires, there is no place for you here,' his previous modelling agent had told him. The words still rang shrill in his ears.

Hussain was dozing off with his head nestled in the book, his arms resting on either side of his head. Ali walked around the dining table, eased him out of his chair, and carried him to the bedroom. In the room, he waited a few moments for his brother to settle down. His mother said that he was better now, but the stump was still bandaged like before, the gauze wrapped tight around the length of his thigh. *Still a long way to go*, Ali thought.

The rest of the day went by in a whirlwind of congratulatory messages, and calls from people he hadn't heard from in years. Majeed called him late in the afternoon when he was at the gym. '*Yaar* Ali, what the hell did you do? You're a bloody sensation!'

Ali laughed as he ran a towel across his forehead. 'I know. I saw the magazine. I honestly don't know how it happened.'

Majeed groaned in mock pain. 'Are you kidding me? You're frickin' famous! That's what happened. Did you know people even congratulated me? Just so I could pass the message onto you. I tell you *yaar*, these people are such hypocrites. Last week they had all sworn you were as good as dead.'

Ali sighed. 'I know, man. But you'll see, these people will forget who I am by next week. That's the worst thing… the speed with which they forget. I'm not pinning my expectations on this crowd.'

'That may be,' Majeed replied. 'But, most people would kill for such a chance. I would!'

As he worked up a sweat on the treadmill later, his thoughts went to the house in Defence he had staked out for himself. That spacious two-storey house with rooms that went on forever, the lush, green lawn with its imported potted plants.

He could see himself buying it.

Chapter Nine

Mona

'Oh for God's sake,' Mona exclaimed as car after car whizzed by the road she stood waiting to cross.

Her driver was useless as ever, parking the car in the remote car park, making her cross the main road in the middle of lunch hour. She was already running late for Nighat's doctor's appointment. She couldn't help rolling her eyes as she imagined her mother-in-law's reprimands.

She stood smack in the middle of the road, atop the one-foot column of concrete that divided the flow of traffic. 'Idiot,' she muttered at the driver, not bothering if her voice carried across to the people who stood waiting with her. A few more cars zoomed by, ignoring the pedestrian crossing sign blinking at them, after which Mona took matters into her own hands, and deliberately marched across the road. *Let them run me over*, she thought, as a bunch of vehicles screeched to a stop, the drivers shouting expletives at her.

She didn't care.

She ignored her driver's pitiful pleading about not reporting this to Bilal. If he thought he would get away with this, he had another thing coming. The punishing sun produced a spattering of beads of sweat over her face, not unlike morning dew. She almost laughed out loud at the analogy. She was still hungover; her searing temper told her that. Last night, there had been another fight. Another turning of the coffee table in their bedroom, the sounds of splintering wood filling the room. She wondered what the servants made of it all: the noise, the mess in the room like the wreckage after a tsunami. She didn't even remember what it was they'd fought about this time, the whiskey had made sure of that. Perhaps something about how she had been avoiding him for weeks.

Had she? She couldn't recall the last time she had been at ease with him – his mood swings didn't allow for that luxury. She didn't need to remember the particulars of their argument. It always came down to breaking things in the room. At first, she'd mourn over the loss of her things for days, but now she had become as flippant about them as he was. She might have hurled an object or two at him last night although she couldn't be sure.

The door to Dr Shafiq's room was locked when she finally arrived in the hospital, hot-faced and sweating. Now it wouldn't open until the consultation was over, when Nighat had once again wrapped her massive folds of fat back in clothes and cackled appropriately at some benign suggestion from Dr Shafiq. And there would be hell to pay later when Nighat relayed it all to Bilal, everything from Mona's tardiness to her lack of enthusiasm for her health. As if Mona could stop her from stuffing herself with food.

After what seemed like an eternity, the door opened and Dr Shafiq emerged, pale and wide-eyed as if he had witnessed something that went against the order of the world. He ran a handkerchief over his face, neutralised his expression and motioned for the nurse to join him inside.

What a family, Mona thought, catching sight of her mother-in-law's sagging face flush with glee as she came out hobbling on her cane. Whether it was motherly affection for Dr Shafiq or something more prurient, she didn't want to think about it. It turned her stomach.

Nighat put up a great show of strength by waving at the nurses, and making loud exclamations, but Mona noticed her leaning on her cane, her whole face glistening with the effort of keeping her enormous body moving.

'Pass me some of the water, would you?' the old woman gasped as she slid her massive frame into the rear seat of the car. 'Ya Allah, forgive me for my sins. This walk was torture. I'm taking the wheelchair next time.'

Mona extracted a bottle of mineral water from the car's cold compartment, twisted it open, and passed it to her. She reached for Nighat's gnarled hand, and enclosed it in her own. Putting on an encouraging smile for her benefit, she asked, 'How was your appointment?'

The sunlight caught Nighat full in the face, and in the unforgiving light, the old lady's wrinkles stood out like an ugly nest. It almost made her look frail – something she definitely wasn't.

'Hmph. No concern of yours.'

'I'm sorry I was late.'

Nighat took a minute to drain the bottle, gulping down the water loudly. After she was finished, she smacked her rouged lips, and leaned back, the loose flesh of her arms wobbling every time as the car drove over a series of bumps. She was weighing her desire to speak of Dr Shafiq against her anger.

Mona knew which would win.

Nighat smiled. 'Well, Shafiq, the darling that he is, says that I should go easy on the oily stuff. At my age, he says the heart's not as robust as it used to be. Nonsense. He made it all sound so pensive. I mean, had it not been for his jokes, I would have gone to sleep then and there. According to him, if I'm not too careful, I may need stents soon.' Letting out a cackle, she patted her stomach 'Bah! As if. He's a dear, and tries to look after me, but he doesn't understand that I don't need any of this fancy gear. We old women… we are made of stronger stuff, you hear. All that home-churned butter and desi ghee parathas in my childhood are what's keeping me going. Imagine steering clear of oily food. He literally begged me to make him a promise not to touch pakoras.'

Mona could have repeated this conversation word for word; she had heard it that often. Every month, it was the same story when Nighat visited Dr Shafiq. Still, out of habit she asked, 'And did you? Promise, I mean?'

'Oh I love pakoras too much to promise any such thing, silly girl. Pakoras will be the death of me, but at least I'll die content.'

'Ah yes, the pakoras.'

For a woman of eighty-three, Nighat still displayed a remarkable strength of character. Her legs had failed her, but her mind was as sprightly as ever. Her small black eyes glittered with intelligence whenever someone struck up a conversation; her statements came soaked with the knowledge that comes from living a long life. 'I may be old, but my heart is young,' she always joked.

The sharp little eyes now swivelled in Mona's direction like black darts. 'Since we're together today, I've been meaning to ask you something. What is all this noise I hear at night of you shouting and crying?'

Mona blinked. 'Excuse me? My shouts?'

Nighat's chin jiggled as she nodded. 'Yes, my dear, these days you seem to be fighting with my son every day.'

Suppressing the anger that rose inside her, Mona focused her eyes on the back of the seat in front of her. Her gaze bored into the porous black leather. 'Your room is miles away from mine, Aunty. You must have heard a neighbour.' The jab wasn't lost on Mona. Nighat had pinned the whole blame on her. Her gaze slid to the murky brown water of the canal, as their BMW shot through the recently widened road. The gentle flow of the gleaming water did nothing to soothe her.

'Lies! Tell me the truth,' Nighat demanded. 'What's all the fuss about? You know how much I hate noise. It disrupts my sleep. Go cry in your bathroom, or wail in your friends' ears, but please for God's sake, don't make life any more difficult for my son. He has enough worries as it is. My poor boy didn't sleep a wink last night. He came to me with such a tired face this morning, his eyes swollen shut. The poor dear.

'Sloppy,' she continued. 'This is what comes from having a sloppy wife.'

And there it was. Mona had suspected Bilal for having put Nighat onto her, but now she was certain. Before she could stop them, the words tumbled out of her. 'It was your dear son who was shouting, not me. Perhaps you should see Dr Shafiq about your ears too.'

In her peripheral vision, she saw Nighat sitting up. The effort cost her a groan, but when her dry hand closed around Mona's forearm, her grip was firm. 'Do you take me for a fool, Mona?'

'No, Aunty, I do not.'

'Then how dare you take that tone with me?' She squeezed her forearm, tentative, but bordering on forceful. 'I may be old, dear, but I am not yet stupid. Don't think I'm like that senile wreck of a mother you had. No Sir!'

Mona squeezed her eyes shut, praying that the tears wouldn't break out. Not in front of Nighat. 'Don't bring my poor mother into this, Aunty. For once in your life, let her soul rest in peace.' She choked the last words out.

'And I've always resented that tongue of yours,' Nighat replied, releasing the grip on Mona's arm, and slumping across the seat again. 'A woman should always know her place, says I. Weak, lustful little creatures women are. Keep them on a short leash or risk finding them glued to the first man available.' She switched to Punjabi, doubtless to drive her point home. 'Back in our day, we earned a clap of a heeled shoe on our buttocks if we badmouthed in front of our elders. A sharp slap on the face too, for good measure. We knew better than to sass-mouth our mother-in-laws after that. Bashir!'

'Ji, Begum Sahiba,' the driver called out.

'Do you people in the villages still give your wives sound beatings to knock sense into them?'

'Indeed we do, Begum Sahiba,' Bashir almost shouted back. 'I've even instructed my mother to beat my wife in my absence so that she doesn't try anything funny. My wife knows the size of our shoes now; she's been beaten so often by them.' Mona saw him smirking to himself in the rear-view mirror. The scoundrel was enjoying himself, and why not? Nighat had given him the perfect opportunity.

Nighat, however, nodded, her expression solemn. 'Good. Your mother sounds like a sensible woman, hardened by some good beatings herself. Good good. You see, Mona, while I don't condone beatings, I do believe these poor people deserve them, imbeciles that they are. Ask them to perform a simple task such as boiling water, and they'd find a way to botch that as well. So, while it may not be proper, a good, sound beating is what people deserve sometimes. Just to knock some sense into them.'

Mona bared her teeth at Nighat in a harsh smile. 'You almost sound nostalgic yourself, Aunty. Do you miss the beatings?'

Nighat's eyes narrowed. 'Watch your mouth, Mona. You don't know who you're dealing with here. Be very careful when you talk to me. Anything you believe Bilal to be capable of, just remember, I'm his mother. I'm capable of far worse. So I suggest you revise your attitude toward me.' Watching the resentful expression on Mona's face, her tone eased. 'I'm not your enemy, Mona. In fact, I'm a strong advocate of women's rights, and perhaps your biggest supporter in the house. But a woman simply cannot be so headstrong. She has to learn when to keep her mouth shut in front of her husband.'

She turned to the driver again. 'Bashir!'

'Ji, Begum Sahiba.'

'Breathe a word about this to anyone, and I'll whip out that tongue of yours, you eavesdropping dog.'

'As you command, Begum Sahiba,' Bashir shouted, his voice thick with reverence.

Mona felt disgusted. Distancing herself from Nighat as much as she could, she forced herself to calm down. She was panting. Beneath the shade of the flowering trees, on the banks of the canal, she watched the women washing clothes. They scrubbed large yellow bars of soap hard on the clothes, slapping the grimy canal water on them to create a rich lather. Some mothers bathed their children with the same water, while others watched as their children swam, pieces of Styrofoam stuffed in their shalwars as they floated around. She tried to lose herself in their small joys.

—

To her utter surprise, things went rather well at dinner. Nighat pulled her long-suffering mother-in-law act quite convincingly, complete with the drawn-out sighs and misty eyes, but Bilal seemed to be having none of it.

'Do you realise that there was another suicide blast in the Northern Areas? Surely, our own grievances can rest for one day. Right, Amma?'

If Nighat was taken aback, she didn't show it. 'Of course, Bilal. Let us take this opportunity to pray for the departed souls.' When they'd all said their prayers under their breath, Nighat rubbed her hands together. 'I sure hope the government is doing something about this situation. I mean, if the terrorists lay siege to Lahore, I won't even be able to run, much less escape.'

'Nothing is going to happen to you, Amma. All I meant was that we should be thankful to God for everything we have.'

'But I heard they are planning to attack Islamabad too,' Mona began, but Bilal cut her off.

'If you must know, Lahore is also under threat. We have had so many bombs going off lately. But that doesn't mean the terrorists will take over the city. It just means that we need to be on our guard. Trust no one.'

'Not even the servants?' Nighat asked in horror. 'You mean to tell me that Bashir and—'

'You can trust your servants, Amma,' Bilal sighed.

Apparently, the surprises for the day weren't over. As Mona stood in the dressing room to remove her earrings, she heard Bilal's familiar tread across the carpeted floor. She thought he was heading for the bathroom, but he shocked her by sliding his arms around her stomach, his body pressed against hers. At first, she didn't know what to think; her body had gone rigid with fear at such close proximity to him, but as the seconds went by and she realised his touch held nothing but tenderness, she relented, and even relaxed in his embrace.

'Sorry about last night,' he whispered in her ear. He wasn't intoxicated. His breath smelled of lentils and mint gum. 'You don't have to go to that party with me. Hell, even I'm not sure I want to go. I just don't know why we fight on such petty issues. It pains me that things between us have to be like this.'

Without intending to, she tilted back her head, allowing herself to be drawn deeper into his embrace. 'It must be the first time in years that you've asked for my forgiveness.'

'You do know how much I love you, right? I did marry you after all.'

That made her laugh. 'Trust you Bilal, to always make the most awkward romantic statements.'

'I'm serious. Why else does one get married, if not for love?'

'For such a successful businessman, you can often be so naïve. If everyone married for love, well let's just say that the world would be a different place.'

'Mmm,' he hummed, already losing interest. His fingers, deft and precise, unbuttoned her dressing gown in a flourish. She felt herself flushing, but quickly reprimanded herself. She was with her husband, not some stranger. How delicate his touch seemed when all she had known in recent years was roughness and pain.

'By God woman,' he breathed. 'You're a wonder beneath the dowdy clothes you wear.' He swivelled her toward him in one fluid motion. 'Is this what I've been missing? I'm such a fool.'

He stepped back from her, his gaze travelling up and down her body. She might as well have been a teenager, the way her heart thudded in her chest. She marvelled at her body's capability to respond to Bilal even now, after all the violence. Maybe a part of her had never ceased loving him, or maybe she was deluding herself. Hadn't he always been like this? Caring for her until it got too old and something else captured his interest. Then there would only be those rows they had, or that emotional detachment with which he treated her, as if she didn't exist. In some ways, that was worse than the rows. She almost wrapped the dressing gown back over her body, but she hesitated for a moment, and that was enough for him to pull it off her. She coloured under his intense stare.

'I'm not too sure about this.'

'The hell you're not.'

She whooped in alarm when he picked her up, the tightness of his grip a promise of the things to come. She closed her eyes and let her head fall against his chest. The earnest beat of his heart was all the evidence she needed of his desire for her. She masked her laughter into a giggle as a thought occurred to her.

'What is it?' he said, as he deposited her gently on her side of their feather bed. The springs creaked from disuse, and she felt a stab of remorse at the countless nights spent in the guest room.

'I'll come to that party with you.'

'That's not what you were smiling about a moment ago.'

'I like it when we're not fighting. Almost makes me feel young again.'

Bilal took her hand in both of his own, cocooning it in their warmth. 'I promise you I'll make things like the way they were when we were newly married. Do you remember our marriage bed?'

She sensed something inappropriate coming on. 'Yes…'

'Well, I'm gonna make sure this one ends up creaking just like that one did.'

Despite herself, she found herself laughing.

'I want you to make amends with Meera,' she murmured, unsure of how he would respond. 'I think we owe it to her after the way we – I mean you – acted at her party the other night. People will be discussing your little tryst with the whiskey for weeks, if not months.'

Bilal paused, his finger poised over the last button of his shirt. A shadow passed over his face. She had said too much.

'Bilal,' she began.

'No, you're right.' He looked up and she saw contrition on his face. 'I acted like a jerk and I deserve all the malicious gossip the rumour mills might churn. But your friend doesn't. I'll figure something out.'

Mona was lost for words. 'Are you under a spell of some sort? What have you done with the Bilal I know?'

'You mean the one on a rampage all the time?' He smiled and she was pleased to see how it lit up his face, making him seem a decade younger. He looked like the man who had brought her that red rose all those years ago.

He grabbed her hand again, and she looked into his eyes. If Bilal had poor romantic timing, she was worse… talking about Meera during a moment like this.

'You still haven't told me what you were giggling about back there.'

She cleared her throat, not taking her eyes off him. 'Well… if you must know, I was remembering the time you surprised my mother with the lunch proposition.'

'Oh that.' He smirked. 'Well, I was honest. Your beauty doesn't hold a candle to your mother's. She was sick at the time, but she knew how to carry herself.'

Mona blinked back tears. 'Thank you for saying that.'

'It's the truth. If you doubt my honesty, you don't know me at all. For example, I think you look irresistible right now.'

'This is honesty mixed with a bit of flattery, Bilal.'

He winked at her. 'Mostly honesty.'

Mona smiled as his lips met hers.

Chapter Ten

Ali

'Crank up the AC, for the love of God!' exclaimed the woman in the back seat. 'We're melting in here.'

Ali looked back, and sure enough, she was addressing him and not the driver. He pursed his lips, swallowing the retort poised on his tongue, and turned the AC on full. Supermodel Iqra... A name that commanded respect in fashion circles; inexperienced models cowered in front of her, and here she sat, a mere three feet away from Ali, fanning her sweating face with a hand, while with the other she screwed and unscrewed the top of her water bottle. She was livid at being made to pick him up from his house.

The car was hurtling down the deserted road that led to the Elahis' grand country house, or 'farmhouse' as people liked to say. They had been on the road for the last forty minutes, and Iqra was still going on about Allama Iqbal Town. Ali was almost at his wits' end.

'As if I hadn't seen enough of that place to last me a lifetime,' she muttered. 'All my life I've lived there, and this woman, this – this Meera has the audacity to treat me like a common chauffeur. If it wasn't for her connections, I would have quit there and then.'

'Now now, Iqra,' the other model, Iman, murmured to her. 'Ali didn't have a choice, did he? Our public transport is woefully ineffective at the best of times, and now when they're on strike? And besides, this is Meera's car. We should all be thankful that we didn't have to beg for a ride to the farmhouse. Even if I had a car I wouldn't have driven that far, not with the current price of fuel. You're just being unfair.'

'I'm being unfair? This world is being unfair with me. I deserve a place in the most dazzling circles of society, and here I am, reduced to travelling in this shitty piece of junk.'

'It's a brand-new Toyota Corolla—' Iman tried to protest.

'Well, I need a Mercedes Benz. I want a BMW. I'm done with this crap.'

The rant went on for a while before she returned to her original displeasure at Ali's presence.

'Why couldn't she come and take him to the damn party herself? Her *star* model. If he's such a star, why pin him on us?'

'Because, she fears that she may not be able to make it to the event and since she has already committed to our being there, she didn't want to go back on her word.'

Iqra spoke in furious whispers, but Ali caught everything and judging by the reddening of the chauffeur's ears, he sensed that he heard everything too.

Ali took deep breaths.

'I expect Sonia will be arriving in a Lexus with that rich boyfriend of hers. That woman is a million years old, I just can't imagine how men are attracted to her. Especially when these days the bombing and terrorist attacks have sharpened everyone's sense of morality, I find people still lunging for her aging flesh.'

'She is pretty,' Iman mused.

'To hell with her prettiness. These men deserve someone better!'

'Like you?' Ali asked her, struggling to keep the anger out of his voice.

'Excuse me?' Iqra's voice rose by several decibels. 'How dare you even talk to me, you vermin? You dare address the reigning queen of fashion this way? Do you even know who I am?'

'Yeah, I heard. You're *Supermodel* Iqra.'

He looked back to enjoy seeing her face transform from chalk-white to an ugly magenta. It was hard to tell her age; her body was svelte without a trace of fat, but her face betrayed her. She seemed to be in the murky territory between the ages of forty and forty-five, when the face just seems to flesh out as if preparing for the oncoming wrinkles. Ali was certain she wasn't a girl. 'If it isn't the virgin's flush on your face,' he sneered.

To this she flushed even deeper, her eyes bulging out of their sockets. 'Why you impertinent little—'

'We're here!' Iman announced with relief as the car leapt over a massive speed bump.

Iqra shrieked at the driver. 'Careful, you fool. You almost ruined my hair. Here, look Iman, has any hair escaped the knot at the back?'

Iman murmured something soothing.

Ali could sense Iqra building up steam about something else, so before she could utter another word, he dashed out of the moving car, and down where the road had dwindled from three lanes to a narrow space barely enough for a single car to go through. It would be hell getting out of this place.

So intent was he to avoid Iqra that he spent more time looking over his back than ahead, so that when he stumbled over a long red carpet that snaked into the large house, he had to grab the nearest thing beside him to keep himself from falling. It was a faux pillar of white plaster that shifted at his weight, sending a large vase of red roses crashing to the floor.

'Now look at what he's done!' Iqra cried from behind him.

Ignoring her, he made his way inside.

Instantly, he was assaulted by bright yellow lights and a whole army of photographers, madly clicking away.

'This is for the *Times*!' one of them shouted.

'The *Daily Lifestyle Magazine*, Ali! Look here.'

Ali stood dumbstruck, his mouth about to fall open.

'Still not used to it?' Iman whispered in his ear and she breezed past him with Iqra in tow. Their presence unleashed a frenzy among the photographers who all seemed to have left the guests at the main events to swarm around the red carpet.

Ali tried to smile as best as he could; the self-confidence he had slowly built up over the weeks wavering at Iqra's recent onslaught. He stood with his mouth stretched until tears came into his eyes. Not knowing what to do with his hands, he thrust them deep into his trouser pockets.

'Together! The three of you together!' a photographer shouted, to which Iqra turned with a gracious expression, all haughtiness gone from her posture, her face bearing an open smile of invitation.

'Ali darling, come here,' she crooned, skipping back to pull his hand from his pocket. Other than her vice-like grip, he detected no animosity from her. She seemed to have transformed in a second.

Positioning herself between Iman and him, she flashed her brightest smile for the paparazzi, drawing Ali's arm around her slender waist. They stood like that for a few seconds, the smile on Iqra's face growing more abnormal as the clicking of cameras persisted. She even swooped down to blow kisses on Ali. 'Make sure it's on the first page, darling,' she said to the photographer for the *Times*. 'Oh, oh look guys, there comes Shahida now.' She broke off the awkward embrace and lunged for the emaciated woman wrapped in a silk sari who had just materialised in the melee of photographers.

With a great deal of blow kissing, they resumed the sideway embrace again, this time with Shahida between them. Ali had his entire concentration focused on keeping his smile afloat. The effect of the camera flashes was dizzying, and he felt the sweat breaking across his forehead. He pulled out a handkerchief, but Shahida stopped him. 'Not now, dear. Focus on the cameras.'

Seeing the models, several people joined in, and it felt like an eternity before Ali was released from their clutches. Before going anywhere, he stopped at the bar thinking he'd have a nice stiff drink only to remember his vow of abstinence. With a tinge of misgiving, he accepted a bottle of Fiji drinking water from the bartender. It tasted exquisite. He allowed the water to slosh around in his mouth before swallowing.

'What are you doing, you silly boy?'

He whipped around to find Shahida Elahi fixing him with a beady stare. A trickle of the water down his windpipe unleashed a severe fit of coughing to which Shahida tutted loudly. 'Well, what else do you expect if you're gonna gargle your water? Water is to be gulped down; drinks are to be enjoyed.'

'Sorry,' Ali muttered. 'I don't drink.'

'Of course you don't. Now come, I want to introduce you to my husband.'

Along the way, they were accosted by several people, most of whom inquired after Meera's time of arrival. Shahida ignored them. She brandished Ali in front of her as if he was a particularly interesting pet she had managed to get hold of, explaining his various achievements in the modelling world, and how he had gained the status of a celebrity in such a short time. It grew tedious after a while, being paraded around as a commodity.

'I am going to kill Meera,' Shahida hissed. 'This is my fortieth wedding anniversary and she was supposed to be here. I paid her to be here, and instead she sends me a group of amateurs.'

Ali didn't feel the least bit affronted. Instead, he said coyly, 'Iqra's a big star.'

'Bah,' Shahida barked. 'Expired meat. Her ship sailed a long time ago. You don't understand how the minds of these high-society people work. You're still a green little boy from the countryside. These people notice each and every thing like a bunch of starving hawks. A single display of weakness or mediocrity, and they'll swoop down on you. I wouldn't be hosting any further events of this magnitude if their belief in my social power wanes.'

Mr Elahi turned out to be a far warmer and more hospitable person than his wife. He dismissed his wife's complaints about Meera with a wave of his hand, and with the other shook Ali's. For a man his age – seventies, Ali assumed – his grip was firm. 'So this is the boy who's been going places? The rising star?'

Ali smiled. 'Hardly, Sir, but you're very kind to say so.'

'Oh enough with the modesty, young man. Do you think my beautiful wife would have invited you to this party if you weren't someone? Even my rheumy old eyes caught the barrage of photographers vying for your photo.'

Ali glanced around the hall, desperate to move elsewhere. He could sense a trick on the part of Elahi, but seeing no one he recognised among the deluge of people pouring into the living area, he stood where he was, helpless to his fate. Soon, however, it appeared that Elahi didn't have a hidden agenda after all. He had just nursed aspirations of becoming a model or actor back in his youth, a line of career that had been instantly and rightfully – according to social conventions – quashed by his father.

'Oh that was quite a time, my boy, quite a time.' Eagerness replaced the wistfulness in his eyes. 'From what I hear, the film industry isn't doing too bad these days. We're well past those days of atrocious Punjabi films. I'm sure you keep up with the times?'

'Of course, Sir,' Ali replied, not certain of where the conversation was veering.

'I have a few friends that work in the film industry, big producers,' – he winked at him – 'nothing that old Shahida knows about. I figured what she didn't know wouldn't kill her. But my point is that these people are not just ordinary producers. They carry a lot of weight, and I don't really have much occasion to meet bright young talent these days, but seeing you here, it just occurred... Oh, well perhaps not.'

Ali's hopes swelled. 'Can you do that, Sir? Introduce me to producers?'

Elahi hesitated. Ali noticed how his eyes wandered over to where his wife stood chattering with a group of ladies. 'We shall see, we shall see my boy. It depends on how good you are at certain things.'

Ali persisted. 'Can I at least have your visiting card, Sir?'

'My what? Oh, yes yes, of course, but I seldom answer my mobile phone. You'd be better off giving me your contact number so that I can contact you if something meaningful comes up.'

Ali dashed back to the bar, scribbled his contact details in a neat hand, and had just handed the piece of paper over to Elahi, when he noticed a change in the air, a break in the conversation. Every eye turned toward the entrance.

'My word,' Elahi breathed. 'She's as beautiful as ever. But what's this precious gem doing with Bilal and his wife?'

'They're close friends,' Shahida whispered, catching Ali by surprise, who hadn't noticed her approach. 'Meera and Mona, they're inseparable these days. Hmph.'

'Bilal's a fair businessman, but I don't like his attitude. He seems to think he's doing everyone a favour just by existing.'

'Mona's no better,' Shahida spat. 'Arriving fashionably late to my party? They can pull these tricks with riffraff like the Kamrans or Subhans, but not us. And look at that conniving thing, Meera. Sending her models ahead of her like sheep for slaughter. The photographers almost ate them alive.'

'I'm sure they enjoyed it. Didn't you Ali, my boy?'

Ali's answer died into a noncommittal noise at Shahida's alarm. 'Your boy? Indeed. Dug your roots nice and easy there, didn't you Ali?'

'I don't know what you mean.' He kept his voice even, but he was liking this lady less and less every second.

'Meet a rich man, and milk him for all you're worth? I'm not sure why I'm even taking offence. That's the way of the world, is it not, darling?' She looped a bony arm around her husband's fleshier one.

'Well at least Meera managed to arrive, Shahida. You have to give credit where it's due. I'll have none of your unjustified wrath against our guests.'

'It would be my last day on earth when I give harlots like her the time of day. Modelling industry, my foot. They're just running a flesh trade in the name of films and shows.'

Ali felt his blood boil, but then a small voice spoke in his head. 'Isn't all that she's saying absolutely true?' He shook his head, a gesture Elahi mistook for vehemence. He looked at his wife in consternation.

'Now why would you say such a thing, my dear? It's a perfectly respectable profession.'

'I would have spat on the ground if we weren't in polite company.'

Elahi's forehead creased with wrinkles and the folds of skin under his chin quivered. Ali's stomach fell. He hoped Elahi wouldn't go back on his promise. It seemed cruel to sow a potential idea only to rip it away soon after germination.

Aware of Shahida's icy stare in his direction, he sensed he had overstayed his welcome standing alongside Elahi, so he turned around to slip away.

A hand on his shoulder held him back. It was Elahi.

'Ah here comes Bilal and his wonderful wife now. Behave, Shahida.'

'Don't I always?' Shahida replied, her feral smile now fixed on the new arrivals.

The man called Bilal strode forward with a broad grin plastered on his face. 'Elahi Sahab!' he cried, embracing Elahi. They broke apart to shake hands. Bilal's wife, Ali noticed, trailed along behind him, her face impassive and unremarkable, as if she were already bored of the people around her...

He realised she was the woman he had seen at the fashion show weeks ago, the mysterious woman whose silence had spoken louder than the banter in the hall.

He looked away when her languid gaze passed over him. He feared she would recognise him although he couldn't be certain what he was scared of. He had just looked at her for a minute (maybe less), and he doubted she would even remember his face. Sure enough, when he looked up again, she had already moved on, folding herself into the extended arms of Shahida. Despite the supposed warmth, Ali caught the friction between the two women, how Shahida enveloped the other woman in an awkward, bony embrace, which the woman reciprocated with a light pat on the back.

Ali was close enough to listen to their stilted exchange.

'How wonderful that you could make it to the party, dear,' Shahida said, her voice like poisoned honey. 'Late as usual though, and not by a few minutes but a full hour. I wonder if the traffic in the city was that bad?'

'You know how it is, Shahida,' the woman called Mona replied, her face tense with the effort of keeping her voice even.

'No, I don't. Please explain.'

Mona bit her lip, her pleading gaze shifting to her husband.

Bilal simply shrugged his shoulders, and leaned toward Elahi's outstretched lighter to light the cigar he held between his lips.

'Well? Is there a particular reason why you and Meera decided to derail my party, or was it just for fun? Let's torment the old couple just because we can. How convenient.'

'I – no of course not. I say, how wonderful the décor is today, Shahida. One can never go wrong with red roses. How splendid.'

'Hmmm. Well, it's J & M, if you must know,' she said with a smug look on her face. 'The best event organisers in town. Now if you would excuse me, I need to go and have a few words with your friend Meera.'

Brushing off the flattery of a tipsy Iqra who attempted to swarm over her, Shahida drew her sari around her thin body with sharpness, and strode toward where Meera stood with a group of admirers. She wore a scarlet gown with her hair thrown across her chest to reveal her naked back.

Ali's attention was torn from Meera by a hard smack on his back from Elahi. 'And this here is one of our emerging celebrities, the famous model, Ali.'

'Ah,' Bilal said, narrowing his eyes at Ali. He was a tall, broad-shouldered man with salt-and-pepper hair slick with gel and sharp, angular features. He gave off an impression of robust health, the way his jacket strained to hold in his frame. 'I think I've seen you somewhere.' His question held genuine curiosity, but it was a lesson in humility for people like Ali. Here was hard proof of how forgettable models like him were. It took more than one show to establish universal recognition. Seeing Bilal's face, straining to place him, he knew how far he still had to go.

He extended a hand toward him. 'I was a model at Meera's inaugural show in Lahore. You may have seen me there.'

'Ah, of course. That's indeed where I saw you. I don't have time to attend many of these parties, but I try to keep myself abreast of the times.'

'Brilliant model, this boy, I tell you. He's a rising star of our long-suffering industry.'

'Yes, I recall the stir he caused during the show. People here don't set much store in male models for obvious reasons, but Ali managed to turn faces in his direction that day.'

'You're very kind,' Ali replied. It was one thing to have female admirers, but to be praised by men… He was still getting used to it.

Bilal's eyes danced with amusement. 'You seem very taken with the boy, Elahi Sahab. Is he going to be your new protégé?'

'Oh, I just like to promote new talent when I can.'

Ali didn't like the way Bilal was smirking. 'Have you met my wife? Mona, come here, love.'

He threw an arm around his startled wife's waist, and pulled her closer. 'We were going to have a nice romantic night at home had it not been for your invitation.'

'Bilal!' Mona's eyes widened. 'Stop it.'

'Come on, love. Don't be so coy.' He turned to Elahi. 'We've been trying to rekindle our romance these past few days. Quite successfully, I assure you.'

'Aha,' Elahi cackled. 'Let us in on the sordid details. It's not like Shahida and I have anything left to boast about. I don't think I even know what she looks like now sans her saris. Probably all skin and bones.'

'Yeah right,' someone piped in, a round-faced man with greasy skin and a bulging belly that he tried to hide with his hands. 'A man as fit as yourself at your age? It doesn't seem worth the effort to maintain your body unless you're scoring some.'

'Jamil, my dear man, who said anything about outright abstinence? The flame of love with Shahida might have gone out, but you can rest assured everything else is in working order, and being used quite effectively.'

'Excuse me, gentlemen.' Mona's face was pink and her hands had gone white from the force with which she held her clutch. 'I just saw a friend of mine.'

'Wait, I'll come with you,' Bilal told her.

'No, it's okay, you stay here.'

'Wait.'

Mona stayed, her head bowed in acquiescence. He felt bad for her. No woman deserved to have the details of her intimate life thrown at other men, especially ones who acted like a pack of rabid wolves.

Elahi resumed the conversation. 'Bilal's been swallowing all my steel, Mona. He's a construction magnate, this husband of yours. You've got twenty projects under construction now?'

'How wonderful,' Mona replied in a small voice.

'Twenty-one if you count the new housing society,' Bilal boasted.

'You don't mean the one near the border? How did you even get the government to sanction that piece? It practically shares its boundary wall with India. You don't want people to think you're colluding with the Indians.'

They shared a good laugh. A few more men, all clad in elegant evening suits, joined them, in a formidable circle of male bonding.

The city's elite in all their glory, Ali thought.

He watched as Bilal ignored his wife, and dived into the latest government scandals that had come to light.

Mona glanced around, ill at ease although she was dressed in a comfortable black shirt that fell to her knees and a loose pair of pants. Apart from a pair of small ruby earrings, she was unadorned. Her face told him how much she yearned to get away from her husband, but he could also tell that she had yet to spot a friend in the crowd. Meera, in her characteristic manner, was chatting away with a pair of photographers, guffawing at the pictures they showed her.

His view of Mona got obstructed as she edged away toward the bar, one step at the time until she melted into the crowd. Elahi once again lunged for him, shoving him deep into the group of men he was chatting with. Bilal's lips twitched at the affection Elahi showed him as if in secret knowledge of something, and in a moment of alarm, Ali shook off Elahi's arm that was draped across his back, and put a respectable distance between them. He may have imagined it, but for a moment, he had felt Elahi's hand hover at the small of his back and then a little further down.

Chapter Eleven

Mona

It was easy getting a glass of diet soda. The bartender didn't give her a second glance as he handed her the innocuous drink. She waited until he was busy serving another customer before topping it up with whiskey. Nobody paid her any attention as she ducked out of the open window and into a large expanse of lawn, lit by outdoor candles and the light coming from the street ahead. She had slid the window shut on her way out, and in the deathly quiet, she looked back at the celebrations inside. It looked like a scene from a movie, just muted. She downed the drink in one gulp and rolled the glass into a nearby flowerbed.

Alia and Shabeena had stood her up again, but was it any surprise? Who would want to attend a party thrown by someone like Shahida unless they really had to? Unlike Mona, her friends had no such obligations. Even Meera had tried to delay her arrival as much as she could, going so far as to endure Bilal's company in the car just so that she could pin the blame on them for running late. She shut her eyes at the memory of Bilal's behaviour in the car, at his lewd remarks to Meera, the looks he gave her, the painstaking care – which was ironic after the way he had flirted with her – he took to be the gentleman for her, going so far as to open the door for her when they arrived. She had to concede that Meera made men go weak at the knees, but why did her husband always act the clown? And if he did it all at his own expense, she wouldn't be bothered, but he had the nagging habit of dragging her into his outrageous conversations. She could have sworn the looks she had just received from Elahi and the men flanking him could have pierced through her clothes. She felt grossly unprepared for the capricious turns Bilal's conversation took, how they veered so close to their intimate lives that it was all she could do not to break into tears of fury while standing there.

A sudden noise of chatter and clinking glasses filled the air before being muffled as the window slid shut. Mona heard the soft tread of someone's footsteps on the grass far behind her, but she didn't pay any attention. She filled her lungs with the warm but not yet humid night air, exhaling each breath slowly. Here at this reclusive farmhouse, far away from the bustling city and its pollution, the air smelled of jasmine and blooming roses.

'It's a beautiful night, albeit moonless.'

Mona's eyes flashed open, and she bit back a gasp.

It was a man's voice.

She gave him a sidelong glance. She'd seen him inside earlier, wedged deep into Elahi's group, probably smirking at her too.

She looked away, and ignored him when he cleared his throat. There was a silence of a few moments, and she was about to put some distance between them when he cleared his throat again, more insistent this time.

'I'm going back inside,' she announced. 'I just came out here for a few minutes to clear my head.'

'People are looking for you inside,' the young man said.

'Is it my husband?' She hated the exasperation that crept into her voice.

'And some other ladies who seem to be your friends.'

'Oh thank God. That must be Alia or Shabeena. Hell, I'd even take Kulsoom if it means escaping Shahida's clutches.'

The young man laughed. 'You hate her too? God, she's oppressive. She just chastised me for enjoying a glass of water.'

'There must have been something you did wrong. Anything less than perfect, and Shahida feels duty bound to intervene.'

'I find most of the Lahori high society operates that way.'

She turned toward him, properly this time. He was younger than she had thought – mid to late twenties – but there was something about the way he carried himself, erect and knowing, that made him look mature beyond his years. It struck her then that she was having a conversation with a random stranger.

She reached for her dupatta, but realised that she wasn't carrying one. Instead, she just wrapped her arms around her chest. 'I'm sorry, I really must be heading inside.'

He looked at her by way of introduction. 'Ali. My name's Ali. I'm a model.'

Ali. Where had she heard this name? Her eyes widened.

'No way! You're the model from—'

'Meera's show, yes. Apparently, that seems to be my identity these days. The model from Meera's show.'

He meant it as a joke, but Mona didn't laugh. The abashment hit her in progressive waves, each larger than the last. How could she have missed him? This was the guy everyone had been raving about for days, the one she had locked eyes with at the show, the one she'd thought would look good with her daughter. Up close, she noticed how handsome he was.

She was aware of her hand clutching her neck in a protective gesture, as if she feared being attacked. Sensing this, Ali took a step back, and the light from the windows and the street fell across his face. His gaze was steady, understanding. It had been years since she'd engaged in a private conversation with a man who wasn't her husband or son.

'Mona,' she murmured, her voice barely a whisper that drew him toward her. 'Mona Bilal.'

Ali cocked his head. 'I know who you are. Meera talks about little else. And I was with Elahi when you came in with your husband.'

'Oh God, don't remind me.'

He apologised, but Mona waved him off. 'My husband is not what you'd call a conventional, conservative Pakistani. He likes to keep things…' she struggled for the word '…interesting.'

Ali scratched his chin. 'I wouldn't presume to be a judge of other people's behaviour, but I believe that in our culture, women deserve a certain respect. In every culture, to be honest. Not that I've ever been out of Pakistan, but from what I've seen on television and generally observed in foreign visitors, they respect their women. People here disparage their culture, their values, but I don't think they're much different from us.'

'You're very wise for someone so young.'

He smiled. It was a bright smile that showed rows of level white teeth, but since he'd stepped closer, his face had once again been shrouded in darkness. 'I'm not as young as you might think. I'm twenty-seven. Practically middle-aged.'

'Then you have no idea what being middle-aged is like. I wouldn't even call myself middle-aged, and my face says I'm past forty.'

'Forty? No way!'

Mona smiled. 'You don't need to flatter me. I'd still say you're intelligent even if you said I looked fifty rather than forty-one.'

'You're the first lady I've met who's this nonchalant about her age.'

'Don't let Meera find out that you know my age.'

In his excitement, he suddenly grabbed her forearm. 'You don't mean you two are the same age?'

He let go of her even before he'd finished his question, his eyes flashing surprise before he lowered his head. 'I'm sorry, I didn't mean to.'

The momentary contact had left them both jumpy. Mona massaged the place where Ali's fingers had made contact with her skin as if she'd been burned. She couldn't quite believe what had just happened. Was her manner suggestive enough for him to reach for her? Was that normal? Immediately, she began erecting the walls of reticence she hid behind in other people's company, and withdrew from the private space they had created between the two of them.

'I'm sorry,' Ali called back, his words sinking into a dull, diminutive whisper that the breeze carried to her ears.

Pausing before the tinted windows, she said, 'Yes, we're the same age.'

It took a little time for her eyes to adjust to the sudden brightness of the function room although it was supposed to be dimly lit. She looked behind her, but it was too dark to make out where Ali might be. She shook her head. It was just an innocuous gesture, something an eager child might do. She remembered her kids used to take hold of whatever part of her they could find, and insist on explanations. Ali had done the same. She had moved among people older than herself for so long that she had forgotten what it was like to be young. Right now, she felt a mixture of exhilaration and despair, as if her mind couldn't quite put a finger on what it wanted to feel. On one hand, it was refreshing to make the acquaintance of someone who so clearly was more interested in her than in her husband's business, not to mention a member of the opposite sex, but there was an underlying shadow of self-doubt that she had felt in his presence, as if she wasn't quite worthy of talking to someone so young. God, what was wrong with her? Was this what being on the cusp of middle-age felt like?

Her friends – Alia, Kulsoom and Shabeena – interrupted her thoughts.

'There she is,' Alia exclaimed, linking an arm through Mona's as the three of them accosted her midway to the bar. Before they could notice, Mona popped a breath mint into her mouth, realising belatedly that Ali must have smelled the spirits on her. He hadn't said a word about it. She looked back at the window, but there was no sign of him, and for a moment she wished she was back there with him. It had felt nice to be heard for once in her life, not having to pretend to be the sympathetic friend who nodded her way through every confession. Judging from Alia's harsh grip, she knew she was about to hear another of those confessions.

And sure enough, having found an inconspicuous corner in the hall, they broke into a barrage of disparaging comments against Shahida.

'She just asked me whether I had the misfortune of arriving in a donkey cart since I'm so late. Are you even allowed to treat your guests like that?' Alia was livid. 'This woman doesn't even have common courtesy. I say we boycott her.'

'She asked me whether there were any hot guys at the Centre that I'm "hell-bent" on visiting.' Shabeena had knitted her eyebrows, but Mona could detect a shadow of a smile on her lips. Shabeena caught her eye and laughed. 'I mean it's just preposterous. Men aren't even allowed into our gatherings.'

'That's exactly what doubles the allure, my dear,' Alia said, in perfect imitation of Shahida.

They broke into a fit of laughter.

'We should leave,' Shabeena said.

Mona glanced at Bilal who was still deep in conversation with Elahi, and judging by his ruddy cheeks, she could only imagine the number of drinks he'd had. Perhaps it would be better to skip the party without him, letting him haul himself back in his drunken state. But they had been doing so well over the past few weeks. Her body's capacity for sex at her age shocked her. Rather than dwindle into a dry state as most women claimed themselves to fall in after the age of forty, her desire surprised her, the mystifying spiral of pleasure that only seemed to heighten the more tender Bilal's treatment of her was. Perhaps this was love, a rollercoaster of bitterness and tenderness, of pain and pleasure. She couldn't leave him here, no matter how drunk or embarrassing he became.

And neither did her friends wish to leave just yet.

Someone with a mic had just announced the arrival of a famous singer from India, which had instantly aroused the general mood of the party.

'Oh look, Iqra has started dancing,' Alia cried. 'Looks like Ali the model is going to be joining Iqra too.'

'Ali? Where? Where's he dancing?' Mona craned her neck in the direction of the dance floor, but the lights had been dimmed further, the flickering disco lights making it even more difficult to see.

'Calm down, lady. Let's get ourselves a little closer to the scene.'

Mona willed her pounding heart to subside – what was wrong with her?

As the Indian singer settled himself into a series of peppy classics from the 1980s and 1990s (aptly chosen to imbue nostalgia and a yearning for youth that caused them to dance and cheer all the harder), Mona and her friends crept closer to the congregation of people surrounding the dance floor. Here, the smell of whiskey, air freshener and sweat had mingled to create an unpalatable stench, kind of like that of cauliflower about to spoil, only laced with a dose of spirits. Bilal was at the other end of the dance floor, his eyes fixed on the dancing forms of Iqra and Meera, both of them involved in a series of seductive dance steps with a lot of hip thrusts and chest heaving. Most of the men had their eyes trained on the dancing couple, both of whom seemed oblivious until Mona detected Iqra's furtive glances in the direction of the men, her eyes never leaving those of a particular gentleman. She took Ali, who was dancing nearby, by the hand, and threw herself against him, wrapping a leg around his hips, a gesture that drew catcalls from the audience. Ali followed her cue, but his mouth was open in wonder as he met each of her erotic steps with a restrained one of his own.

Standing next to Mona, Shabeena drew a sharp breath. 'Astakfirullah! What in the name of God is your friend doing? And her models? Look at that harlot and Ali. If not for their clothes, they might well be engaged in that unspeakable act reserved for the bedroom.'

'God forbid the thought of something as offensive as sex enter your mind, Shabeena,' Alia spoke in mock horror, winking at Mona. 'It was the stork that brought you your babies, right?'

Shabeena was poised to retort, but Mona cut her off. 'Please ladies, act like ladies for—' but before she could finish, someone grabbed her by the arm and pulled her forward.

Instantly, she found herself on the dance floor face to face with Meera. 'I thought you could use some fun tonight,' she said, bumping her hip against Mona's.

'Oh Meera, now really.'

'Here, dance with my most prime model, Ali. I wouldn't suggest going near Iqra as she's on a rampage, but Iman isn't bad. And then there are some of the others who've arrived, but I don't remember their names.'

Mona stood still, her heart pounding against her ribcage. 'Meera, I can't. Bilal's watching, but in spite of that, I cannot dance with a person I don't even know.'

'But we do know one another,' Ali spoke up from behind her. 'We met outside on the lawn while you people were busy partying,' he explained to Meera.

'Well then, what are you waiting for? Knock yourselves out.'

Meera vanished somewhere in the dense crowd, leaving Mona alone with Ali who very gallantly extended an arm in her direction. 'If I could tempt you with a dance, my lady?'

His attempt at a British accent made her smile. So many people had closed in on the dance floor that Mona had a hard time spotting her husband, but when she did, her blood ran hot. Iqra had her arms drawn around Bilal's neck, her head bunched together with his, as Bilal ran his expansive hands down her back and around the curve of her derrière.

Mona forced herself to close her open mouth, and unclench her bunched-up fists. After taking another moment to compose her expression, she smiled at Ali, and took his hand. 'It would be a pleasure.'

His hand was warm and dry, so large that Mona felt it enclose hers completely. Her breath caught in her chest as Ali ran one hand around her back. For the first few seconds, she was on edge, but Ali's hand never wandered. It remained fixed on her lower back. In time, she relaxed and allowed herself to enjoy the dance. They were doing a slow version of the traditional waltz, but she didn't dare put her own hand over his shoulder. It was still an awkward dance, with her hand slunk on her side, but when someone from the crowd signalled at the singer to crank up the pace and volume, and the singer launched into a fast track that made the waltz look useless, Ali removed his hand from her back and with one hand, twirled her, his lips murmuring the lyrics of the song. Mona thought to stop him, but the light-headedness was a welcome relief and she found herself panting when they both arrived at the edge of the dance floor.

'Wow, you can really dance,' Ali shouted in her ear over the noise. 'I swear even Meera cannot match your grace.'

Mona felt her face flaming under his gaze. 'You did most of the work. I merely stood there.'

Ali reached forward and pressed her hand, once. 'You sell yourself short. You're beautiful, Mona.'

Mona met his eyes, properly, for the first time that evening. In the flickering light, she discovered that his eyes weren't jet black after all. There was a smattering of deep hazel in his irises that she hadn't noticed in the darkness outside.

'Thank you,' she replied.

—

'Meera's party again? I'm not sure I like the sound of it.' Shabeena's sternness floated in from the cordless phone. 'I've heard some pretty nasty rumours regarding her so-called parties. Apparently, no one's up to any good there. Dancing, you say? Ya Allah! I think I had enough at Shahida's little get together the other day.'

Mona almost laughed at Shabeena's euphemisms. Curling her legs beneath her on the couch, she leaned back, the phone glued to her ear. She flicked on the television to prevent anyone outside from eavesdropping. God knew how many servants Bilal had recruited to spy on her. It had been three weeks since the party and she knew she was being watched like prey. Suffice to say, Bilal hadn't been pleased to hear she had danced with someone; Mona was thankful he hadn't actually seen her or he might have had her shackled to the couch. Still, simple fear of Bilal's displeasure was no reason to skip a party – a party well within the bounds of decorum.

'It's just a party, Shabeena,' she reasoned. 'Like the ones we have all the time. The only thing that will be different is that there will be some new people there. People we don't usually hang out with. Younger people, I guess.'

Shabeena sucked in her breath. 'So the rumours are true then. They say that the Colonel's wife was wooed by a young man at one of these parties. I didn't believe it at first, but now… One of my friends at the Centre tells me that after her husband discovered the affair, he drained all the money from his wife's account, and now she's back at her parents' abandoned house, broke and humiliated.'

'My God, Shabeena, that woman must be like sixty.'

'Exactly,' came back the terse reply. 'These single men are known to play with older women's feelings, and after extorting every single cent out of them, they abandon them.'

Mona felt it was the other way around these days. 'Maybe it's love,' she thought aloud.

'Mona! How could you? Have you forgotten we're Muslim women? Once married, we're supposed to stay with our husbands – for better or worse. We can't even think these thoughts. It's *haram*. Having an affair, why that's akin to killing someone.'

Mona switched the phone to her other ear, and got up to pace toward the window overlooking the lush gardens of her mansion. Despite Shabeena's chastising, she was at ease – as tranquil as a lake. 'Let's not be melodramatic, Shabeena. We are drifting away from the topic here. I just meant that if a woman has a chance at finding true love – even after marriage – then why shouldn't she take it up? What's the harm? And besides, divorce is allowed in Islam.'

'It is frowned upon.'

A stab of annoyance imbued Mona's calm. 'Well, so is inebriation. I see your husband does plenty of that.'

'Mona… Let's not go there.' Shabeena's tone was icy.

Mona rued her decision of confiding in Shabeena – a religious woman of all people. But what would she have done? Alia was in Spain with her husband, and instead of speaking about this with Kulsoom, she might as well announce it to the world. Kulsoom wasn't known for her discretion. That left Shabeena.

When Mona spoke, her tone was placid. 'Shabeena, listen to me. I'm not a child. I think I'm capable of making it through a party without sleeping with a guy half my age.'

'Don't go,' Shabeena pleaded. 'Not when there's been that dreadful blast in Peshawar last week. Lahore might be next.'

'If I let the bomb blasts dictate my life, Shabeena, then I'd be stuck at home for a very long time. And besides, attending these parties is my way of standing up to these terrorists.'

'But you don't know,' Shabeena insisted. 'The women at the Centre told me, oh the sins unsuspecting women have committed, you have no—'

'Oh please, not the Centre again, Shabeena.' Her patience, already worn thin, had snapped. 'Those women are hypocrites; you know they are. Desperate old bores lusting for a fling, but too self-righteous to admit it.'

Shabeena's silence told her that the hit had struck too close to home. Mona cursed herself inside, before taking a deep breath. 'Look, Shabeena. You're one of my best friends, and that's the reason why I confided in you about the party. I didn't ask for your opinion. I simply needed a friend, not a lecture. And about the Centre, I'm sorry. That was uncalled for. Can you forgive me?'

But Shabeena had hung up.

'Great!' What a useless bunch of friends she had. For once she needed these women, and this was how they repaid her kindness. Had Shabeena forgotten the hours Mona had spent with her as she nursed the wounds she had suffered from her husband's drunken beatings? Where were her religious friends then? And Alia? Ten days, and she hadn't even bothered to grace Mona with a phone call. And the less said about Kulsoom, the better. It was just like talking to a ten-year-old. Disgraceful – the whole lot of them.

Mona turned away from the window, and flung the phone toward the couch. It hit Bilal's treasured Lalique crystal vase instead, and both things shattered on the wooden floor. 'God!'

She flung her bedroom door open, and yelled for Shugufta. She'd be damned before she allowed Bilal a chance to complain about this too.

Satisfied with Shugufta's reply of 'Ayi Bibi!' she retreated back into the room, and stepped into her walk-in wardrobe. Today was Tuesday, and the party was supposed to be on Saturday. *Excellent*, she thought as she rummaged through her wardrobe for suitable clothes. Bilal would be on one of his little clandestine excursions, the ones he thought she didn't know about. Making an excuse for work on Saturday, he would drive off to Johar Town to meet one of his darlings. He tried to mask the scent of women by drenching himself with cologne, but Mona knew. She always knew, but never said anything. Their attempt at rekindling their romance had only lasted a few weeks. Mona was back to drinking in the guest room to drown her anger, and lately, indifference in the clichéd bottle of rum.

Not anymore.

He didn't even deserve her indifference, especially after he had continued his affairs despite their so-called romantic reconciliation. It had just been an excuse to get her more passionate in bed, and it had succeeded. Thinking too highly of him, she had abandoned keeping tabs on his whereabouts, and convinced herself of his love for her. And then, just like delicate china, the dream had shattered into a million shards after she went through his mobile phone one night when Bilal was in the shower and discovered not one, but three girls he was in a relationship with.

Her eye caught a flashy red dress with a provocative slit that showed a considerable amount of leg. Bilal had gifted it to her in one of his rare acts of contrition, or more likely when he hadn't found satisfaction outside, and came looking for it at home.

She hugged the dress, and admired the effect in the mirror. It looked splendid, and would look even more so with some red lingerie. She'd have to get some from the store, but that wasn't a problem. Nobody would raise an eyebrow. Who would even think of faulting a dutiful wife striving to please her husband?

A crackle of laughter burst from her mouth at the thought.

Over the past few weeks, she had surprised even herself with the sudden shift in her mood, and behaviour. There was an unyielding need to follow Meera's example, to revive her beauty again. She had begun to live again, to breathe again.

'Thank God for you, Meera,' she murmured, spraying one of her old perfumes in the air in anticipation of the reek of sweat and unwashed clothing that always accompanied Shugufta.

Chapter Twelve

Mir Rabiullah

The girls undressed without making a sound. They shrugged out of their dull wool dresses, revealing bodies charming enough to melt a rock. The headscarves were the last to go. Mir Rabiullah watched them hoping that this time he'd experience something even close to excitement.

But nothing. It seemed like he had finally arrived at an age where the allure of the female body melted away into nothing. He covered himself with a sheet and ordered them to leave.

'But, Mir Sahab, we've been instructed—'

Rabiullah slapped the girl. She crumpled to the ground. 'You dare speak up to me? You foul-mouthed bitch. Get out of here.'

'They'll beat us if we leave now,' another girl whimpered. 'They'll know we didn't do our job.'

The girl looked to be no more than fourteen years old. *And already in the flesh trade*, the Mir thought. No wonder the government was gaining ground on them. He could feel a headache coming on, and if he didn't get rid of these girls, he would end up strangling them.

He hated being old.

Someone coughed outside his tent.

'Come in,' Rabiullah said, throwing on a kameez over his body.

It was Usman, one of their more senior recruits, about to head out on a suicide mission. He lowered his eyes when he saw the naked girls cowering in the corner. 'The Leader has asked for you, Mir Sahab,' he said.

Rabiullah had a sudden idea.

He spread his arms. 'As a token of my appreciation for what you're about to do, Usman, you may spend some time with these girls. Bring your friends too.'

'But Mir Sahab,' one the girls gasped, 'they are animals. We were only instructed to—'

'Silence,' Rabiullah shouted. 'You will do as I say or I shall have you stoned to death. And not a word to anyone.'

Usman's eyes went wide with hunger. Rabiullah patted his back as he exited the tent.

Usman kissed Rabiullah's hand. 'Mir Sahab, I thank you.'

As Rabiullah walked away from the tent, he spotted four other recruits rushing inside.

He smiled.

He was panting by the time he arrived at the Leader's tent.

Inside, everyone was silent.

One of the men rose from his place to offer his seat, but Rabiullah brushed him away. His place was next to the Leader. He navigated his way through the bamboo mats, careful not to step over bowls of porridge that people were having. In the middle, on a large, patterned cushion, sat the Leader. His eyes were closed and even at this age, he held his back straight, his entire posture erect. *He probably had no problems in bed*, Rabiullah thought, surprising himself at the bitterness he felt.

He thought of Usman and the boys ravaging the girls and he shivered with pleasure. He lowered himself in front of the Leader and kissed the hem of his kameez. 'You called me?'

The Leader didn't open his eyes. Rabiullah noticed that he had applied kohl to his eyes, something he only did on special occasions.

'What has happened?' he asked the person seated next to him.

He shook his head. 'The Leader has received word about our newest recruit, the one Samiullah had trained.'

'The one we sent to Karachi?'

'The very same.'

'Indeed,' Rabiullah replied, his throat going dry. 'And the word is?'

'Failure,' the Leader said, opening his eyes.

The gathering quailed at the anger in the Leader's voice.

'Samiullah has failed me. The recruit was arrested before he could perform his duty. The Karachi centre might be under threat.'

There was a collective intake of breath around the room.

The Leader held up his hand to the gathering of people. 'But no matter. Samiullah will pay for his mistakes.' His gaze turned toward Rabiullah. 'Did you enjoy the gift of girls I sent you?'

Before Rabiullah could reply, the Leader continued, 'Good. I want you to flush everything out of your system so that your devotion to the cause is complete.'

'When has it ever been in question, Abuzar?' Rabiullah whispered.

Rabiullah relished taking the Leader's name, something no one else in the camp could boast of.

'Good,' the Leader replied, his eyes dancing with intrigue. 'Because I have a plan.'

Chapter Thirteen

Ali

Ali blew out a thin cloud of smoke into the air. His throat itched from the cheap fag. Stubbing the cigarette butt in the crystal ashtray, he grimaced at the bitter taste in his mouth.

Majeed, however, seemed to be enjoying himself. Leaning back against the bamboo wicker chair with one arm thrown around his new girlfriend, Rubeena, he puffed thick plumes of white smoke in the air. She would have been desirable if not for the ripe smell of her. Ali sat with his head tilted back to avoid the overpowering stench of sweat mixed with damp clothes that Rubeena exuded. The fact that she had doused cheap perfume over herself did nothing to alleviate the raw smell, but instead heightened its pungency.

The days were longer now in May, and uneasiness seemed to fill the air. With the rising heat came the easily provoked Lahori tempers, the streets serving as ludicrous scenes for frequent brawls between people. The resentful middle class held the air-conditioned cars of Lahore's minuscule elite class in unwavering contempt, and in their frustration, they launched on each other, out on the streets for everyone to see. Muttering curses as they boarded sweltering, overcrowded buses, their faces wore ugly looks as they fell into a renewed clamour for a seat on the bus. The lucky ones, like Ali, owned motorcycles. Anything was better than the buses and rickshaws, the slow and systematic descent into dehydration.

Safe inside the air-conditioned café now, the mad scramble of traffic seemed harmless. The new motorcycle had taken a chunk out of his savings, and unfortunately, that wasn't the only extravagance he had been able to afford. With money came an inexplicable power, a forceful urge to spend, rise, and dominate. His mother only had a hint of his improvidence, and yet, the way her blue eyes bored into him assailed him with guilt. He shuddered to imagine what she would say if she knew the full extent of his flagrant disregard for money, the truth about his visit to the car dealer yesterday, followed by a negotiation with the bank to take out a car loan. And there was still the matter of Hussain's prosthetics to consider. The doctor had quoted a cost so staggering that Ali's mind had reeled. He needed money for the procedure, but then, he also needed the car. How could Hussain ever hope to get anywhere without a car?

Majeed made a noise somewhere in his throat, and Ali started. He fidgeted in his hard seat, coaxing his butt out of its deep slumber. His efforts were rewarded by the familiar tingle of nerves awakening to the restored blood supply.

Throat cleared of phlegm, Majeed leaned in toward Rubeena for a kiss.

Ali averted his gaze and he saw Gul, Rubeena's sister, do the same.

Majeed didn't just go for a peck.

Rubeena gave Majeed a playful shove, her face ablaze. 'Haye Ji, get off me. What would your friend say? This isn't something respectable girls of our society do. And out in public, no less.'

The irony wasn't lost on Ali.

Rubeena's sister, Gul, gave a solemn nod. 'Indeed. These things are best left for the bedroom, to be done after marriage.'

Giggling, Rubeena loped her arm through Majeed's, and rested her head on his shoulder. She spoke Urdu with a thick Punjabi accent. 'Gul, you're absolutely right. I'm not some Heera Mandi trash, okay? I'm from Samanabad. Our father is a highly respected businessman, and we live in a *badi haveli.*'

For all her self-righteousness, however, Gul couldn't keep her eyes off Ali. He noticed her suggestive smile; the bobs of her head that stirred the tendrils of curly hair that hadn't been sprayed into a hard clump. Her smile revealed teeth stained with red lipstick that she quickly wiped when she saw his alarmed expression. At least she didn't stink. That was all Rubeena.

'You've been awfully quiet man,' Majeed observed, having received a temporary reprieve from the clutches of Rubeena.

'My thoughts exactly,' Gul remarked.

Ali gave a noncommittal shake of his head, and took a heavy drag on his cigarette. He hadn't spoken a single word throughout the meeting.

Rubeena's eyes narrowed. 'What is it, pretty boy? We look like cheap company to you?'

Ali met her blazing stare. 'Did I say that?'

'Well, you implied as much, didn't he, Gul? I tell you, we are respectable girls from Samanabad, and we live in a—'

'*Badi haveli.* Yes, I got that part.'

'Huh! Make fun of me all you like, but the fact is that we are old blood. Our ancestors were *from* Lahore, not some filthy inbred migrators from faraway lands. At least we aren't like the trash that parades around this city these days, passing off as "elite" class. Hmph! Stark naked both physically and morally.'

Gul sniffed. 'They really do cross boundaries. Imagine Rubeena, they hire models for dirty work. The shame. When the escorts can't sate their appetite, they turn to models. Pay them by the hour from what I've heard.'

He felt the colour rise in his face, and for a horrible moment, he thought they knew about his past – his humiliation. His suspicions were dispelled when Rubeena said, 'Sure enough. We read about it on the internet. Disgusting little tarts these rich women are. *Kharaab*, every one of them. What's the name of that new woman flaunting herself on magazine covers with a brigade of her junkie models? Maira, is it? No, Mala...'

'Meera,' Ali said, relaxing in his seat. Except for their ridiculously high opinion of themselves, these girls were harmless. Cruel, but harmless.

'Exactly!' Rubeena straightened her hair, and smacked her sticky lips where the lipstick had congealed. 'At least you got something right.'

She rummaged inside her handbag, and produced an ancient lipstick thick with grease.

Rubeena began a monologue on the indecency with which Meera carried herself as she lathered some lipstick on her already gleaming lips, and while Majeed and Gul listened to her with rapt attention, Ali found his thoughts wandering. If this was Majeed's idea of decent and 'youthful' company, then Ali was glad to be single.

Maybe he was damaged by his exposure to the fancy rich ladies, but he just couldn't imagine himself going out with one of these girls.

His thoughts drifted toward Meera's parties where the ladies had smelled like an assortment of flowers in a bouquet. Most of them were too old for him, but some retained a lingering vitality. Their posture suggested a peculiar yearning, of dreams unfulfilled, and of nights not slept. Mona's face flashed in his mind. So beautiful, and so unaware of her own beauty. Ali wished to see her again. Meera had mentioned some new, private party she was organising for close friends, but he didn't know if Mona would attend. Something told him that Mona wasn't like the rich ladies he knew. She seemed pure, unadulterated, like the pristine water of the Himalayas. Her flickering gaze and almond-shaped eyes were enough to drive anyone crazy.

'Ali! What do *you* think of Meera?' Rubeena suddenly asked him, a smirk crossing her lips. Her lips replenished with plenty of red, she looked like a hungry vampire.

Dazed from thoughts of Mona, Ali hesitated before replying, 'What can I say that would do justice to that brilliant woman? She gave me work when I was at my worst. She's a life saver, a wonderful human being.'

'*Acha?*' Rubeena's gaze bore into him. 'Well then, why hasn't she offered any help for your brother's treatment?'

He froze for a moment before setting down his teacup back on the table gently. 'What is this, Majeed?'

Majeed looked at him pleadingly. 'Man, listen. It's not the way you think it is. Just hear me out.'

'Yes,' Rubeena exclaimed, a smug look on her face. 'Majeed told us everything about your brother and that filthy woman's insensitivity.'

Ali would realise later how hard his fist had struck the table. His teacup and saucer flew from the table, smashing into pieces a foot away. Gul clutched her own drink in alarm. All three of them flinched. 'How dare you bring my brother into this?' He could hear his teeth grinding. 'And how dare you tell them about my personal life, Majeed?'

Majeed lowered his head in shame. 'I know this is no excuse, but I'm worried about Hussain too.'

'Oh yeah? You show up in my life after three years, and all of a sudden you're interested in what happens to my brother? Just admit it, Majeed, you were having a laugh with these girls at my expense.'

'No wait, this isn't what Rubeena meant,' Gul began, but Ali rose from his seat.

'I'm out of here.'

The three of them rose with him. Gul touched his arm. Ali sprang back as if bitten. 'Don't touch me.'

'Oh for God's sake, be a man,' Rubeena spoke up. 'At least listen to what Gul has to say. No wonder this country is going to the dogs when our patience has shrunk to the size of a bean.'

Ali was breathing hard. 'Just keep my brother out of this.'

'There's a person,' Gul spoke hurriedly, her hands clasped in front of her so that she wouldn't reach out to touch him again. 'Mir Rabiullah. He runs a charity organisation that helps victims of bomb blasts.'

'A charity,' Ali echoed, his voice rising. 'A charity? Go find somebody else to shower your altruism on.'

Rubeena pressed her fingers into her temples. 'Does this guy even have a brain?' She rounded on him. 'Wake up and smell the coffee. Seeking help from someone who offers it willingly isn't charity. Prosthetics and post-operative care for amputees is notoriously expensive, not to mention frequently botched in Pakistan. Do you really want your brother to end up nursing a stump for life?'

'Why do you care?'

'Because I work for the Mir,' Gul replied. 'For the past three years, I've been a member of his organisation. He's an excellent human being, and he's got aid coming from all sorts of places. When Majeed mentioned your brother, we thought we might be able to help. Rubeena was just trying to tease you with the earlier conversation. We would really like to help... in any way we can.'

'At least think about it,' Majeed said in a small voice.

Ali's rapid breathing had subsided. Only yesterday, his mother had asked him about hiring a physical therapist and the possibility of prosthetics. It didn't help that Hussain had developed a severe infection in his stump that had induced a flurry of hospital visits, siphoning off money from his savings. He needed help; he knew that.

'And suppose I meet this Mir,' he started, 'what then? What does he ask in return?'

Gul was quick to reply. 'Nothing.'

'Nothing?'

'All he asks for is prayers for the wounded and unfortunate.'

'Sounds like a trap.'

'We can visit him today if you wish. I've told him about your case, and he says he'd be glad to help. He'll meet us in person. He doesn't do that for everyone.'

Ali narrowed his eyes. 'I still don't understand why you're helping me.'

Gul smiled. 'Because you're Majeed's friend, and if you weren't blind to what's in front of you, you might notice that my sister and your friend are a thing. He will be my brother-in-law—'

'Whoa, easy there,' Majeed said, but Ali noticed that his ears had gone red, and he was smiling – widely.

'So, that being the case, in addition to my being a member of the organisation, I thought it only proper to mention my offer to you. Why else do you think I've been sitting here, enduring their kissing sessions? Contrary to what you might have perceived, I have better things to do.'

His earlier rage having evaporated, Ali now felt shame spread through him. When had he become so wary of women, of friends?

Rubeena held up a hand before he could open his mouth. 'Not another word. I'm going to have an ice cream after the way you just grilled us. And you'll pay. We can chat later.'

–

Mir Rabiullah lived in the outskirts of Lahore, somewhere in Bedian – mainly a rural area that had recently been taken over by the elite who, ignoring the dilapidated roads and open drains, had erected large farmhouses, some of them so large that they could easily have housed schools and colleges. The Mir's home was nothing extravagant, but it was very large. Nestled in a small hamlet off Bedian Road, his compound stood on an unpaved road littered with trash and detritus. However, as the tall, mud walls of the compound came into sight, the street became notice-ably tidier. Gul drove a small Suzuki Mehran, gifted to her by the Mir for her exemplary dedication toward his cause. After a few days of futile reflection, Ali had given into her offer after a horrid night spent listening to Hussain's sobs. To his relief, he found that he could face his family in the mornings now, something he hadn't been able to do for the last few days as Hussain's condition had deteriorated, and Ali had been helpless, at the mercy of the doctors who either wouldn't or couldn't tell him about anything that would alleviate Hussain's pain. 'The bane of public health-care,' Gul had called it, when they were on the phone last night. 'Choosing not to give a shit about people. That's Pakistan for you. I promise you Mir Rabiullah will treat Hussain like he would his own son.' After that, there was nothing more to be said except make plans for the visit to the Mir the next day.

'Helping people financially is only one aspect of the business,' Gul explained as she navigated a bunch of potholes. 'Mir Sahab also believes in psychologically rehabilitating people affected by tragedy and trauma.'

When Ali voiced his confusion regarding the term, Gul smiled. 'Classic big city thinking, Ali,' she chided. 'I don't mean that these people are crazy or something. Psychological rehabilitation is making sure the survivors of bomb blasts are able to function in society after the trauma they've suffered. In our tribal areas, especially Waziristan, where bombs go off nearly every day, people not only lose their limbs, but sometimes their entire families. Entire communities wiped out of existence at the mere whim of a single person controlling a drone. It's as if we're as irrelevant as flies.'

Ali was impressed by her enthusiasm, and a little disgusted at his lack of empathy for his own people until now. It was funny, but it had never struck him that the tribal areas might have been a part of Pakistan. Sitting here in Lahore, Waziristan might as well be as far as Antarctica, and as unapproachable too.

'I'm ashamed by how I judged you the other day. You and your sister. This world has been so unforgiving toward me my entire life that even when kindness was right in my face, I refused to acknowledge it.'

'Don't mention it.' Gul drummed her fingers on the steering wheel, tilting her head to look at the looming compound. 'Well, here we are.' She hitched up her scarf (she was wearing a scarf today and a long shirt with full sleeves) so that her hair was hidden from view and with a thumb and forefinger, she rubbed at her lips to wipe away any remnants of lipstick. 'Mir Sahab never objects, but it's not proper decorum to appear before him in make-up and inappropriate clothes.'

Ali raised his eyebrows as Gul flagged down a man in an ordinary shalwar kameez to open the solid metal doors.

'Why does Mir Sahab need all this?' He gestured around the men with Kalashnikovs strung around their shoulders and the ten-foot high mud brick walls. 'The presence of so many weapons is alarming for a charity organisation.'

Gul parked the car under the shade of an ancient acacia tree, and stepped out. 'With the kind of people we're helping, we are a major terrorist target. The local police don't care, but that doesn't mean we can't do something about it ourselves.'

Apart from the bunch of men milling around the gates, the place was deserted at this time of the day. The sun beat down mercilessly on their necks and Gul ushered them into what seemed like a large two-storey structure with an old wooden door that creaked when she opened it. For the headquarters of a major charity organisation, the building was woefully unequipped. The entrance hall was lit by two bulbs, which dangled by their naked wires from the ceiling. Ali noticed that the paint on the walls was peeling and a damp odour permeated the place.

'Mir Sahab has the walls drenched with water every two hours to help keep the place cool. He hates spending money on extravagance.'

'You mean air conditioners?'

'Exactly.'

His shirt clung to his back with perspiration, and as Gul knocked on another wooden door that seemed to have seen better days, Ali raised each arm to sniff his armpits. He was fine.

'Come in,' came the genial reply from behind the door.

Fixing the scarf on her head once more, she ushered them inside. '*Asalam o alaikum*, Mir Sahab,' Gul said, lowering her head in deference.

Ali repeated the words, his own head lowered too.

'Close the door behind you, my daughter.'

Ali looked up to examine the room. It was a large space, probably big enough to accommodate a hundred people. An ancient ceiling fan whirled slowly overhead, doing a futile job of circulating the muggy air. The Mir, however, seemed unfazed by the heat. Seated on a maroon and black patchwork spread on the ground, he indicated two nearby stools. 'Have a seat.'

As they drew closer, Ali thought he heard a chorus of bright voices from beyond, as if there was a congregation gathered. Gul broke into a gushing torrent of words as soon as they were seated. She began by describing her various achievements over the past few days, her remorse over the fact that she couldn't bring her famous *kheer* for the Mir to eat considering how busy she was, ending her monologue with a fascinating retelling of Hussain's tragedy with his leg.

The Mir held up a hand. 'Is this the boy's brother?'

Gul nodded.

He extended a large, fleshy hand in Ali's direction. 'They call me Mir Rabiullah.'

'Of course,' Ali replied, shaking his hand with vigour. 'I've heard all about you.'

Mir Rabiullah laughed. 'Gul does get carried away with her approbation of me.'

He was a stocky man of about seventy years of age with a formidable mane of white hair that he kept partially hidden under a small, white cap. He sat with his legs crossed so it was difficult to tell his height, but judging by the firmness of his grip and the clarity of his eyes, the Mir was in robust health. His beard that reached to his chest was henna-dyed to a bright orange. His palms, Ali noticed, were also faintly orange, the colour more pronounced in his fingernails. He remembered the old midwives who came prior to Hussain's birth had similar hands. They would mix water into henna powder, making a thick, dark-green batter which they gathered into their fists and went to bed holding it, letting it dry in their hands. The next day, their fingers would be sore, and it would be a time-consuming task of washing off the rock-hard substance, but Ali remembered how, once the gluey substance was gone, their hands glowed a deep orange, their fingernails stained almost dark brown. They would then be purified to deliver the baby. The Mir seemed to have done the same thing, but his colour seemed a few weeks old.

'So, my son,' he began, fixing his bright green eyes on Ali's face. 'Gul has told me all about your brother, and before I say anything further, allow me to convey my deepest sadness at the turn of events. It is deplorable that our country has come to this, that a brother will now so ruthlessly take another brother's life.' He sank his head as if shamed. 'Islam does not teach us this. The Holy Quran does not teach us this. These people are barbarians.'

His voice had a melodic quality, kind of like the beady thrum of the sitar, pleasing and yet resonant in his ears. Ali could tell that Mir Rabiullah was a great speaker. The conviction with which he said each word made Ali want to believe him – in him. He nodded. 'Thank you, Mir Sahab.'

'Just look at me, how ill-mannered I am. I forgot to order refreshments.' He turned around to a door-less frame at the back of the room. An old bed sheet covered the entrance, fluttering in the air from the ceiling fan. 'Usman beta, please bring two cups, no, three cups of tea here.'

They heard a sound of assent, followed by the clanking of metal utensils.

'He makes excellent tea, just you wait.'

The tea was indeed different. It had bits of crushed almond mixed in it and an undercurrent of something spicy.

'Cinnamon,' Gul whispered to him.

Mir Rabiullah enquired briefly about the nature of Hussain's injuries, before nodding gravely. 'Such a tragedy for someone so young… May Allah give him strength to bear this. However, the nature of his injury is something we have a lot of experience in. Unfortunately, there have been enough bomb blasts in Pakistan that I have person- ally witnessed over a hundred such cases. Amputation is a serious business. We, being healthy individuals, don't understand the agony that the person affected with this goes through. Prosthetics offer relief as well as admittance back into the real world, but they have to be handled expertly. There are many doctors here in Lahore that would charge you a fortune, but will still attach a prosthetic that causes so much bleeding that the person returns to crutches.'

Mir Rabiullah's chest swelled and his eyebrows knotted together in a tight frown. 'I don't have words to condemn these terrorists, but I assure you, my son, that my organisation will bear all expenses that are incurred during the course of your brother's treatment. He will be treated privately.'

Ali felt Gul nudge him, and he hurried to close his gaping mouth. 'I – I don't know what to say.'

Mir Rabiullah smiled. 'There is nothing to say. This is what we do. We have a panel of philanthropists both home and abroad who work tirelessly to bring in donations. Coupled with how tightly I control the budget of this establishment,' – he indicated the shabbiness of the room – 'we just about manage to help more people than the budget would have allowed otherwise. I'm usually too busy to meet with individual people, but since Gul requested that I assuage any fears you had about the organisation personally… Well, suffice to say, I can never say no to Gul.'

Gul giggled. 'Mir Sahab, you spoil me.'

'But there must be something I could do in return,' Ali persisted. 'I don't want to exploit your organisation. I can manage to contribute toward the expenses. I have some money stashed away.'

Mir Rabiullah fixed him with a solemn stare. 'This is just a preliminary meeting, my son. If you wish to contribute, by all means, please do, but it is not necessary. Our accountants and managers at the office in the city will figure it all out. Today was just meant for us to get to know one another. Perhaps it was God's will.'

Ali felt some of his self-control return. He could still be of some use to his brother. 'Thank you, Mir Sahab. I don't have the words to thank you.'

A magnanimous smile broke across the Mir's face. 'Just pray for our country, our poor, long-suffering people.' He rose to his feet in a swift, balanced motion that defied his age. 'Now, before we get lost into the web of paperwork, allow me to offer you a glimpse of the kind of work we're doing here.'

With a friendly arm around Ali's shoulder, Mir Rabiullah guided him back into the poorly-lit entrance hall ('Something I've been meaning to fix, but never find the time,' the Mir remarked) and into a large, bustling courtyard full of children, probably hundreds of them. That was where the noise was coming from. They were seated on jute mats, but their clothes were clean and they seemed well kept. Cool air blasted through the cheap, locally made coolers that used water circulation to cool the air before releasing it. They were crude and loud, but did the job of keeping the temperature bearable, almost pleasant. 'I make sure not to forget my humble beginnings,' Mir Rabiullah added. 'But that is no excuse to let the little ones boil in the heat.'

He motioned toward more doors at the back. 'There are more classes being conducted down the hall while the seniors are taught upstairs. We keep juniors and seniors separate to best promote a healthy and stress-free environment.'

He stopped in front of a row of children – around the age of nine – scribbling furiously into their notebooks. 'And what did Mir Ikram teach you today?'

'Fractions!' they shouted in unison.

The Mir laughed. 'Then you're already smarter than I am. I never got the hang of mathematics. I'm more of a philosophical person.'

'What is philosophy, Mir Sahab?' A child asked, looking up. He too had the tell-tale green eyes and fair skin of the people of the tribal areas.

'All in good time, my little lamb,' Mir Rabiullah chuckled. 'All in good time.'

They passed the children and ducked into another large room, this one thick with the scent of cooking. Ali smelled the wonderful smell of roast lamb and mint chutney. 'We had a foreign dietician here once who drew up this chart for us. We try to follow it, striving to provide balanced meals that foster growth and health among our students. However, sometimes we have dinners of *nihari* and sweet cakes, all of which is quite unhealthy, but then what's life without a little indiscretion?' He squeezed Ali's shoulder. 'Of course, you two are staying for lunch.'

Ali felt assailed by a wave of gratitude so strong that he felt his heart constrict.

Chapter Fourteen

Mona

It was midday when Mona's eyes flickered open. For a dazed moment, she thought she was late to wake up the kids for school; she was about to jump out of bed when the inevitable reality hit her – they were far away in college.

'Oh.'

She groaned, clutching her head in her hands. A searing headache pounded her skull.

'Crap,' she cried, whipping the sheets off, and ducking her head under the bed. The half-empty bottle of whiskey was nestled deep in the shadows under the bed, out of sight.

Relieved, she sank back into the soft warmth of her pillow, and tried to calm her racing heart, summoning up the faces of her two beautiful children in her mind. Their bright, young faces always infused her with strength, a sense of awe that she had brought them into this world – such precious children. And how they had grown! Like eager teenagers, Farhan and Aimen had wasted no time in abandoning her in favour of the delightful life in Canada.

Still, they had to come back. Bilal expected Farhan to take over the family business, and as for Aimen, well, Aimen had to be married off soon. Already, they were flooded with potential suitors. Every weekend, new colourful families visited their home, each of them different in appearance, but all of them the same: avaricious, calculating people who lavished attention on them in the hopes of securing a bright future for their sons.

Mona watched with increasing disbelief as middle-aged mothers breezed in wearing their best diamonds for a simple house call. She had grown accustomed to the way the women displayed their jewellery to the maximum effect with the careful positioning of one hand over the knees so that the solitaire ring glittered, the way they threw their heads back to reveal the magnificent necklaces, and with hair made up in delicate chignons to reveal the expensive earrings. Things sometimes missed her scrutiny, but never her mother-in-law's. Nighat's shrewd gaze caught even the most clandestine ornament on a woman, and if there was one thing Mona could rely on Nighat for, it was her uncanny ability to weed out the useless *naway khan* (nouveau rich).

'They just try too hard,' Nighat would reply if someone questioned her about her incredible observation skills. 'And they don't have tact. Gaudy little bloodsuckers trying to get into the old crowd. Hmph!'

If nothing else, Nighat guarded her family like a faithful old bulldog, barking away the snivelling stooges. Mona stifled her mortification at the analogy, clamping a hand over her mouth to silence the snort that was about to burst out. She ran an anxious eye over Bilal. He was still asleep, *thank God*.

He had shattered her feeling of well-being last night. She hated the constant nudges to live the way he demanded, the result of which was an inevitable row.

She thought back to her conversation with the model Ali – probably the most engaging conversation she'd had with a man in years. Usually she only met the shameless friends of Bilal, many of whom considered the wives of their friends their personal property, a veritable butt of their jokes.

But Ali had been so gentle, so anxious. It had reminded her of her own youth, the constant urge to tiptoe around conversation, the need to apologise, the hesitation before speaking. It had been refreshing. She wondered when she'd see him again.

Watching her husband sleep in such joyful peace now, she wanted to pour water over his face.

With the caution of a deer, she pulled back the quilt, and attempted to rise from the bed unnoticed. While she had been adrift in thoughts, Bilal had managed to somehow throw one arm around her waist, and just as she was trying to wriggle out of his grip, the bed creaked.

Shit! she thought. The damn bed. Bilal's eyes flew open, and he sat up in bed like an electrocuted man. 'What is it? Are you okay?' His voice was thick with sleep, and his tousled hair spread over his forehead like a spray of black and white. He jerked his head back to set his hair in place, and attempted to open his eyes wider. 'It's Sunday. Why are we awake so early?' he asked again.

'Because it's almost one o'clock in the afternoon.'

'Damn, really?' Running his fingers through his hair, he looked around for his shirt. 'Slept like a log today.'

He seemed to have no recollection of last night's massive row, the row that had led to her inevitable binge on whiskey. Mona had even thrown half a glass of juice in his face – she was so angry – and to her horror, he had licked the liquid off his stubble like a hungry dog. After leaving her for the comfort of his study, he had crept back sometime in the night, and cuddled with her.

As if nothing had happened.

As he stumbled around the room now, looking for his lost shirt, the afternoon sun peeking through the curtains illuminated his body. The pyjama bottoms hung tight on his waist, exaggerating the amount of fat around it. Even though Bilal tried to keep fit, the years were taking their toll on him. His tummy had begun to sag.

However, in spite of the deterioration, his body still retained the image of brute strength, his barrelled chest and muscular arms testimony to that. He looked like he could overturn a bull.

Finding the woebegone shirt hidden under the couch, Bilal threw it on, and opened the door. Mona knew this routine: he would bark at his personal attendant to iron him some fresh clothes, bark some more about the kind of breakfast that should await him, and if the orders weren't understood, he would even step outside to give the attendant a good kick in the shins. Mona preferred the more subtle way – the intercom. Picking up the phone, she rang the kitchen and asked Shugufta for some tea and toast in bed.

Hearing the receiver being set down, Bilal turned from where he was castigating his poor assistant, and frowned at her. 'There's no time for tea in bed. The guests will be here any minute.'

Mona blinked. 'What guests?'

'God, lady, do you have no sense at all? Didn't Amma tell you last night? A very rich family from Vehari is coming for Aimen.'

'Oh please! Not again. Are you two out of your minds? For God's sake, the girl isn't even here, and we're choosing a husband for her? Without her even getting a chance to see him?'

'She can meet him when she comes.' He narrowed his eyes, his hand still on the doorknob, the door half-open. 'She's not like you. My daughter actually trusts me.'

Whoever was standing outside must have heard what Bilal had said. A violent urge to fling the lamp at him rose inside her, but Mona stood her ground, bunching up the cotton sheets in her hands. With a supreme effort, she quelled the storm of anger inside her. 'When exactly do they arrive?'

Poised to retort, Bilal was surprised to hear the evenness in her tone. A smile broke out on his face when their eyes met. 'Now, *that* is how a wife should behave. Delicate and subservient. Why, you almost look like the woman I married.' Laughing, he continued, 'They are due to arrive at one-thirty, and since they're from Vehari, I don't want to see you wearing anything inappropriate. Make sure you're fully covered. And wear a dupatta, for God's sake.'

'But I don't understand why you want to get Aimen married off so early. She just turned eighteen.'

Bilal shrugged off the shirt again, and tossed it on the bed where Mona sat. 'For an intelligent, educated woman, you're often quite obtuse.' He leaned down, looking her straight in the eyes. 'Aimen gets married as soon as she gets back from Canada, and if we don't start looking now, that is never going to happen. I don't want her to get involved in the wrong crowd, and get fancy ideas of building a career for herself.'

She could smell the morning breath on him. Wincing, she replied, 'Can you even hear yourself? What kind of antiquated thinking is that? Not build a career… What is she, a show piece to decorate the house?'

Bilal sneered. 'Worried she might end up like you?'

'Oh, get out of my face.' She pushed him aside, and rose from the bed. 'And brush your teeth while you're at it. It smells like something died in there.'

'Aww. You used to love my morning breath. Remember all those times we used to get down and dirty right after waking up? What happened?' Tossing the shirt at her, he forced a kiss on her lips, and started for the bathroom. 'You can take a shower in the guest room. It's practically your second home.'

Mona massaged her temples, as the sound of running water filled the room. She would choose the most obscene dress she possessed, and flaunt it in front of those people from Vehari. Let them see what a true urban socialite looked like. She flipped through a barrage of homely attire, and proceeded to unzip a figure-hugging dress with diaphanous Chantilly lace that left little to the imagination. Sure, she would be covered from head to foot – in lace – and yes, she would wear a net dupatta with it. Even better, she would drape it over her body in such a way so as to make it even more risqué.

With a smirk, she looked around, and hearing the reassuring sound of the shower running, she thrust the dress into her armpit, and stole into the adjacent guest room. Shugufta was waiting for her there, having no doubt heard every single word that had passed between Mona and Bilal. *Bloody servants.* Shugufta's eyes widened at the dress, but she pursed her lips, and lowered her gaze. Mona tipped her head up. 'Don't just stand there, Shugufta. Have this pressed, and then help me put it on. And I haven't hired you to have opinions about the way I dress.' She rolled her eyes at the feeble protests. 'Your expression was enough, Shugufta. Now get to work.'

By the time Shugufta had zipped the dress over her back, it was well past lunchtime. In her desire to shock, Mona had forgotten to watch the time. She slipped her feet into a pair of towering golden heels, threw the net dupatta across one side, and made for the door.

Animated voices came from the drawing room, and Mona had no difficulty in catching the unmistakable nasal twang that was native to the people of Southern Punjab. A chorus of laughs followed. *God, how many people are in there?* she thought.

'Move aside,' she ordered the maid who stood guarding the door with a rag in one hand. Mona paused, holding the shiny golden door handle, and levelled her gaze at the kitchen maid. It was Ruqayya, one of Nighat's best eavesdroppers.

Ruqayya's gaze travelled from her face, pausing somewhere around her chest after which her face reddened, and she bowed her head.

Good, Mona thought, as she pulled open the drawing room door.

The chatter ceased, as everyone turned to see the latest arrival. They were seated on the turquoise sofas at the far side of the room, beside the largest window that afforded the best view of the lawns. Nighat sat in an armchair, and Mona was pleased to see her mother-in-law's jaw drop open. So did Bilal's, who was seated in the adjacent armchair, massaging his mother's back. He withdrew his hand and clenched his fists in his lap. His eyes blazed.

Meeting his gaze for just a moment to exhibit her triumph, Mona turned away from her husband, satisfied at the impression she had produced. She moved toward the supposed mother of the groom, a stout fifty-something woman, whose expression revealed a mixture of awe and disgust. She was wearing a shocking pink silk suit underneath her embroidered white *chaddar*, her henna-coloured hair peeking from where the chaddar didn't cover it. She may have been beautiful once but age and weight had robbed her of any lingering attraction, transforming her into a shapeless bulk. Mona stepped closer, and the woman rose to give her a one-armed hug. '*Assalam Alaikum*,' she drawled, her body smelling of cheap perfume and old sweat. 'They call me Saeeda, and this is my husband, Sardar Wazir.'

'*Walaikum Salam*,' Mona replied, nodding at the white-bearded husband who gaped at her like she was an extinct species suddenly reappeared. Sardar Wazir muttered a scandalised '*By God, the women of today*' under his breath, but his gaze remained fixed on her.

Her skin crawled. Saeeda's son and daughter made no move to greet her. She ignored them, taking her seat in a lonely armchair, away from the odd family but right opposite the piercing stares of Bilal and Nighat.

An uncomfortable silence followed.

'Ahem,' Saeeda said, twisting the heavy gold necklace around her neck. 'We were just talking about Aimen. Studying in Canada, is she?'

Mona nodded, still unsure how to proceed.

'In New Yaark, right?'

For a moment, Mona just stared before recovering herself, and muttering, 'Toronto.'

Nighat gestured toward the pastries and nibbles laid out on the coffee table. 'Have some more, Saeeda, Wazir Khan. The frosted pastries are simply exquisite.'

Sardar Wazir picked up a pineapple-glazed pastry, and bit off a sizable chunk, chewing noisily. 'Tasty, but I like my kheer and *jalebis* more. Aunty *Jaan*, do you know we have entire herds of buffaloes in Vehari? The milk they produce… exquisite. You'll forget this Gora food once you have some of our desi food.'

Mona felt nausea clawing her throat. *Buffaloes?* These people had herds of buffaloes. 'And where do you people live?' she asked.

Saeeda looked stricken. 'Why Baji, we live in our haveli among our farmlands and animals. Sardar Sahab and I would die before we leave Vehari to live someplace else. Our land is our livelihood. Even Ubaid here agrees with us. After studying from Landan, he came right back to Vehari, to live with us.'

Mona cringed.

'London, Ammi, London,' Ubaid corrected her.

Ubaid leaned forward, his chubby face shining as if he had polished it with oil. His greasy hair had been swept back giving him the impression of a well-groomed pig. 'Indeed, Ammi *Jaan* is right. I missed Vehari so much while I was in London. There is something inherently wrong with a place that doesn't have cow dung drying on its walls.'

'Well said, beta,' Sardar Wazir boomed as Saeeda beamed at her son. Ubaid's face broke into a crooked smile, resembling a cat in possession of its favourite cream.

'Impressive,' Mona said, glancing at Bilal who looked like he had swallowed a bunch of stones. He met her gaze, and she saw revulsion mixed with grudging appreciation in it. He knew she had been right in questioning these people from the get-go, and she knew he would never admit it. Still, there was a certain perverse pleasure in seeing Bilal so uncomfortable.

Vehari? Buffalo farms? What had he been thinking?

Saeeda chattered on, recounting Ubaid's many qualities while Sardar Wazir nodded with his head held high. Their meek daughter (Mona never learned her name) sank lower and lower into the couch, her face veiled behind a crimson dupatta. She hadn't spoken a single word the entire time.

'Why are you so silent, beta?' Mona asked her, partly to shut Saeeda up, and partly because she was curious.

'Girls from good households don't run their mouths like a clutch of hens,' Saeeda remarked. She looked at Nighat, but if she was hoping for the old lady's approval, she was mistaken.

Nighat edged forward from her seat, her back straightening to accommodate her vast body. 'What do you mean?' she asked testily.

Saeeda seemed unperturbed. 'I said that good, sensible girls don't go talking nonsense. A girl's job is to respect and honour her husband by staying silent, and doing as she is told.'

'Always?'

'Always. To utter even a single word of disagreement is akin to committing adultery.'

'Really?' Nighat seemed to swell, her chest rising and falling in rapid bursts. 'What makes you think that? While I agree that arguing with your husband is fruitless, not saying anything at all, even when you're in the right? Why, you must possess a type of patience we're not aware of, Saeeda. Do you think I reached where I am today by keeping silent?'

Bilal put a hand over his mother's, but otherwise remained silent. Mona knew this gesture well; her husband put up this nonchalant face whenever a storm was breaking out inside him. She breathed in with satisfaction, and crossing her legs, leaned back on the soft velvet-backed chair. There was no way this *rishta* was happening.

A flicker of genuine fear crossed Saeeda's features, and her eyes darted toward her husband who was pretending to be busy examining his nails. Saeeda hastily attempted to backtrack. 'Of course, I didn't mean you, Nighat Baji. You are an elderly woman, and we should all treat our elders with respect and kindness. I only meant that independence and audacity are things that a girl should set aside once she assumes marriageable age. I mean, there are only so many well-to-do families in Lahore who would be willing to take a girl who is known for her uncontrollable mouth. Even in old age, and by that I don't mean you Baji, I believe it is better for a woman to be humble and contrite rather than risk societal expulsion by being a big mouth.'

She seemed to be going from bad to worse, and with each word, the grimace on Nighat's face deepened. 'Brashness and public speaking are not for girls,' Saeeda continued. 'Our job is to manage the home, and take an active interest in the welfare of our husbands. The thoughts of working somewhere other than home, and building a career, well it does sound preposterous if you know what I mean.'

Some amends, thought Mona, a smile threatening to break across her face. She bit it back, as Bilal stared daggers at her. The hand he had extended to cover his mother's was white with pressure to the point that Nighat freed herself from him with a reproachful glance.

The old woman now directed the full extent of her fury on Saeeda.

'You mean to tell me, Saeeda, that you'd rather shut your daughter-in-law in the home than allow her to be honest, and speak her mind? You would shut my grand-daughter in that farm of yours. Not to mention, you like relegating older women to some obscure corner of the house to lose their minds to senility in peace?'

'Of course not, Baji, I—'

'You do realise this is the twenty-first century? My granddaughter is studying in Toronto, not Vehari. She is an independent young woman who will most likely work after marriage.'

'Work?' Saeeda and Wazir Khan sputtered in unison.

'Yes, work!' barked Nighat.

'But that is simply not acceptable,' Wazir Khan exclaimed, bunching his snow-white beard in his fist, then straightening it in downward motions. 'No daughter-in-law of mine will work in the barns or factories like some farmhand.'

'Farm?' Nighat boomed.

A snort escaped Mona before she could stop it.

Bilal closed his eyes.

Shaking with rage, Nighat pushed herself out of the armchair, a formidable force. 'Get out. The whole lot of you. I've heard enough. What kind of old-fashioned thinking is this? Are you people rich agriculturists or stupid pinheads? Who let you in the house?'

Saeeda replaced the chaddar back on her head in haste, and looked at her husband for directions. Ubaid glanced at Aimen's photograph on the side table with a glum face, and pushed himself to his feet when he saw his father rising.

'*Chalo* Saeeda,' Wazir Khan said, his walking stick quivering as he absorbed the amount of disrespect ladled on him by a woman. He strode out of the room with the gait of a man much younger, the walking stick being dragged along like a rag doll.

Saeeda and her kids also departed without a word, scurrying out when they saw that no one had risen to see them off. The maid closed the drawing room doors with a resounding boom as if to emphasise the significance of what had happened, leaving Mona alone with Nighat and Bilal.

Clearing her throat, Nighat leaned back in her seat, and pulled a plate of soggy pakoras toward her. The room was so silent that Mona even heard the smack of Nighat's lips as she bit into the sweating pakora. 'Now,' she said between bites, 'before any of you pounces on me, remember that I did the right thing. There was no way in hell that those people would have kept Aimen happy. I just did you all a service.' Brandishing the pakora in Mona's direction, with bits of onion and green chilli flying out of her mouth, she added, 'Having just made this speech about women's rights, it does sound a bit ironic to say this, but I do not want my daughter-in-law to appear like this in public. Ever.'

'Get dressed,' Bilal breathed, not looking at her. With his elbows on the armrests, he was watching his fingertips as they touched. His voice was so low that Mona had to lean forward to make out what he was trying to say.

'Sorry?'

'He said that you should get dressed,' Nighat replied on behalf of her son. Licking the sticky oil off her fingers, she pointed at her. 'That Wazir Khan almost passed out at the sight of you. I repeat, don't wear this dress in front of these people. I don't care what you wear to your parties, but in this house, my rules still apply.'

Mona bristled. 'There is nothing wrong with what I am wearing, and considering the fact that I'm fully covered, I don't understand what the fuss is about.'

Nighat gave out a bark of laughter. 'Covered, indeed. That is a great improvisation of clothes if I've ever seen one.'

'I am wearing a dupatta, aren't I?'

Bilal slapped his hands on the wooden armrests of the armchair. 'Don't make me say this again. Get dressed! Now.'

Mona folded her arms, and sank into the armchair. 'Or what? And, why should I dress right in front of *paindu zamindaars* (backward feudal lords) you insist on inviting to see our daughter. Do you really want to show the world how desperate you are? The more you invite these nonentities to this house, the worse off our daughter will be. Do you honestly think that a racist, self-deprecating cow like Saeeda will keep her happy? Poor Aimen would have died of suffocation.'

'She does have a point,' Nighat remarked, sucking on a juicy chicken bone. In between the slurping noises, she patted her stomach, and moaned with satisfaction.

'Still, this shouldn't have happened,' Bilal said. 'These people have long roots in Southern Punjab, and who knows what kind of damage they may inflict upon our reputation there.'

'Oh, who cares about Southern Punjab!' Mona stamped her heel on the marble. The whole room rang with the sound of steel on stone. 'For God's sake, Bilal, let it go! Whatever happened, happened for the best.' She took a deep breath. 'You shouldn't have invited them here in the first place. We'll find a decent *rishta* for Aimen. When the time is right.'

Nighat burped loudly, and covered her mouth as she fell into the throes of a huge yawn. 'Oh well, seems like the day has come to a fantastic end before it even began.' She scanned the room for her maid before heaving herself from the armchair. The seat cushions plumped back as air rushed into them.

Ruffling Bilal's hair with a wizened hand, she added, 'You guys enjoy yourselves, and mind you, don't fight too much.'

Mona watched as her mother-in-law laboured across the vast space between the armchair and door, her numerous folds of fat wobbling as she complained about her knees.

Bilal seemed to have taken no notice of his mother. His hair still stood up at the odd angle where Nighat had ruffled it; he seemed unperturbed by it, a fact that intrigued but also worried Mona.

She pursed her lips as the door clicked shut. Sensing Bilal's simmering gaze on her, she clucked her tongue. 'Oh God, I'm starving. Did you have any lunch?' Hands on the armrest, she leaned forward to heave herself out of the chair. 'I think I'll just see what's left in the kitchen—'

'Sit down.'

'But—'

'I said *sit* down.'

His eyes looked murderous.

Without a sound, Mona sank back into the armchair, the softness of the foam encasing her rump – a difficult position to rise from in case he launched himself on her.

Bilal crossed, then uncrossed his legs, watching her from his heavy-lidded eyes, the afternoon light reflecting a macabre glint off them.

He meant business today.

Her heart began thudding painfully in her chest, but she struggled to keep her breathing even, her face impassive. She knew the drill – any sign of weakness from her and Bilal would pounce on her like a hungry lion, and devour her inside out. It had happened many times before.

She had been at Gymkhana, sipping coffee with her friends when the idea to leave for Malaysia unannounced sprang up. Mona had been married for only two years.

'Why should men have all the fun? Why can't we just run off to Malaysia? Just like that!' Shabeena had said, snapping her fingers. This was back when she was younger, and playful enough to care about what others thought of her.

Within minutes, the rest of them had agreed to the idea, and in a matter of hours maids had been forewarned to care for the kids, cash was withdrawn, and tickets were booked that would take them aboard a Pakistan International Airlines jet to Kuala Lumpur via Karachi.

'Imagine! We don't even need a visa,' Kulsoom squealed, clapping her hands together in the plane while they were leaving for Karachi. 'It's visa on arrival for Pakistanis, and I've heard one of my friends say that it's magical. Like a paradise on earth.'

Mona had called Bilal from her hotel room in Karachi that night. She had already alerted Farhan's maid regarding her departure, and since Bilal wasn't at home, she had thought she'd wait until late at night to call him.

Tilting her head sideways to balance the phone receiver between her ear and shoulder, she lathered moisturiser on her legs, a wistful smile on her face as she heard her husband's gruff 'Hello'.

'It's me.'

A pause. 'I know.'

Mona frowned at his tone, and her hands paused in their kneading of her calf muscles. 'I called Zafreen earlier, but you weren't at home. It's sort of crazy actually, and please don't laugh at me, but the girls just made a plan for Malaysia at lunch, and I sort of went with it.' She let out a nervous laugh, half expecting him to break into fits of laughter, and badger her for leaving her toiletries behind.

He didn't. A huge chasm of silence filled the distance between them, and all she could sense was his increasing heart rate as his breaths came out in short pants.

'Uh, Bilal. Are you there?'

'You fool.' The words sounded like nails on a blackboard as he ground them out of his mouth. 'What kind of a stupid mother leaves her child in the hands of a maid she hired yesterday. What the hell are you smoking, woman?'

His words took her by surprise; her mind whirled. In those early years of marriage, the fights were rare. She didn't know the drill; she had no idea how to respond. Instinctively, the words 'I'm sorry' escaped her lips.

That is when the tirade began.

'Sorry? Sorry? You think your measly little sorry covers your gaping blunder? You know Amma's in Multan, and still you left the kid alone without a second thought? Who does that? Those bloody contractors… They left. I had to leave my meeting because of your insufferable childishness. Leaving the child alone in the house. Do you know how much this has cost me? Do you?'

The phone receiver slipped from her shoulder. She caught it, abandoning her legs, pulling them beneath her. Tears slid down her cheeks in parallel lines, pooling in the nape of her neck as she kept repeating, 'I'm sorry. I'm sorry.'

Those weak, useless words rang in her head today, as she looked at her husband. The years came unravelling back at her, the undulating waves of abuse that had never tapered off, only climbed in their intensity. She could feel the heat rising from her skin as Bilal rose from the armchair and advanced toward her, his teeth bared. The rug absorbed the sound of his footsteps, and since Bilal had always been a light walker, it seemed as if he was gliding, not walking. The silence unnerved her even though she knew what to expect. This was the chase, the inevitable dance of pursuit that allowed Bilal to assert his dominance, his supremacy.

'You did this on purpose. Even after I strictly told you not to, you wore these filthy clothes in front of the guests. Are you a common slut now? Have you degraded yourself to that status?' He stopped in front of her, his leather moccasins stepping over her front toes as he leaned forward to face her.

She gasped in pain.

'You disgust me.' His shoes pressed hard on her toes, squashing the nails so that they bit into the soft flesh underneath. His breath smelled of fresh mint and Colgate, his clothes of the Mont Blanc cologne he loved.

'You're hurting me,' she cried, trying to push him off, but it was like trying to shift a bull. Her hands fell back in her lap, defeated.

She averted her eyes as he unbuckled his belt.

'Deep inside, you know you deserve what's coming,' he said as he straightened himself again. 'Who knows, a pervert like you might even enjoy it.'

'Bilal, please.'

'Shut up, Mona. You should have thought of this before you disobeyed me.'

Mona braced herself as the first blow rained down on her cheek.

Chapter Fifteen

Bilal

He splashed water on his face to hide the tears. What would his mother say if she found him weeping like a little girl?

'You are a little sissy,' she'd say, her tone brokering no argument. 'You're not your father.'

He scrubbed hard at his hands, as if cleaning them would wipe away the proof of his savagery, his inhuman nature. He'd beaten her more today than he ever had before. The thought made him want to vomit, but he forced the bile back down his throat.

She had forced his hand. She always did.

He had tried to stop himself when he saw how her body shuddered under his hand – his kicks. Her whimpers had pierced him, but it was as if a frenzy had gripped him, a longing to exact vengeance for all those years of her ineptitude as a wife.

'Why can't you understand my love?' he shouted, bringing his fist down on the mirror hard. Shards of glass flew everywhere. His hand came away bloody, but he didn't feel a thing.

This wasn't what he had bargained for. He thought he'd married a living thing, but it took him exactly a year to realise that he'd married a stone. She had no feelings, or if she had, she kept them masked from him.

Her indifference to his business affairs, his preferences, hell, even their children alarmed him. It was as if she just pretended to care, the way she went through the right motions like a bloody robot. He didn't *know* her. Even after all these years, he didn't know her. Sometimes, he caught emotion on her face – real emotion – like the first time she had discovered that he was seeing another woman. It was after Aimen had been born, and having fallen prey to post-natal depression, Mona had distanced herself from him, sleeping in the guest room adjacent to theirs. Looking back, he knew that this depression was what really brought that wedge between them. They'd never been the same again. He had never known then just how many nights she would come to spend in that horrible room. If he'd known, he would have had it demolished.

She had discovered lipstick marks on his collar – stupidity on his part – and that being his first real affair, he had floundered when she had questioned him. Unable to properly answer her questions, he had seen the realisation dawn on her face, the hurt of his betrayal manifest in those almond eyes of hers. Her mouth had tightened, her eyes narrowed as she fought back tears, hands bunching up the shirt she held.

'Why?' she said. 'We were so happy.'

The statement infuriated him. 'Were we?' he had replied. He had shaken her by the shoulders, shouting the same thing again and again.

And then the light had gone from her eyes, and when the first slap landed on her cheek, she didn't flinch. That made him hit her more – the first time he had ever raised his hand to her.

'Women are wanderers,' was the first thing his father had told him when he was old enough to understand. 'Keep them shackled, and they'll stay loyal to you. Let them roam free, and they'll find a man faster than you can blink your eyes. That's the greatest lesson of life that I can teach you as your father.'

Nonsense, he realised now. His father had been a miserable masochist, too caught up in the cruel little world he had created around himself to care about anyone. It was a wonder his mother had emerged from that abusive relationship the way she had – unharmed and full of strength.

Not like Mona, who cowered under his hand. At times, he almost wished she'd hit him back. To give him what he deserved.

God, he loved that woman – more than anything in life. But she had never been his. She didn't want to be. No matter what he did, it wasn't enough. He wasn't enough. There would be months when everything would be normal again, they'd be happy again, and just when he would begin to hold out hope that there really was love between them, something would shift in her. He'd lose his temper at the smallest thing, and she'd take it as a personal affront. And the same vicious cycle would commence again.

She would punish him by lying in bed like an unresponsive statue. It made him furious.

Her trembling body came into his mind again, and he rushed out of the bathroom to the guestroom. He needed to make amends. He couldn't live with the remorse.

He twisted the door handle.

Locked. He was locked out of the guest room just like she'd locked him out of her heart. He raised his fist to the door, but changed his mind. Instead he pressed his forehead to the cold wood, trying to breath evenly through the pain exploding in his hand. He deserved it after what he'd done to her.

'Beat her, did you?' his mother asked him as he passed her room the next day.

When he didn't reply, she changed tack. 'What happened to that hand of yours?'

'I don't know what you're talking about, Amma,' he replied, keeping his voice even.

She laughed, but there was anger there. Her eyes blazed as she watched him, her hands gripping the armrest hard.

'One of these days, she will leave you, Bilal. She will leave and never look back.'

It was his turn to laugh. 'She can try.' He turned away from her to hide his face. His heart was pounding. 'She can't leave me,' he said aloud, as if saying it would somehow make it all true.

'I think it's safe to come out of that delusion, my dear. We live in the twenty-first century. She can do as she bloody well pleases. I might not like her guts, but I don't like the way you treat her either. She doesn't deserve it.'

'And me? Do I deserve to be treated like this?' It was a whisper, but his mother had heard.

'Oh, you men and your arrogance. You're so much like your father, and yet so different. You have a heart, Bilal, even if you don't know it yet.' Her voice hardened. 'Do right by your wife, Bilal, or I promise you I will assist her in getting rid of this violent marriage. If she wants out, I will make sure she gets out.'

Bilal didn't turn around to face her. He couldn't let her see the pain on his face. 'I don't care, Amma. She can do as she pleases.'

'But, you do care, my son.' His mother's voice was soft now. 'More than anything. You love her even more than your own mother.'

As he walked away, he knew she was right.

Chapter Sixteen

Mona

The swelling on her face had subsided a bit, leaving behind an ugly shade of purple on her right cheek. There were black circles around her eyes, where the skin felt like a child's playdough. She wondered if her foundation would manage to conceal it.

She felt a sudden longing to speak to her mother. In Mona's younger, more disruptive days, it was often up to her mother to force her to sit down and take a breath. Mona would only have to put her head in her mother's lap, and listen to her soft voice, and the fight would leave her. She would become the meek and dutiful daughter her mother always wanted her to be, not the wild, unkempt urchin she usually was.

Her mother had been a kind soul, but practical. Long before Mona's father had made it big in the stock market, back when she had been a young girl, they were poor. With her father's meagre salary, they would struggle to make ends meet. Food was scarce, meat even more so, and vanities like watching movies in theatres or buying make-up were inconceivable. Her mother would buy that cheap one-rupee kaajal from a street vendor, and getting back home, she would mix some ash from the firewood in it, just to make it last longer.

They used to wear ash in their eyes.

Mona remembered how delicious meat would taste on her tongue in those days; the way it would just melt in her mouth with those rare buttered *rotis* only her mother knew how to make.

Chicken would be even more elusive. They could eat it only as an infrequent treat: on birthday dinners or special occasions, like when she had emerged first in her Grade 6 writing contest.

Life had been brutal in those days, an unceasing cycle of hardships, empty stomachs, and cruel landlords. But even then, Mona remembered those days as full of love and happiness.

'One day, you are going to get married, Mona, and then you will understand the joy of being a wife, of being a mother.'

Marriage. Joy. Motherhood.

What had happened? How had things come to this? Each day unfolding to reveal the same perpetual sorrow, a lifetime of misery that clung to her soul dragging her deeper into the abyss. Her feelings seemed to have been swept under the expensive rug of prosperity. 'When you have money, who cares about happiness?'

That is what people said; that is what she used to believe when she was poor.

But not anymore.

She was scrolling down her Instagram feed, in admiration of flawless women, when the door to the guest room opened.

'Mona darling!'

Mona froze, the phone falling on the floor with a loud crack, splitting open to reveal its battery.

'Oops. Didn't mean for that to happen,' Bilal said.

He was smirking.

Don't overreact, she told herself, as she caught Bilal's reflection in the mirror, approaching her. She noticed his right hand was heavily bandaged.

She ignored it.

For a moment they watched each other, sizing each other up, Mona's gaze fierce, Bilal's placid, almost amused. It had been a week. His temper had cooled, but Mona was still angry; angry enough to hurt him.

After what seemed like a minute, Mona vacated the stool to squat on the floor, picking up the debris of her phone, and shoving it into her handbag. Her ears burned with anger and apprehension, her heart fluttering inside her chest like a frightened bird. Deliberately, she slowed her movements to stop her hands from shaking, and convinced that she had retrieved all the contents of her mobile phone from the floor, she straightened, and made her way toward the door.

She walked straight past Bilal without once meeting his eye, and had just begun experiencing a steely triumph when Bilal grabbed her hand, spinning her back toward him. There was no escaping this conversation.

'What?' she asked him.

'I'm sorry. There, I've said it. Don't make me say it again.'

'Excuse me?'

'I just asked you not to make me say it again.' Bilal's eyes crinkled with amusement, as if this was all a big joke, a charade created to entertain him. That more than anything angered Mona: the presumption that she was so easy.

'I don't have time for jokes,' she replied, her voice terse. 'Let me go.'

She pulled her arm back, but it wouldn't budge; Bilal's grip was strong.

'Look at me. No, stop struggling. Just look at me.'

The amusement left his eyes. All of a sudden, he seemed dead serious. Mona found herself unable to return his stare, so she lowered her eyes. She tried to prise his fingers off her wrist with her other hand, but soon gave up. His grip was like iron.

'Let go. You're hurting me. Haven't you hurt me enough already?'

Bilal's head tilted to one side. 'Why are you being like this? Didn't you just hear what I said? Here,' – he dug his free hand into his pocket, and pulled out a small box – 'this is for you. I know I shouldn't have raised my hand against you, but you just... You force me. You can be so implacable at times. I mean, why dress so provocatively? It's not like we were doing something wrong by inviting people over for Aimen's *rishta*. Then why sabotage the entire thing deliberately? Don't you want your daughter to get married? Now that bastard Wazir is telling the whole world that I'm married to a slut.'

Mona listened to the tirade, her eyes downcast, her hand going numb from the restricted blood flow. 'Do you even hear yourself? If this is your idea of contrition then I'm sorry to inform you that you suck. Just go to hell, Bilal. Do I look like I care what that loser Wazir says about me?' Her breath caught. 'You are my husband. You're supposed to protect me, not beat me.'

'Oh Mona, you know how it is. When I saw you dressed up like that, with that cleavage, and the improper fitting, I almost had a heart attack. The fact that my wife could dare wear this attire in public was more than I could bear. What were you thinking? What the hell were you—'

'You raised your hand against me.' Mona's voice was low, almost a whisper.

'What was that?'

'You raised your hand against me.' Mona raised her eyes to meet his. He blanched at her expression. 'You kicked me, the mother of your children. You kicked me until I collapsed, and if that wasn't enough, you then abandoned me like a dog. That is not okay. That is not okay.'

She was shouting now.

'You left me for dead, Bilal.'

Bilal's grip slackened on her wrist, his mouth open in wonder. Blood rushed back to Mona's fingers, tingling her extremities. 'And now you have the nerve to ask me for forgiveness.' She took his hand, and thrust it on her right cheek. 'There. Feel it? Do you feel the swelling? This purple gob of meat used to be my cheek. You kicked me in the face, and here you stand like nothing's happened? Do I look like I care about your petty gifts? To hell with you. I don't ever want to see your face again.' She said the last words in a measured, but murderous tone.

Bilal's mouth was still open when she pushed past his shoulder, and strutted out.

'What has got into you?' he called out from behind.

She turned to face him from the doorway.

'Sense.'

'Where are you going? We're not done here.'

'Go to hell, Bilal!' Mona shrieked, not bothering if anybody could hear her.

She needed to get outside. This house was toxic.

The furious shades of colour on her face caused her no end of trouble when she sat down to apply make-up. Thankfully, a headscarf hid the strangulation marks around her neck and she wore her Chanel shades to mask the purple bruises. She was far from her normal self, but at least she looked presentable.

Despite her best efforts, Meera's jaw still dropped when she saw her at the charity fundraiser that afternoon. 'What the hell happened to you?'

Mona tried to smile, but it still hurt. 'Fell down the stairs,' she murmured. Her tongue felt thick and sticky in her mouth, like a foreign object. 'You know me, clumsy as a clown.'

Meera slid her forefinger under Mona's chin and lifted her face. Mona's hand shot to her neck to keep the head-scarf fabric around it in place.

Meera immediately pulled at her headscarf. 'What's this foolishness? Why are you wearing a headscarf? Are you going all Islamic on us?'

'Meera, please—'

Mona tried to prise her friend's fingers away from her, but they came away with the fabric. She felt the touch of the air conditioning on her warm neck and knew her secret was exposed. She hadn't bothered to lather any make-up on her neck.

As quickly as she had removed the fabric, Meera fixed it back around her neck, her eyes wide and frightened.

'Is that bastard hurting you?'

Mona looked at a spot on Meera's shoulder, too afraid to meet her eyes. There was some dust near the collar of her navy-blue jacket. 'No,' she said in a small voice. 'I fell down the stairs.'

'Oh my God.' Meera's hand shot to her mouth briefly before she looked around and neutralised her expression. 'Come with me.'

She led her into a corner behind a large, concrete pillar. The only people around were waiters setting the lunch table. They stole a few looks, and then scurried away.

Meera's words came out slurred as if she were drunk – drunk and angry, a horrible mixture. 'You can't let him get away with this? This is absurd. No, I don't think I even have a word for this. This is cowardly abuse, worse than what the tribal men do to their wives. At least they own up to it.' She shook her head. 'I am going to kill that bastard.'

'Stop it, Meera. I don't want to create a scene. I didn't come here for this.'

'So this is why you haven't been returning my calls and are missing all the society parties. Shit. I had thought the worst that could have happened was that you got an abortion. That's why I didn't pry.'

Mona laughed, briefly, before clutching her jaw again. 'Ow.'

'Is he at his office at this time? I am going to go see him right now. Right this moment. There is simply no excuse for this kind of abuse. What is he, an animal? Hell, even animals have limits. And what was your rhino of a mother-in-law up to while he shredded you into pieces?'

'Please Meera, if you so much as say a word about this to anyone, I will never talk to you. Promise me.'

'No. Absolutely not.'

'Promise me! I need to handle this my own way.'

It took two more attempts before Meera agreed, grudgingly. 'This isn't over, you know,' she muttered, folding her arms across her chest. 'I would have divorced the bastard if I were you, and then sued him for domestic abuse. I would have dragged him through the streets if he'd so much as lifted a finger to me. Pakistan is not the country it was twenty years ago, Mona. Today, we have rights – frail, meagre rights, but they are something.'

'Hello, stranger,' someone said.

Mona jumped at the voice.

It was Ali.

'Jesus Christ in heaven,' Meera exclaimed, her hand on her heart. 'You scared the life out me.'

Mona clutched the right side of her face and allowed herself a short laugh. The pain singed through her bones, but she forced herself not to wince. 'Wherever did you learn that phrase?'

Meera gave her a half-smile. 'It was this American I married once. It was a disastrous three-month marriage that culminated in us threatening to shoot each other in the head, but he taught me a few choice phrases. Care to learn them, Ali?'

Ali held up his hands. 'No thanks.' His eyes fell on Mona, and he took a step back. 'What happened to your face?'

Mona sighed. 'Is it that obvious? I thought I didn't look conspicuous.'

'But what happened?'

'Damned if I know,' Meera replied, her mood darkening once again as she drew herself up to her full height and walked away. 'Ask her yourself.'

There was an awkward pause as both of them stood facing each other, Mona glancing at the ceiling as she tried not to catch Ali's eye. They both spoke at the same time.

'I'll go get some coffee—' Mona began, while Ali started by asking, 'So what really happened?'

Finally she caught his eye, and they both laughed. With his hands in his pockets, his eyes dancing, the Adam's apple bobbing up and down, it was the first time he looked like the carefree boy he should be, considering his age.

'I'm sorry,' he said. 'I didn't mean to pry. I just hope your injuries aren't too painful.'

'Oh, I just fell down the stairs,' Mona lied.

'It's the heels. I keep telling my female friends to ditch them for something flat, but do you women ever listen?'

'Oh please, heels are a woman's prerogative. Without heels, there is no woman.'

'Now, you're just being sexist. Wow Mona, I didn't know women could be sexist too.'

'Yeah, I've always been a weird one.' She felt her hunched shoulders relaxing. 'Thanks,' she said. 'For making me feel better.'

'And for not prying, right? Because, I've had my fair share of falls down the stairs, and this doesn't look like one.'

Mona gave him a lopsided grin, the best she could do with her current working muscles. 'Yes, and for not prying.'

They proceeded back to the main hall where the ladies were getting ready for the roll call for the charity auction. Mona was surprised to see a couple of Birkins up for grabs on the main table. Shahida, of course, was one of the organisers of the event. Next to her, Meera sat in her prim, tailor-cut navy suit, riffling through some pages in front of her. Every few seconds, she looked up to glare at Mona.

Mona stood with Ali at the back of the hall, behind all the other society ladies who were scrambling to pick the best seats, putting on their best poses in front of the photographers.

'I'm surprised to see you at this boring event,' Mona said to him. 'I have to attend these because I'm a member.'

Ali shrugged. 'I make it a point to go wherever Meera invites me.'

'Ah, being the leading model and all.'

Ali shook his head, smiling.

'Going to buy anything?' he asked her. 'I can see quite a few things up there. And is that an—'

'Ivory elephant, yes. You underestimate our delusions of grandeur. Those poor elephants who died to create this monstrosity.'

They went on about the injustices performed against elephants, before Ali shifted the conversation to a new topic.

'So, are you coming to Meera's party?'

Mona raised an eyebrow. 'Don't tell me another party is in the works. I don't know what I'll do with my husband. Perhaps I should dose him with Valium before I come,' she muttered under her breath.

Ali's breath was warm in her ear. 'I'm gonna pretend I didn't hear that.'

Mona shivered. She could smell the musk of his cologne, he was standing so close to her. She took a step back. 'I'm afraid I've lost count of Meera's parties. Maybe I'll attend, maybe I won't.'

'The Elahis are going to be in attendance though.'

Mona could catch the sarcasm in his tone. 'You bet your ass they will. Shahida is not one for missing out on the attention. Look at her perched on the stage like a mother hen looking over her flock.'

Ali's body shook in silent laughter. 'Now that you mention it, there is something bird-like about her. Suppose she pecks at her food?'

Mona looked at him. 'You're going to find out soon enough.'

It was weird, but she didn't need to worry about watching her mouth with him. She realised that there were men in the world with whom she could be comfortable. Just standing there, making pointless conversation, doing nothing felt refreshing, like a swim in the ocean. She didn't want to think why she felt so at ease with a man who was practically a stranger, but Ali was the first person who seemed genuinely interested in her as an individual, and not as a commodity. He hadn't asked her once about what Bilal did, or how much money she had stashed away in her accounts, and just now his blissful avoidance of the issue of her bruises.

She looked at him, and knew he had been watching her the entire time. The thought sent shivers down her body. Maybe it was all a game for him, but the fact was that a man more than ten years her junior stood next to her, hanging on to her every word. If that wasn't a boost for her ego, she didn't know what was.

'So Ali, being a dashing young man, you must have a host of admirers.'

He laughed, but she persisted.

'Is there anyone special in your life right now? That is, if you don't mind me asking, since I seem to be breaking one of our unspoken rules about prying.'

She sensed him going very still. 'No,' he said finally. 'But—'

'But?' Heavens forgive her, this time she was hanging on to his every word.

'There used to be at one time. More than one.' He thrust his hands back into his pockets and lowered his head. 'It's a part of my life I don't like to remember. But to answer your question, no. There is no one at present.'

'Oh,' she said.

'And you? Do you love him?'

'Him?' she echoed. He had stepped too close for comfort. She could see the individual hairs of his stubble. Her breath constricted in her throat. 'Of course I love him.'

'In spite of the fact that he beats you?'

His gaze bored into hers. She couldn't look away.

'You weren't supposed to pry.'

'I can't help it,' he whispered.

'He's my husband,' she found herself saying. 'I have to love him.'

'You don't have to do anything, Mona. That's the beauty of life. You always have a choice.'

Mona attempted to laugh, but a hollow sound erupted from her throat. 'My choice is my husband,' she said, trying to convince herself more than anyone.

'Of course it is,' he said, stepping back.

The spell broke.

Mona looked down at her hands. They were shaking.

'Funny how time passes,' she said, checking her watch. 'I didn't realise I'd been here an hour. I need to run an errand.'

'Don't leave on my account,' Ali said. 'Half the time, I don't know what I say.'

'No Ali, it was really great chatting with you, but I really need to head out.'

'Well then at least allow me to escort you to the lobby.'

She looked at his hazel eyes, innocent and earnest, and found herself nodding. 'I guess.'

In the lift, they found themselves bunched together with a group of other people. Ali nudged their way to the far end where they stood side by side. Her shoulder dug into his bicep, and when a man tried to move closer to Mona, Ali laid a protective arm around her, and shifted her to the wall. His fingers pressed into the soft flesh of her bruised upper arms, and she winced, but what took her by surprise was the tingling that ran across her body. In that brief moment, the lift jolted, and Mona crashed against his chest. She closed her eyes at the impact, and almost burst out laughing at the cliché: a weak woman, injured and helpless, falling into the arms of a strong, younger man. It felt like something out of a romantic novel, not that she didn't enjoy reading them from time to time. She flushed at the thought, but when she opened her eyes, the moment had passed, and she was a sad-looking middle-aged woman in the mirror across from her, wearing a printed hijab to conceal her husband's abuse. All of a sudden, she felt sick to her stomach. Her momentary desire, no matter how innocuous, disgusted her. The fight with Bilal must have addled her mind. How could she act so weak and defenceless to thoughts and desires that weren't just immoral, but forbidden?

When the lift halted at the ground floor, Mona pushed her way through the throng of men and ran out into the lobby, ignoring Ali's calls.

Chapter Seventeen

Ali

They were in Mir Rabiullah's sitting room again – if a bunch of cushions thrown together around a large stool could be called a sitting room. The Mir lay sideways with a cushion thrown under his arm to prop himself up. In one hand he held a glistening jalebi while his other bunched up his beard. He ran his fingers through the wiry tufts of hair. Despite the nonchalance, Ali sensed something, as if the very air was charged with anticipation. Rabiullah wore a large frown on his face, his gaze intent on the half-eaten piece of jalebi he held between his fingers. His lips smacked from the sticky syrup.

Gul sat on the cushion across from Ali, her eyes lowered, her hands on her knees. Things were tense between them. Gul was finally beginning to grapple with the knowledge that her affection was one-sided. Ali felt for her like he would for a friend, but nothing more. To be honest, he didn't believe anything he said to her could change the situation. He didn't love her – that much he knew. The sight of her didn't cause his mind to spin. He wasn't even sure love or lust even produced these feelings, but whatever emotions it aroused, indifference wasn't supposed to be one of them. Because whenever he laid eyes on her, he felt the familiar blanket of indifference settling in on him, like during his modelling days. He wished it didn't have to be like that. She had helped him out with Hussain and he was thankful to her for that, but that was the extent of his feelings for her.

Apart from enquiring about Hussain's progress, Mir Rabiullah had been mostly silent.

'You're making sure he isn't playing any sports yet, aren't you?' he asked suddenly.

Ali started. 'What? Oh, you mean Hussain? He couldn't play even if he wanted to. He's still getting acclimatised to the prosthetic leg, and with that botched amputation, he continually runs the risk of contracting an infection. But apart from that, he's improving. The doctor said that the way things are, he can see Hussain leading a very normal and healthy life in future.'

Mir Rabiullah nodded. 'That's good to hear. Of course, all of this must be such a relief for your poor mother. Your modelling assignments are going well? Do you need any support?'

Ali flushed before clasping his hands together. He could feel himself sweating with shame. No matter how benevolent the Mir was, Ali didn't think he'd ever get over the shame of taking someone else's monetary help for his family. There was nothing more degrading. 'Work is going well,' he mumbled.

'Good, good.'

The Mir sat up straight then, crossing his legs together on the stool, and fixed Ali with an intense stare that seemed to peer right into his soul. 'I'm not sure if Gul has mentioned this to you, but there is – ah – something I need help with.'

'My help?' Ali was incredulous.

Gul cleared her throat, looking up for the first time. 'We haven't had a chance to talk yet.'

'You just made a one-hour journey together to come here. You're telling me that a young couple sitting together didn't talk?' The Mir's eyes narrowed. 'Unless all is not well between you two.'

Gul smiled, her full sparkling smile. Ali was astonished at how convincing she looked. 'No, Mir Sahab. We were just too busy discussing today's weather and although I try not to be so interested in showbiz, I just can't help quizzing Ali about all the latest happenings.'

Ali stared at her. They had spent the entire journey in silence, Gul's eyes fixed on the road while he played with his hands. He could recall every single cuticle around his nails, he had spent so much time studying them.

Mir Rabiullah laughed. 'That's what I like about you, Gul. You're so smart, but also such a girl. It's good to be reminded of that. By the way you work, I sometimes forget.' He turned to Ali. 'I'm sure you have a busy schedule ahead of you, so I'll try to keep this short.' He waved down Ali's protests. 'No no, trust me I know how busy you are. And it's pretty simple, the thing I want you to do for me.'

Ali leaned forward in anticipation. 'Sir?'

'There is a new sponsor who has been in touch with us for quite a while now. A big sponsor. You know, a man with deep pockets. He had promised me a chunky donation in exchange for a few services I rendered for him. Now as it happens, it's been a few months since I was promised the money, and although I'm not short on cash,' – he held up his hands to God – 'it's just that I'm not sure whether he has reneged on his promise or our deal still holds.'

Ali raised an eyebrow. 'I'm not sure how I can be of assistance in the matter, Mir Sahab.'

'If there's one thing that distresses me in this world, it's unfinished business.' The Mir spoke his next words slowly, as if he had chosen them with care. 'I want you to help us remind him about his promise.'

'You mean like barge into his office or something?'

Mir Rabiullah laughed. 'Oh nothing as dramatic as that, my dear boy. All I want is for you to get us access to him at a party. I would like to send a couple of my accountants to go over the matter with him personally as he's been evading our requests to meet him at his office. All I want is for my people to have a chance to ascertain whether the deal is off or if he still plans to give us the donation eventually.'

Ali gave a short laugh. 'With all due respect, Mir Sahab. I don't think I can help at all. I'm just an ordinary model. I don't get invited to business dinners.'

'If I'm not mistaken, your good friend Meera is hosting a party soon. In the Walled City?'

Ali bit his lip. 'How did you find out about that?'

'Your friend isn't exactly known for her discretion.' It was Gul who spoke this time. Ali was surprised and a little hurt at the derision in her tone. 'All Mir Sahab needs is a small favour. You should be proud, Ali, proud.'

Ali turned to the Mir. 'Yes, Meera is having a party, but it's going to be strictly private. You can't enter without an invite.'

Mir Rabiullah cocked his head. 'Are you telling me that you cannot persuade your friend to let you invite a couple of friends to the party? If my sources are correct, it's quite a big party.' He heaved himself off the stool, and began pacing around the room. Ali noticed that there was a limp in his leg that hadn't been there before, as if he had had a bad fall. 'I hope you realise this, Ali, that I use this money to help people in need. Money doesn't fall from trees, you know. There is a certain limit to how altruistic a person can be. After a point, people simply won't hand out their money for free. You do them a favour, and only then they'll pay. Of course there are certain people who don't pay even then. In that case, all we can do is talk to them and remind them of how their money will be utilised for a good purpose.' He stopped walking and held up his hands. 'That's all I ask. Just get two of my people access into the party. We don't know for sure when that person might be seen in public again. His office staff knows about us so we cannot reach him there.'

Ali looked at the Mir and saw a sad, old man in shabby clothes and a tatty cap on his head, his bright green eyes imploring him. He felt disgusted by his indecision. This was Mir Rabiullah – the man who had saved Hussain. Ali rose and took the Mir's hands in his own. They were dry and callused. 'Of course I will help you, Mir Sahab. May I ask who this person is?'

'Chaudhary Hussain Elahi from Elahi Steel Mills.'

The shirt suited him well. A jacket didn't seem necessary, but what if the event was formal enough to require it? Would they kick him out of the place just because they could?

He snorted at the thought. Not only was he on the guest list, he was taking another two people to the party under his name. Meera had been more than accommodating. 'Two people? Why not invite a hundred, Ali?

There's more than enough food to go around.' She had waved the bagel she was eating at him. 'Don't invite a hundred people. I'm serious – the food would run out. Imagine the horror!' They'd laughed together at her imitation of a rich society lady with an empty plate. 'Just ring up Shahid on your way out, and tell him I've approved two more guests. Give him their names.'

His phone beeped as he was driving a comb through his slick hair.

It was another message from Ahmed, one of Mir Rabiullah's accountants. *We've arrived at the venue. Waiting for you.*

Damn.

He sank in his mattress, and looked around for his shoes. He was eyeing the drawer in the dresser for shoe polish when he heard a soft knock on the door, followed by a dull creak, and the unmistakable tread of his mother's footsteps.

'May I come in?' she asked, pausing in the doorway.

He spread his arms wide. 'You already have.' It gladdened his heart to see her laugh. 'But I'm gonna have to run in a moment. I'm already late.'

Instead of coming right inside, she leaned against the corner of the wall that opened up into the room. 'Busy, busy.' She looked him over once, nodding in approval. 'Looking dapper!'

Ali thanked her, and busied himself with his shoes, lowering his head so that it touched his kneecap. Usually, his mother left at this point after making a couple of vague remarks about his clothes or shoes. She had never asked him where he went or what he did.

After tying and re-tying his laces, he looked up, and found her still standing there with an unreadable expression. 'And where is it that you're headed?' she asked him.

He lowered his gaze. 'To a party.'

All of a sudden, she started laughing, and seeing his shocked expression she covered her mouth with one hand, and with the other held up a finger. 'Excuse me,' she panted between gasps, 'but I'm surprised you held it in this long.'

Ali was perplexed. 'Held what?'

'Oh come on. Drop the charade already! I know what's going on. I'm your mother, remember?' Padding up to the stool in front of the dresser, she sank into it, and wrapped her arms around her legs. 'So, who is she?'

Ali rose from the bed. Had Gul reached out to her? Or had she, with a mother's shrewd understanding of her children, somehow figured out his repressed but undeniable feelings for Mona? With a level voice, he managed, 'She?'

'Oh Ali! I wish you would trust me just a little. You don't think I'm a total dingbat, do you? I mean, I've been looking at your dazed expression in the mornings, your nightly absences, the way you make an extra effort to dress smart every morning.'

The knot of unease that had risen up to his throat loosened a little. She was grasping at straws. 'I'm a model, Mom. It's my job to dress smart, and work late.'

She flapped a hand at him. 'Oh come on! You think I wasn't young once? I understand what's happening all right, but until now I had decided not to say anything. I mean, I can see you're still uncomfortable in owning up so I won't push you – oh my God, look, you're blushing!'

'I am not! And I'm not seeing anyone, Mom, if that's what you mean. At least not yet,' he added.

'Oh, so there might be someone in the near future? Interesting.'

'Oh God.'

His mother's face grew serious; her sky-blue eyes that were dancing with delight moments ago were darkening now. '*Dekho* Ali, I would never presume to interfere in your life, you know that, and God knows I don't have the right to after all I have put you through, but bear in mind this little piece of advice I'm giving you.' Her gaze locked level with his. 'Always play fair when you can. Your personal life aside, you are a rising star today. Soon, people will throw themselves at you. The world will be open for you. If you're serious about someone, just go for it, take it to the next level, but just make sure that person is worth it. The world is already a sad place without us making stupid mistakes only to regret them later on. And the grief of a broken heart, Oh Ali, that is something else altogether.'

Ali stared at her. 'Do you regret marrying Abbu?'

She hung her head as if at a loss for further words, before glancing up at him. 'Just be careful, won't you beta?'

He didn't know what to say to her. Instead, he asked her about Hussain.

Her eyes lit up at that. Jumping up from the stool, she dropped a quick kiss on his forehead, and turned for the door. 'Hussain's started taking baby steps on the prosthetic,' she said looking back at him. 'I'm so thankful to Allah! Life is getting better, and all because of you. Do thank that gracious man from me.'

'Who, Mir Sahab?'

'Yes yes, the one who paid for Hussain's prosthetic leg. What an angel. Do take me to meet him sometime, won't you?'

Ali assured her he would, but something about taking his mother down to the Mir's abode didn't seem right, like he would be crossing a line. He couldn't quite put a finger on the feeling except that he'd have to think things through before he could even hope to introduce her to Mir Sahab. *Not that I'm a bad guy*, he thought, determined not to let anything taint the saint-like image he held of the man in his mind. His request to meet Elahi was a reasonable one, and Ali was glad to be of some use to him.

Getting out of Iqbal Town during rush hour was another matter though.

Two men in black suits and what looked like very expensive silk ties approached him when he finally climbed out of his car. 'Ahmed Raza, Sir,' one of them, a burly, bearded man said to him, extending a hand.

'Jamal Abid,' said the other one.

Ali shook both their hands, sizing them up in the process. Their grip was strong, their hands rough and callused – they definitely didn't seem like the hands of accountants who spent their entire day behind a desk. A prickle of unease pierced him.

'You guys work out much?'

'Indeed,' Jamal Abid said, his eyes gleaming as he ran his fingers through his fashionably tousled hair. These men seemed to be dressed for the Oscars, not some random party in Lahore.

Ahmed Raza exposed large, neatly filed teeth. 'Every single day. You'd be surprised at how boring a desk job can be.'

They were just accountants, but with a penchant for muscles. Mir Rabiullah sure seemed to know how to intimidate people. Of course, Ali berated himself. How else would he be where he was today if he didn't know how to work the magic of intimidation.

'Let's go,' Ali said, gesturing them to take the lead. 'We're late already.'

Meera agreed with his observation. 'You're late,' was the first thing she said as she stood to greet guests at the entrance to the magnificent haveli. 'For a moment, I thought you were a no show.' She rolled her eyes upward as if berating herself for even entertaining such a thought, before her gaze landed on the men with Ali. Meera let out a low whistle. 'Well, well, who do we have here?'

Ahmed and Jamal both introduced themselves with their first names only, glossing over the fact that they were from a charity organisation. Ali didn't press them on the subject as revealing their true identities would just serve to alert Elahi.

He felt a savage delight in the plan to take Elahi by surprise. Elahi hadn't got back to him regarding the offer for movies or introductions with directors. And after he'd heard the rumours that Elahi swung both ways, he had given up trying to contact him. *Good riddance*, he thought.

Meera's eyes sparked in mischief, as she tugged on the shimmering black blouse of her sari to reveal more cleavage.

'Stop staring,' she quipped, catching where his gaze had drifted. Ali brought it back to her face. Meera's eyes were fixed on the two handsome men. 'Make yourselves at home, gents. We have enough drinks to last us a lifetime. And food too! Not that you seem to require sustenance. What are you, beasts?'

As Ali led them away, Meera widened her eyes at him, and gave him a thumbs-up, mouthing something that sounded strangely like 'Hook me up!'

Wasn't she already married? Or was she between husbands at the moment?

Unsure of how to reply, Ali hung his head low, and entered the expansive courtyard of the haveli. It was something out of the Mughal era with its elegant courtyards and towering arches. Ali understood then why this place was such a haunt for the elite of Lahore; it was a careful mix of old-world charm splashed with the amenities of today. Standing erect at three storeys high, the building possessed enough magnificence to enchant even the most detached observer.

Ali was amazed to see couples kissing openly, something unheard of in Lahore. From the excited whispers of the men that passed him, Ali gleaned that a *mujra* was going on inside one the haveli rooms.

'Dancers from Heera Mandi itself,' Jamal remarked, fixing his red silk tie in place, an avid expression on his face. 'This woman, Meera, has some balls. You don't get to see courtesans dancing every day.'

A group of younger men and women sat huddled together on the porch overlooking the courtyard. Even from afar, Ali caught the sweet, cloying smell of their weed as they threw their heads back, taking turns to smoke a single roll-up. From the jaded look on some of their faces, Ali guessed the involvement of other drugs. His suspicions were confirmed when a man from the group sprinkled something on a small table, and lowered his head to snort it up.

Cocaine. He quickly looked away.

'There's a dance floor too, look!' Ahmed exclaimed, nudging Jamal, and pointing to a space that had been cleared in the middle of the courtyard where a raised dais had been put up. A bunch of technicians squatted on the glass-floored dance floor, testing strobe lights. Ali slowed his pace. Due to the careful, studious way in which the accountants spoke, he had assumed that they were native Urdu speakers, but just now in their eagerness, their accent had slipped. It didn't really mean anything. These men could be from elsewhere in Punjab. He shook his head. Why was he on edge? Was it the sight of the cocaine that had thrown him off like that? He needed to get Mir Rabiullah's work done and then cook up an excuse to leave. This party was not healthy for his vow of abstinence. Already, he could feel the sweat trickling down his neck.

A woman in a long, flowing black gown caught Ali's attention. She was ambling along the edge of the court-yard, just short of where the garden began. The decided restraint in her walk, the delicate waves of the luscious brown hair... She looked like Mona.

'Hey, where's Elahi?' Jamal asked, but Ali ignored him and strolled toward the woman in black. 'Mona?'

What if she refused to recognise him? He wouldn't be surprised after his behaviour at the charity event the other day.

She turned, but it wasn't her.

It was a haggard old woman, her ancient face full of lines. It was Shahida Elahi, he realised. 'Mona?' Her voice was as sharp as a whip.

Ali winced.

'Why would you be looking for Mona now?'

'I'm actually looking for Elahi Sahab, your husband.'

Shahida's eyes narrowed into slits. 'Really now? Why would that be? Has my husband been feeding you that cock and bull story about his long-unfulfilled desire to enter the film industry, his friendship with film directors, because I would advise you to save your breath. None of that will happen. My husband simply needs fresh fuel to feed his perennial delusion about the film industry.'

'I wanted to see him about something else,' he said when he was sure his tongue would bear the weight of his words.

'Hmmm, well don't ask me. Elahi will be where the girls are. Or the boys. I tell you, there are days when I can't figure out whether I married a hetero or a homo.' She waved a hand at him. 'Go ahead and call me a homophobe. I can proudly say that I am.'

Ali returned to the two men, shaking his head.

Jamal's shoulders shook with silent laughter. 'His wife, I presume. The old bat. Mir Sahab has a special dislike for her.'

At least there was one thing in which they saw eye to eye, Ali thought.

He gestured toward the place where the mujra was in progress. It was anybody's guess how they were going to weave their way into the thicket of men surrounding the stage. 'Let's start there.'

Ali noticed how Ahmed checked his watch furtively. 'Ten-thirty. It's getting late, Jamal.'

Jamal looked back at Ahmed, his smile as wide as ever. 'No, it's not. Not unless we find Elahi in good time.'

Before Ali could ask what this little exchange meant, they were swallowed into the crowd of men. The smell of their sweat and cologne came in heavy waves, causing tears to erupt in his eyes. Ahmed and Jamal were shouldering their way deep into the crowd, Ali barely managing to keep up. They elbowed and kneed people in the gut giving the impression of a couple of crazed tractors crashing around a field of tender wheat. People tipped and bent out of their way, some deferentially, others painfully as they got hit somewhere tender.

'Ali!'

Ali turned around to find himself face to face with Mona. He blinked once, before letting his gaze travel all over her body. The dress she wore hugged her body in all the right places; a slender silk ribbon was tied into a bow around her waist, drawing attention to how slim it was. Ali was certain it would fit in his two hands. It was a wonder this woman had borne two children. He wondered why she hid herself beneath loose kaftans and baggy shirts.

'Wow, you look...' It was quite the cliché, but he wanted to say 'sexy'. He felt himself going red. 'I meant to say that you look fantastic.'

It was her turn to blush. She put her hand on his shoulder and leaned toward his ear. He felt an involuntary shudder pass through him. Perhaps he was destined to fall for women many years his senior. Right now, all he wanted to do was... he was embarrassed to even think of what he wanted to do.

He focused on what she was saying. 'Everyone knows young people fake their admiration for the middle-aged. You don't need to flatter me to be my friend. I'm not one of those women.'

'I never lie about my admiration,' Ali quipped.

She gave a short laugh, shaking her head. 'Something tells me I should trust you.'

Ali shrugged. He couldn't take his eyes off her waist. He shoved his hands deep into his pockets to make sure they didn't act of their own accord. Slowly, he levelled his eyes with hers. A series of fine lines crinkled around her eyes when she smiled. He still found her irresistible. He gulped, mustering a gob of saliva to wet his parched throat.

'Rather claustrophobic in here, isn't it?' Mona remarked, eyeing the rowdy crowd of cheering men around her. 'Someone told me Meera was here, but all I can see are drunk men. Drunk and' – she cleared her throat – 'lusty. I've been groped three times tonight. I think it might be a record.'

'You look beautiful, Mona.'

'Why, *thank you* Ali for saying it again.' She lowered her gaze. 'You look pretty dapper yourself.'

He thanked her.

'You're not angry about the other day, I hope?' he said all of a sudden. 'I shouldn't have questioned you about your private life.'

Her face assumed an impassive look. 'I don't know what you're talking about. And besides, you could never hurt me. You're too sweet for that.' She looked past his shoulder. 'Hey, are those men with you? They're pointing at you.'

Ali whipped around, and saw Jamal and Ahmed waving and pointing at him. They looked comical with their flailing arms and serious faces. When they were sure they had his attention, Jamal pointed at something to his right. Ali followed his finger with his eyes, and saw that he was pointing right at a tight clump of men, Elahi planted firmly in the middle.

Ali looked back at Ahmed's raised eyebrows and nodded. It was Elahi, all right.

'Wow, your friends sure know how to dress up. Those silk ties, my my.'

When Ali didn't smile, she broke into laughter. 'Oh, to be young and full of such conflicting emotions. I only meant it as a mild compliment, Ali. I think you look much better in your red shirt. It's silk too, isn't it?'

Ali still didn't reply, but this time a genuine smile crossed his lips as he closed his eyes. Better, but her way of speaking to him was still detached, like she was talking to a child. Maybe it was all in his head. It wouldn't be the first time. He thought of holding her hand, but she grabbed his with such ferocity that Ali's eyes opened in surprise.

'Oh my God,' she whispered. 'Oh my God.'

The next few seconds passed in what seemed like a flash, and yet Ali saw every minute detail of what happened as if someone had played it in slow motion. He was still reeling from Mona's touch, her icy hand in his, when the unthinkable happened. With the flourish of experts, Jamal and Ahmed drew revolvers from inside their jackets, and aimed them at Elahi and his group.

Nobody else had noticed them; they were all busy admiring the dancing courtesan. Mona screamed, but nobody heard her. The shout building in Ali's throat died there. He knew his voice wouldn't travel. His muscles flexed in anticipation of action, but before he could so much as lift a foot, the sound of shots rang in the air. The men around Elahi fell like a row of dominoes, one after the other, until the only one left standing was Elahi himself. Ahmed's back was turned to him, but Ali heard his savage laugh in the chaotic noise as he aimed the gun at Elahi's forehead and pulled the trigger.

Elahi crumpled to the ground, his face bearing a look of utter incomprehension. He had been too surprised to even shout for help.

Finally, as if awakened from a feverish reverie, the people around them turned their attention to the spreading pool of crimson on the concrete, the jumble of bodies lying one atop the other, limbs spread at inhuman angles. The courtesan herself seemed to have paused mid-air, too scared to move a muscle. What followed were a few moments of silence where the people knew that something terrible had happened, but their minds hadn't had the chance to process the severity of the event to initiate an appropriate response.

Before they could spring into action, a deafening boom sounded somewhere near the entrance of the haveli, followed by a rain of concrete and earth.

Chapter Eighteen

Mona

'Bomb blast!' someone screamed.

'Duck!' Mona shouted, plunging Ali to the ground with her, as a spattering of hot concrete fell on their backs. Before her eyes, a flying steel rod drove straight through a man; launching itself into the ground like a flag post, the man hanging like a grim trophy.

Women screamed, men shouted. Beside her, Ali sucked in a breath as someone ran over his back. People were rising to their feet, and she knew what would be next. A stampede. They had to get out of here.

'We're going to get minced if we stay on the ground like this,' she growled, the grit thick on her tongue. She tasted ash and terror. Her gaze drew a blank across the courtyard. There was nowhere to go. Everywhere she looked, dozens of puzzled eyes stared back at her, the realisation of what had just happened dawning on their faces. The place was going to fall into bedlam in seconds. 'Get up,' she urged Ali, who seemed to be lost for words. He would widen his eyes, blink furiously and then repeat the same gesture.

'I can't believe it,' he said, his head resting on his arm.

The smell of burning wood reached them.

'Well, neither can I,' Mona replied, pulling herself to her feet. She didn't want to get burnt alive. Perhaps that's what kept her head clear. From the expression on Ali's face, she knew he had gone into shock, as had many other people who stood with creased eyebrows, unable to move. She looked behind to find the wooden entrance on fire, the flames licking their way toward the haveli proper.

'Get up!' she shouted at him. She nudged him with her foot; she'd worry about improprieties later. Ali barely noticed, his wide eyes looking up to her in puzzlement.

'My God,' he whispered. 'What have I done?'

His friends, she realised. Of course! They were the ones who had fired at poor Elahi and his group. But this wasn't the time to think about them, and besides, those men were gone. She glanced around to confirm her suspicion. There was nothing except the burning haveli, and a bunch of people who were fast approaching hysteria.

'Ali,' she warned him, 'if you don't get up this instant, I will leave you here to get trampled. I swear.'

Ali looked at her with large, plaintive eyes. He seemed unwilling or unable to muster the energy to rise from his place on the ground, his shoulders hunched and turned into his chest. He wanted to make himself appear as small as possible.

Mona's stomach lurched as the wooden section of the courtyard came crashing down, the eager flames latching themselves onto the unharmed wood. If it went on like this, the whole building would come down.

A stiff breeze brought a cloud of ash in their direction, filling her mouth and nostrils with smoke and grit. Her eyes watered as indecision weighed heavily on her. As if on cue, police sirens rang in the distance, gaining momentum as they approached. Mona had never been so relieved to hear the police. The weight of terror clutching her heart, the fear of being trampled alive mellowed down as she watched screaming police vans halting one after the other before the burning gate. Several ambulances followed, their rotating lights casting a peculiar hue over the raging fire. The puzzlement and indecision gave way to a burning desire to get to the police – to safety – as the people made a beeline for the entrance.

To her surprise, Ali shrank back in horror as a couple of policemen approached them. It took her an instant to understand. They would arrest him in a second if they realised he had known the assailants.

A man in a torn tuxedo following the policemen pointed at Mona and then Ali. 'They were there when the men got murdered. They saw it. They screamed. They knew what was going to happen. They knew!'

Far from showing them any kindness, the officers pulled Ali to his feet roughly, pushing and shoving him in the general direction of the flickering lights, while a lady constable arrived to escort Mona out. She was a short, dumpy woman with a pinched expression, and small, merciless eyes. Her nails dug into the flesh of Mona's arm as she guided her through the wreckage. Mona stumbled twice, but the constable pushed her on. There wasn't so much as a break in her stride as she kicked aside loose rocks and pieces of steel to make way. Mona felt the calluses on the constable's hand as the grip on her arm intensified.

Her heart sank as she saw Ali being thrown into a van, a gleam of triumph on the face of the man wearing the torn tuxedo who had now turned his attention to the flock of cameras and media persons that had appeared at the scene. A blinding flash and Mona felt her photo being clicked.

She struggled against the woman dragging her toward a waiting police van. 'I'm not going to jail. Leave me alone.'

'You have been identified as being present on the scene of the crime. You are now a person of interest.' The constable's voice betrayed not even a hint of emotion. She might have been reading a catalogue.

'No, I'm not. Let go of me.'

The media's attention had turned from the man in the tuxedo to Mona. Sensing their curious gaze, Mona abruptly righted herself. She dug her heels in the ground, and pulled back with all her might. 'I will not go. Let the media see how you're treating the victim of a bomb attack.'

Irritation stirred the features on the constable's face. 'You rich society ladies and your tantrums. You're coming to the police station to answer for your involvement.'

'Let her go!' Ali called from his van. Before he could say anything else, the door shut on him.

Suspicion snaked its way into Mona's head. The police vans bore no emblems of Punjab Police, neither did they say which station they belonged to. That meant only one thing: this was the elite force reserved for special circumstances. 'Where are you taking him?' she asked a group of tall, burly men once they had reached the van she was supposed to be packed in. 'Where are you taking me? This is illegal. You are not within your rights to apprehend a respectable woman.'

'A woman who comes to watch mujras, dressed like a whore herself,' snorted one of the men, burying his mouth between his hands as he lit a cigarette. 'You're coming with us, lady, whether you like it or not.'

'The hell she is.'

She recognised the voice before she spun around to see the face.

Bilal.

At that moment, had they been alone, she would have kissed him. Never before had she felt such a rush of affection for him. She could imagine the number of favours he must have asked to make his way here, right into the middle of the bomb scene. And sure enough, there seemed to be a high-ranking police official striding beside him as he rushed to where Mona stood.

He took her in his arms, that single gesture conveying his worry, love and agitation. She could hear his rapid heartbeat, his murmurs of consolation, and beneath it all, the charred taste of antagonism. She felt it again as his arms closed around her back tighter, crushing her. She struggled against his chest to break free, but he pulled her closer. 'Don't,' he whispered. 'We need to show a united front.'

Only when the police official who had arrived with Bilal cleared his throat did Bilal release his vice-like grip on her. Mona sprung apart from him in a single fluid movement. Her back thrummed with the pain of his powerful forearms.

Bilal turned his attention to the police official. 'As I explained before, my wife was here at the express invitation of Ms Meera, the lady who runs a modelling agency. If there are any questions, she is the perfect person to go to.' He took Mona's hand. 'Now, if there's nothing else, I would like to take my wife home. She has endured enough horror for one day.'

The lady constable bristled; she wrung her hands at her senior. 'What is this, Sir?'

'Not now, Andaleeb.' The police official nodded at Bilal. 'Your wife is free to leave.' He inclined his head toward the waiting van in which Ali sat shackled. 'What about him? He was discovered with your wife. Do you vouch for his character too? If you do, we can let him go as well. The matter of fact is, Bilal Sahab, that we have dozens of suspects in custody now, almost all of whom will turn out to be victims, not perpetrators. If you can get any more people off our hands, we'd appreciate it.'

Bilal's eyes found Mona's. He arched an eyebrow, his unspoken rule of enquiry. Mona gave a brief nod, her heart hammering in her chest. Poor Ali, he was traumatised enough as it was. He didn't need the additional torture of spending the night at the police station.

Bilal's lips curled as he gazed at his wife. Without missing a beat, and without even looking at Ali, he turned to the police official. 'I have got nothing to do with this man. Do with him as you will.'

Mona's eyes widened. 'Bilal, no! Ali's innocent too.'

But neither Bilal nor the police official were having any more of it. And there was something in Bilal's eyes, a glare that melted the words in her mouth. She felt as if her tongue had turned to jelly such was the ferociousness of his gaze. Without another word, she seated herself in Bilal's BMW.

And she waited, willing herself not to burst into tears at the sad sight of Ali, shackled and despondent in the police van. The murderers might have been his acquaintances, but Mona knew it in her heart that Ali wasn't involved in any of it. If he were, she wouldn't have been able to attract his undivided attention with her red dress. There is something about the eyes that gives a person's feelings away. And this evening, Mona knew from Ali's eyes how happy he was to be with her. That kind of happiness doesn't come when a person's half-planning to blow up a bomb.

Her feelings for him might be a jumble, but at that moment, Mona felt a crushing helplessness at not being able to do something for Ali. She averted her gaze as the van left a cloud of dust in its wake, speeding down the narrow gravel road.

Bilal shook hands with the senior police official, and opened the door to the BMW.

They drove in complete, suffocating silence, the earlier screech of the tyres the only indication of Bilal's anger. Mona refrained from uttering even a single word, terrified at the prospect of Bilal getting a gist of the tumultuous storm inside her. She wasn't sure what it was that she was feeling, so far from making stabs at conversation or attempting to discern the reason behind Bilal's anger, she focused on keeping her lips pressed together. Tightly.

When they arrived home, they climbed the stairs together. Despite everything, he had come to save her. If it hadn't been for him, she would have been in police custody. She would have got out by morning, but by then her mortification would have been complete. The whole city would have found out, and Mona knew her acquaintances. They wouldn't have let go of this particular scandal for years.

She extended her hand to take his, but at the precise moment, as if anticipating her movement, Bilal flung his hand away from her reach. He pressed her against the wall of the corridor, holding his forearm against her neck. She choked at the sudden force on her windpipe.

'Bilal,' she rasped. 'Stop.'

Bilal edged his face closer to hers so that all she could see was the malevolence in his eyes. 'I told you not to go to the party. You never listen, do you?'

She attempted to speak, but no sound came out. She gasped for breath.

'Do you know what that bastard policeman charged me for carrying you away from the crime scene? One million rupees and a week's supply of whores. He's made a pimp out of me. Do I look like a pimp to you?' He pressed harder against her windpipe. 'Do I?'

But Mona couldn't even breathe. She struggled in vain, her fists pummelling his broad chest. When her breathing turned into a loud rattling sound, she saw the alarm cross Bilal's features. He removed his forearm from her neck.

She crumpled to the floor in a fit of coughing and gasps. The air flooded into her lungs again.

Bilal crouched down next to her. The hand he ran over her hair was shaking. 'Why do you force me to be hard with you?' he said. 'If you'd only listen to me and do as I tell you, none of this would happen. You know how disobedience brings out the worse in me.'

Mona clutched her searing neck. 'I was about to thank you,' she whispered.

Bilal leaned closer. 'What?'

'I was going to thank you for saving me,' Mona cried loudly, 'before you pounced on me. You bastard.'

His hand on her head went rigid. He removed it, using it to tip her chin up. His eyes sparked, but his mouth wore a cold smile. 'If you think you can act like a harlot for the world to see, you are mistaken, my dear. Hanging out with riffraff like that bitch Meera and her insufferable models. Have you lost your bloody mind? I save you from that lunacy, and you thank me by turning your nose up at me.'

He flexed his fingers, but didn't raise them to beat her any further.

'They're not riffraff, Bilal. Your dear friend Elahi was there too. The poor man lost his life, and—' She was about to confess to having witnessed the murder of Elahi, but she bit her tongue.

Bilal laughed, a self-satisfied grin spreading across his features. 'Good riddance, I say. I'm certain that procuring steel from his dumb son will be infinitely easier now. That bastard had a habit of charging a premium, not to mention his unbearable, never-ending dreams for filmdom. Glad he's gone.'

Mona shook her head. 'You're an animal.'

Bilal laughed, his Adam's apple bobbing up and down. 'Am I? Well, I'd say that little piece of filth you were hanging out with at the party is a more fitting candidate, since I'm sure that's how the police would be treating him. Like the animal he is. Funny how the world works.'

As he rose, he reached out to ruffle her hair like he would a dog's. 'Sweet dreams, my love. I would wait for you in bed, but at this point, I think we can rest assured that you'll be retiring in the guest room. It's a pity since I relish angry sex.'

'Go to hell,' Mona spat back.

'I suppose all of your friends will be here to sympathise tomorrow, so mind you don't drink too much so that it shows on your beautiful face. Let it be our own dark little secret.'

With that, he left her sitting on the ground with her knees pushed up against her chest, and her hair tousled. He was whistling by the time he closed their bedroom door. Mona remained seated there for a long time, thinking of nothing in particular, her mind running around in circles, before she dragged herself to the guest room.

—

Bilal was right about one thing. As soon as Mona stepped into the drawing room, she got engulfed in a mass of limbs. There were too many women trying to get a piece of her, making it impossible for her to recognise any of them.

'Oh, you poor dear.'

'Haye Allah, the horror you've endured. How are you even standing? Lie down!'

'Someone bring her a wet towel. She's sweating like a pig.'

'A pig? Now really, Jamila.'

'Lime water and honey is the perfect remedy for stress.'

The ladies spoke on top of each other so that Mona only caught snatches of conversation. She was alarmed at her sudden popularity. She tried to edge back into the foyer, out of the hungry clutches of these foreign ladies before a familiar voice boomed from somewhere in the room. 'Ladies! Quiet down and take your seats.'

Nobody listened. They continued to pepper Mona with questions and home remedies for injuries she hadn't sustained.

'Ladies!' It was Alia, and from her tone, Mona knew she was really pissed off. 'If you don't get away from Mona this instant, I shall have security guards throw your asses out. Like Meera did.'

That did it.

The women fanned out, muttering to themselves, some throwing Alia dirty looks.

'Aha!' someone called from the far end of the room. 'There she is.'

It was Nighat, seated in one of the few armchairs that could support her weight. She beckoned her with both arms.

Mona blinked her eyes once at Shabeena as she passed – their secret code for conveying frustration – before kneeling down in front of Nighat. Her mother-in-law gave her a long look, her eyes travelling from her feet to her face, resting for several moments on the angry purplish bruise on her neck where Bilal had tried to strangle her last night. Nighat pursed her lips, and Mona quickly covered her neck with her dupatta.

'All seems to be in good working order.' Nighat winked at an anxious Kulsoom who stood on the balls of her feet, bending forward to get a closer look. 'You have been incredibly lucky, dear. There have been so many casualties; it simply boggles the mind. So much grief, and for what? So that the women of this country can be wrapped in those ugly burqas, and the men can roam free with weapons on the street, doling out punishment as their hearts desire? God damn them. They'll have to kill me before I allow a damned burqa on my head. I'd prance around naked just to spite them if I wasn't so fat.'

Some women chuckled, a dry, half-hearted sound.

'Why, this is hardly anything to joke about, Aunty,' Shabeena spoke up, her eyebrows knotted together. 'To think that Elahi Sahab and his friends would have been alive if we just had the prudence to take the headscarf.'

'You think they would stop at the headscarf? They'd wipe that bright red lipstick from your lips, probably slice your lips off in the process. Then they'd shroud you in a burqa and so many layers of clothing that you'd be unrecognisable. And when all of that is achieved, they'd bend you over on the couch in the privacy of their homes, spread your legs and take you then and there. That's the way they like their women.'

No one laughed this time. The room rang with silence.

Shabeena had her hand on her chest. 'Oh my God, your language. Being older than me doesn't give you license to deride me like that—'

'It's my house!' Nighat boomed. 'I'll talk the bloody way I want. Condoning terrorism – why Shabeena, I thought you were better than that. Over thirty people have died. And all of them educated and from good families. Imagine! Rich people!'

'I would never condone terrorism, but if we're going to sit here and pretend that rich people's lives are more valuable than poor ones, I'm sorry but I'll have to leave,' Shabeena replied.

'As well you should,' said a woman Mona didn't know from next to the sofa. There were so many of them she didn't know. Where had they all come from? 'If somebody spoke to me like that, I'd commit suicide.'

'Do it. Less burden on this poor planet to be rid of your idiotic brain,' Nighat shot back.

'Well you have a point,' another woman, a half-starved thing with grizzly black hair said. 'In my opinion, it's the elite class that's carrying the country forward. I for one will have to side with you, Nighat. My grief at the loss of such valuable lives is inconsolable. Why couldn't it have happened in a place like Anarkali or Lohari Gate?'

'Okay, stop it. Everyone.' Mona rose from her crouch. She straightened her hair, shot a warning glance to Nighat who simply shrugged her shoulders and pretended to examine her nails. She continued staring at Nighat. 'Aunty...'

After chewing on a cuticle for a long while, Nighat spoke up, 'Okay fine, you win. I'm going out. My friend Shabeena here seems to have a short fuse.'

Shabeena grimaced. 'I'm not your friend.'

'Shabeena,' Mona said sharply. She turned to the swarm of ladies she had no recollection of ever meeting. *Who let them all in here*, she thought briefly before pointing – literally pointing – to the door. 'I'm so thankful for your concern, but as you can see, I'm completely unblemished. Not a scratch. So, if you all could please...'

They were rich society ladies. They didn't need to be told twice that they were now unwanted. They rose in a great cloud of anger and huffed their way out.

Alia giggled. 'There will be hell to pay, Mona. Most of these were Shahida's minions, out to get any scrap of information they can to report back to the old crow. Her husband is dead, but Shahida's game is still going strong.'

'Who's going to his funeral?' Kulsoom piped in. 'Please, I don't think I can take all the pressure of weeping ladies. I don't want to go.'

Alia groaned. 'Oh please! I've been dying to see that bat in agony since the day I laid eyes on her! I'm going.'

Kulsoom recoiled. 'How mean!'

Alia mimed hugging Kulsoom from the distance. 'Why honey, there wasn't anything left of Elahi to bury. Apparently, he got crushed into pieces under the rubble.'

Kulsoom's eyes widened. 'Actual pieces?' She placed a fluttering hand over her head and sank into a sofa. 'Oh God.'

Alia smirked at Mona.

Mona stood with her hands on her hips. 'Well? Were any of you going to ask whether I'm okay?'

Shabeena rolled her eyes. 'Do you think we braved your mother-in-law's fury to make small talk? We called your husband a dozen times, begging him for information since you were so conveniently asleep. He said that apart from some pressure you sustained on your neck, you were unharmed. And would someone tell me why Bilal's tone is always so clipped with me? As if he's doing me a favour just by speaking to me.'

'Don't mind him,' Mona said, her hand travelling to her neck. It still stung to touch the tender spot where Bilal had tried to strangle her last night. 'He has his phases. You'd be better off not talking to him entirely.'

'Speaking of attitude,' Alia said, edging forward, her fingers tapping the glass-fronted coffee table. 'Has any of you spoken to that Meera? From what I've heard, it's as if a demon's possessed her ever since the blast. She even looks the part. All swollen eyes and tousled hair.'

Mona's heart skipped a beat. She hadn't checked her phone all morning. She had downed two Valiums in one go to induce a slumber so deep that she wouldn't have to think of Ali in jail or lay seething in hatred for Bilal. The tablets worked, but there was a strange emptiness in her head, a vast void where thoughts used to be. It was only now that things were starting to trickle back into her mind: her phone, Bilal's silence after their fight, Meera's condition and most of all, Ali's fate.

'What happened to Meera? Her models? Damn, I have to check my phone. There must be a billion missed calls.'

'A bunch are rotting in jail from what I've heard,' Shabeena spoke up. 'Can't say I blame the police. These people should be imprisoned for life for possessing such questionable morals.' Her eyes met Mona's. She sighed. 'Meera is fine. Alia is exaggerating as usual. The poor woman is just having a hard time getting her people out of jail. I guess this is the time when contacts count.'

'Sure do,' Alia said, watching the gardener outside watering the rose bushes. 'I say Mona, I never noticed. Your gardener here looks like a version of Al Pacino. How hot is that?'

'Ugh.' Shabeena shook her head at Alia.

Mona wasn't paying attention. Her mind was transfixed on the earlier information. So, Ali was still in jail. If she had learned one thing from Bilal over the years, it was his repeated conviction that the jails in Pakistan were the most awful places you could ever find yourself. 'I wouldn't even wish it on my worst enemy,' he used to say.

And yet, he had so willingly allowed Ali to be carted off to the lockup, without even a second glance. How he had changed. Sometimes she'd watch him for hours, amazed that she had married such a monster, such a misogynist.

Ali. Even his name had an unfathomable effect on her, a shiver that ran through her whenever she heard it. What was happening to her? Two kind words, and here she was melting like wax. *Get a grip on yourself*, she thought.

Alia's mobile rang. Alia frowned. 'Unknown number. Huh.' Her expression changed when she put the phone to her ear. 'Oh hi! How are you... as a matter of fact yes, we're with her. The princess has finally awoken.' She looked at Mona, drew the phone away a few inches, and mouthed 'Meera'.

Mona sprang into action, rushing to take the phone from Alia.

Alia dodged her. 'She's all right... maybe in a little shock, but physically fine. And she's dying to talk to you.

Here.' Alia thrust the phone into Mona's hand, and withdrew, shaking her head.

Mona held the phone to her ear. 'Hello?' Her voice came out timid and breathless. Her heart thudded painfully in her chest.

'Mona, oh thank God. This is such a relief. You weren't picking up your phone since last night, and although I called your home earlier, I didn't get a very definitive answer. Your husband was so curt, which shouldn't surprise me, but I was thinking that if there was a time he could be more friendly, this was it.' Meera was speaking without pause. 'Of course, I have never expected anything better from that ass crack, but, oh God, I am rambling. How are you, Mona? God, I am so sorry for inviting you to that party.'

'Slow down, Meera, please. Breathe. I'm fine.'

'With half of my models behind bars – both male and female – I swear I have had no time to visit you. I knew you were somewhere in the vicinity of where Elahi got shot. Thank God they didn't get you.'

Mona refrained from mentioning the fact that she'd seen the killers. 'How are your models?' she asked instead. Her voice rose in pitch. 'How is Ali?'

Meera groaned. From her breathing, Mona could tell that Meera was pacing across the room wherever she was. 'Don't ask. It's an absolute nightmare. The police questioned poor Ali for hours last night. It wasn't until I gave them a piece of my mind did they finally relent. I mean, for Christ's sake, he's a model, not a terrorist, but you couldn't tell that from the way they were drilling him. The poor man was as pale as a ghost.'

Mona felt something squeezing her heart. Tears came into her eyes as she recalled Ali's face when he had seen her last night. Life could be so cruel. She didn't know what kind of connection he had with those two charismatic murderers last night, but whatever it was, she was sure Ali wasn't to blame in the least. 'Where is he now?' she asked, suppressing the crack in her voice. 'You made sure he got home safely, right? His brother is quite sick. His family must be beside themselves.'

'I've got bigger fish to fry, Mona. They still have that courtesan under custody. If word gets out that she's been moonlighting as an escort under my watch, they'll have me in prison in a blink of an eye.'

There were close to a hundred text messages on Mona's phone, most of them from her children, none of them from Ali. She scrolled through the list of missed calls. Apart from her friends, there were a few unknown numbers, but still no Ali. She was quite sure they had exchanged numbers at some point in the past, and yet he hadn't reached out to her. Maybe he hated her for leaving him the way she did last night. She didn't blame him; she hated herself.

Looking back to ensure her friends were busy with their phones, she sneaked a quick message to Ali: *Hey, didn't hear from you. Horrible night! Hope you're doing okay. Let me know...*

Five dots. If there was a way to scream desperation, this was it. Before she could change her mind, she typed *Waiting!!!*, and pressed send a second time. At least now she knew there was no margin of doubt that she was desperate. The two messages in quick succession said as much.

For the next thirty minutes, her thumb clicked on the button to light up the screen in the hopes of seeing a message from Ali, but none came. She got excited a couple of times when a few messages arrived, but they turned out to be from the phone company she was subscribed to. She wanted to scream. On top of everything, Kulsoom wouldn't stop yapping about her fear of seeing Elahi's dead body at his funeral. After a while, even Shabeena got annoyed.

'For the last time, Kulsoom. Stop acting like a baby. There is nothing of that poor man for you to see. You just need to pay your condolences to Shahida, although why you're so keen on visiting that old hag, I'll never understand. But then, I could ask myself the same question.'

'Social rejection is not an option for me, sorry,' Alia piped in. 'Besides, imagine watching Shahida cry. I'd sell my body on the streets for the chance.'

Elahi's house looked like a war zone. There were cordons everywhere, starting from the entry into Cantt and ending at the gates where several security men with their many dogs examined each car before approving entry. Mona had only agreed to accompany them because it had suddenly occurred to her that Meera's house was within a stone's throw from the Elahis' place. As soon as she had said some fake words of consolation to Shahida, she would leave for Meera's. She hoped to find the whereabouts of Ali, at least get a chance to talk to him. She didn't know about him, but it had been years – ever since she had fallen out of love with her husband – that she had felt this way for someone. It was like her whole body was crackling with electricity, her limbs rigid with the pain of separation, of the uncertainty of what had become of him. She didn't know how she'd react on seeing him. She wanted to prepare herself so that she wouldn't fall to pieces. She took a deep breath and followed her friends into the shadowy reception area of Elahi's mansion.

Inside, it smelled strongly of incense and roses, the white marble floor sprinkled with rose water and sandalwood oil. The thickness of the perfume choked her nose. She breathed through her mouth. Before entering the room from where the wailing ensued, they all covered their heads.

Instantly, Mona's heart went out to Shahida. She felt no satisfaction in seeing her frail body hunched over the *charpai* bearing her husband's body, her thin shoulders shaking as she wept into the hard wood, a dozen women trying and failing to pry her away. Some pushed water to her lips while others hitched her flailing dupatta back onto her head. In a short moment of lucidity, Shahida regained her composure, straightened her shoulders, and ripped the dupatta off her head. 'Nobody touch me!' she warned them, her voice savage and absent of grief.

Then she crumpled over the charpai once more, sobbing bitterly. 'He would always come back. Always. No matter how much we fought or how long my parties would last, he would always be waiting for me in bed at the end of the day with a cup of green tea in his hand for me. Who will bring me that tea now? Where will I turn to for warmth in the cold night?'

'As if it ever gets cold in this place,' Alia murmured, but Mona sensed her half-heartedness, the futility of her remark. The truth was that grief in any form was intolerable, even that of enemies.

Mona brushed her lips against the top of Shahida's head – it smelled of age and baby shampoo – and withdrew, intent on getting away from the place as soon as possible.

She looked around as she ducked under a tray carrying bottles of mineral water, held aloft by a harried waiter. As she righted herself, her eyes fell on the men's area and she froze. There, only a few steps away from her stood Ali. His head was bowed to his chest, but she knew it was him. The way in which his hair divided in the middle, and fell in delicate cascades on either side of his scalp; it was unmistakably Ali. She wanted to rush to him, to take his hand, but she forced herself to stop. She couldn't enter the men's sitting area. Not unless it was an emergency.

Who cares, she thought, crossing the threshold and entering the congregation of men. All conversation ceased as heads were drawn in her direction. She stood there, feeling the flush rising up her neck. In her nervousness she wrapped the edge of her dupatta around her fingers. She didn't want to look at the men staring at her. Her eyes were fixed on Ali's bowed head.

After what seemed like a minute, an elderly man with a kind face rose from his seat and approached her. Mona tore her gaze away from Ali, and looked at his ancient face, the pale blue, watery eyes that must have seen many decades.

'Is there anything the matter, my dear?' the old man said. 'If you are lost, allow me to guide you to the women's section. It's not proper to stand here in the middle of so many men, especially when there's a dead body in the house. The men should be paying their respects to the dead, not staring at women.' The old man smiled, revealing gums absent of teeth.

'I – I'm not lost,' Mona stuttered.

She saw Ali's head snap up. She met his eyes, and saw surprise transform into confusion, and finally what looked like a mixture of anger and concern. He gave his head an infinitesimal shake. Mona blinked her eyes, once, before pulling the falling dupatta back over her head, and withdrawing from the room. 'Sorry, I'm not lost. Just got distracted.' She had done what she had come for.

'If you're not lost, my dear, why on earth did you come prancing in here? The ladies of today... I tell you, Zafar, if this had been my daughter...' the old man called after her until he was out of earshot. *Not so kind after all*, she thought to herself.

After ten minutes of waiting on the far side of the tent that had been erected to cater for more people coming in to offer condolences, she saw Ali's tall form emerge from the house. He shielded his eyes from the glare of the sun and searched for her. She didn't raise a hand in acknowledgement, but he spotted her, and began to make his way toward her. That gave her the opportunity to watch his body move, the broad shoulders more pronounced in his loose-fitting white kameez. She admired the way his arms worked in synchrony with his legs, the perfect fall of his feet, one right next to the other. He didn't seem to have sustained any external injuries; his face as he drew nearer was unmarked and there was no evidence of a limp nor did any pain contort his features. Even in this funeral attire, he seemed ready to light the ramp on fire.

When he saw her watching him, a brief smile played on his face like a sudden refreshing breeze before it was gone. He was sombre once again when he halted in front of her.

'How are you?'

'How are you?'

They both spoke in unison.

He waved his hand. 'You first, please.'

Mona shrugged. 'Lucky for me, I was carted off by my husband at the most opportune moment. Women like me, we come close to suffering, but never seem to touch it.'

'Stop it. You endured your share of horror last night. All because of me.' His face broke into a despairing frown as a solitary tear dropped from one eye, blotting his kameez. He had begun to let his chest hair grow, Mona noticed. 'It's difficult to imagine oneself being such a source of horror. I should be serving a life sentence for what I did. I deserve capital punishment, but instead I let Meera rescue me from the lockup, as if I were an innocent who didn't know the first thing about what happened.'

Mona exhaled in relief. So he hadn't blurted anything out about what they had witnessed last night. Good. 'It wasn't your fault, Ali. Terrorism is nobody's fault.'

A wry smile crossed his lips. 'You honestly believe that? Didn't you see me bring in those two men at the party? I'm an accomplice to a most heinous crime.'

'You didn't even seem to know those people! What are you talking about?'

A shudder ran through him, and Mona quelled the urge to take him in her arms. Her nails dug into her palms as she stuck her arms on either side of her body.

'It's true that I didn't know them. I had only met them last night for the very first time, but I should have known. From the way they were asking about Elahi, I should have known. I was just so caught up in... in—'

He shook his head as if the thought tortured him.

Mona's breath caught in her throat. 'Caught up in what?'

Ali's gaze drew level with hers. 'In you. It's probably the last thing you want to hear, and honestly, I don't know what's got into me. Even now, with this mind-numbing guilt assaulting my senses, I cannot help but think about you. When you came into the men's area, I was about to pass out with depression. You brought me back to life.

Standing with you here, I am aware of my guilt, of course I am, but somehow, it isn't as crushing as when I'm alone.'

'Ali—' Mona began.

'I don't know what I'm feeling, Mona. I know this is wrong; everything about this is wrong. I don't even know you properly. How many times have we met? A handful? More? And yet, I seem to know you more than I know those tiresome models I see every day. With you, I can let down my guard for just a moment.' He laughed. 'Of all the scenarios I had pictured myself saying these words, this one never occurred to me. A man has died – several men have died – I am more or less an accessory to murder, and here I am confessing my feelings to you. How strange life can be.'

'It's not your fault, Ali.'

'I know it's my fault, Mona, but I will learn to live with it. I will have to repent, and God willing,' – he had a faraway look in his eyes – 'I will soon learn how to avenge this assault on my trust, this misuse of my confidence in someone. It is my fault, Mona, and I know it.'

Mona shook her head. She spoke the next words before embarrassment gripped her. 'I mean to say that it isn't your fault that you feel this way. About me.' She searched his eyes for a reaction. 'And neither is it bad to feel this way.'

A spark crossed his eyes. 'Mona?'

She wanted to take those words back. She had no right to utter them. She was a married woman. And besides, he had enough to deal with. She knew she was only a passing attraction for him; a life boat in his sea of troubles just because she had shared the unfortunate moments of the bomb attack with him. Events like that, they bond people. She wasn't even sure if it was attraction or an innocuous need for companionship. But she knew that she needed him. Whatever he might feel.

'I – I just…' she began, 'I wanted you to know that I feel the same way. I shouldn't, but I do.'

'Mona,' he repeated.

'Mona!' someone shouted.

It was Kulsoom.

Before Mona could so much as attempt to retrace the conversation, to steer it into calmer waters, Kulsoom wedged herself between them, feet firmly planted on either side. 'Oh, nice to see you again, Ali,' she said over her shoulder before dragging Mona back toward the house.

Mona turned around, and their eyes met. She saw the disappointment of the unfinished conversation in his eyes, but there was also a glow on his face that she had seen once on Bilal's face, during the early years of their marriage. She recognised it as love, and her heart sank and rose. Dread and excitement assaulted her in equal measure.

Chapter Nineteen

Ali

Ali paced the room over and over. The movement did nothing to calm his rapid heartbeat. His heart seemed ready to leap out of his chest. Although the days had gotten very hot, the stone floor was so cold that he could feel the chill seeping into his feet through his rubber soles.

After weeks of chasing after Gul, he had finally managed to catch her as she exited her one-room apartment, in a place where only hooligans would dare venture. He had no idea that the area had fallen into such disrepair. Once, it had been the pride of Lahore, but now, it was just a crumbling old building with dodgy people wandering in the shadows, and dolled-up women as ancient as sin eyeing young men for a chance encounter in the alleys, all for a measly hundred rupees or so. The badi haveli that she supposedly lived in had been a farce.

Gul had yelped in surprise, her eyes immediately flitting toward the nearest exit as she smiled at him, pulling a headscarf from her handbag and covering her heavily made-up hair. 'Fancy seeing you here,' she said brightly.

She hadn't closed the door to her apartment, and Ali had simply thrust an arm against her neck, and driven her back into the room, muffling her scream with his other hand. He had no time for her nonsense.

To his relief, it didn't take him long to get Gul to spill the beans.

'I didn't know the entire plan,' she gasped, her hand clasped around her neck where an ugly maroon bruise had started to appear. 'I swear to God, Ali, I didn't know the man would blow up the whole place. I simply thought he wanted to get rid of Elahi.'

'So you did know that there was a plan?' Ali wanted to strangle the breath out of her. Did she have any idea of the guilt he was wracked with?

As if reading his thoughts, Gul's frightened eyes met his. 'I know how you must be feeling. Believe me, I have personally experienced the same. I've been used by the Mir before, but never in this way.'

Ali's rage mounted. He took a step closer. 'You knew what he was like, and still you took me to him, allowed him to lure me into his disgusting trap? What kind of woman are you? What kind of human are you?'

Gul flinched. 'I never thought he'd go to such lengths. I've only ever helped him in single murders. I had no idea he was involved in this terrorism thing. Why do you think I haven't been answering your calls? I've been trying to keep a low profile in case someone tracks it back to us. Your being here is a great threat to us both.'

'To hell with you,' Ali had shouted.

And now, here he was, pacing the Mir's visiting chamber, Gul having vanished somewhere inside the building to fetch the man. They had come uninvited; Ali had dragged her here without her consent.

After what seemed like hours of waiting, the door creaked, and Ali caught the tall silhouette of the Mir as he stood in the doorway. He looked like a new man, standing erect with his chest thrown out, a bright red chaddar thrown across his shoulders, his white shalwar kameez gleaming in the darkness.

Stepping into the room, he spread out his arms. 'My boy. My dear, dear boy.'

In spite of the revulsion at seeing the broad smile on the man's face, Ali couldn't help but admire the sheer charisma of the man. If he hadn't known he was capable of such crimes, he would have happily fallen to his knees and kissed the hem of his shirt. Ali shuddered at the scale of this man's hypnotic power.

He allowed himself to be swept into the Mir's embrace for only a moment before he jerked back, the horrors of that night flooding back into his mind.

'You betrayed me,' he said, avoiding meeting the Mir's eyes. He rested his eyes instead on the brooch he had pinned to his chest. It was a crude metal thing, with a single ruby shaped like a drop nestled in the blackened steel. 'I trusted you, and you made me a pawn in your horrible scheme. You have the blood of dozens on your hands.' His eyes finally met the Mir's. He was shocked at the calm radiating from them. He took a step back. 'How can you live with what you've done? How can you live with yourself?'

The Mir's grin widened, the wrinkles around his eyes standing out in sharp relief. 'Live with myself? My boy, how can *you* live with yourself? How can you not feel the exhilaration that comes with the deed you've performed? Has God deserted you so completely?'

'You call killing dozens of people God's work? You are no better than the common thief who justifies his deed as necessary for feeding his family. Except you're even worse. You don't even have a family. You just kill innocents for fun.'

'Infidels! The whole lot of them. Infidels! Not inno-cents.' The indulgent grin had gone from his face, replaced by a smile that exposed his yellowing teeth. He looked scary.

Gul took several steps back. Before Ali had time to process what was happening, the Mir had leapt forward to grab his wrist. He pulled him toward the door that led deeper into his compound. 'I don't have a family, do I? You think I've tricked you into performing some unforgivable deed, that I didn't have the resources to have someone else do if I wanted?' He shot Ali a dirty look. 'You fool. I did it for your own benefit. Let me show you how.'

Ali struggled against him half-heartedly. He was being taken upstairs – the mystifying place where all the sounds had come from during his first visit – and he really wanted to see for himself what happened there. He was aware of the gentle tread of Gul's footsteps behind him. The Mir's grip on Ali had loosened as he struggled up the steep flight of stairs. Ali could easily break free and make a run for it if he wanted, but somehow he knew that the Mir wouldn't hurt him. If he had wanted him gone, he could have asked his cronies to get rid of him at any time after that incident. His heart hammered in his chest as they drew closer to the rickety door that stood at the end of the stone steps, patches of light showing through the slits in between what seemed to be hastily put together wooden slats.

'I don't have a family, is that right?' the Mir murmured again. His fingers unlatched the door, and he pushed it open. 'Here, Ali, see my family.'

Ali's eyes snapped shut in the sudden glare of lights. Behind him, Gul gasped.

He forced his eyes open. He stood looking for a long time, blinking only once when the pressure on his eyes became unbearable. In front of him was a large hall, rectangular in shape with a high ceiling below which hung dozens of high voltage bulbs that lit up the hall with the brightness of many suns. What captivated his attention, though, wasn't the brightness, but the rows of men, all standing in precisely straight files, clad in black, their faces and heads concealed behind thick fabric, the halls ringing with the stamping of their boots. The way they would jump in the air, rolled face-down across the ground and rose up once again with a jump implied that they were engaged in some kind of training activity.

Kalashnikovs were laid out next to them on the floor. They proceeded to pick them up, and pretended to fire them in the air.

'My God,' Gul murmured behind him, her voice a whisper of fascination.

The Mir stepped into the room and turned around to face Ali. He clasped his hands around his waist. 'This, my dear boy, is my family.'

Ali stood on the landing, his tongue growing thick in his drying mouth, his senses too overwhelmed for him to utter a sound.

'This is just one compound, Ali,' the Mir said. 'There are several more across the country, containing hundreds more, and then there are ones in the tribal areas. Some are special women's training institutes. So, when I said that I asked you to perform that favour, it was for your own benefit rather than mine.' He gestured to the men behind him. 'As you can see, I have more than enough people who would have been willing to barge into that event and open fire, invited or not.'

Ali cleared his throat, and forced his lips apart. 'How is this country still standing if you have people like this at your disposal?'

The Mir adjusted his turban, which had gone slightly askew. 'What a silly question. A few hundred won't stand much of a chance in front of the force of this country. However, the question you should be asking yourself, dear boy, is whether you are going to inform the government about this?'

Chapter Twenty

Mona and Ali

Text Messages, June 1

Ali
Saw something unreal today. I don't know
how to process it. I feel lost.

Mona
You need company. I wish I could meet
you right this moment.

Ali
So do I. I hope soon. When can I speak
with you?

Mona
Soon.

Text Messages, June 7

Ali

I've come to meet you. Standing outside
your house now, chatting with your guards.

Mona

OMG, are you serious? Why are you here?
Leave at once. I'm with my family.

Ali

Kidding.

Mona

Honestly! You're such a boy. Am I to
believe from these humorous messages
that you're finally getting over that woeful
incident?

Ali

Kind of. Your words helped. I don't know
why I get so awkward when you're with
me. I just feel unable to express myself.

Mona

I've been told I have that impression on men.

Ali

Someone told me you have a thing for younger boys.

Mona

Not funny. You make me sound like a cougar. I'm busy with my husband. Will chat later.

—

Text Messages, June 8

Mona

Hi

Ali

'Lo

Mona

What's up with the despondent greeting?

Ali

I thought you were busy with your husband. I would hate to disrupt the cosy night of a lovestruck couple.

Mona

By busy, I meant I was at dinner. Trust men's minds to travel to the darkest places.

Ali

Intimacy is a dark thought for you? How shocking! I thought society ladies had a colourful life. At least the ones I know have. No torrid nights in Paris for this lady?

Mona

Paris, sure! Just not with Bilal. He's driving me nuts. How goes the modelling world?

Ali

Thinking of leaving it. I don't enjoy the constant glare of the camera, and I cannot suck up to the designers anymore. Sorry.

Mona

Should I speak to Meera?

Ali

Why do you care? Concerned, are we?

Mona

Of course I am, Ali. And even if I didn't know you personally, I'd offer the same advice. Don't leave a job just because you don't enjoy it as much as you should. Life is never as enjoyable anyway. Look at me. Look at the luxuries I enjoy every day, and yet I take it all for granted. They don't make me happy.

Ali

Even an unfeeling rock could tell that you're unhappy. I wish I knew how to make things better. And this is not a joke.

Mona

Sigh...

Ali

I have an idea. Coffee? Just the two of us.

Mona

Enticing! But I'm not sure I'd like being spotted in the company of a handsome young man.

233

Ali
Aha! Handsome. Thanks

Mona
I wish things were different. Besides, people would just call me a crazy aunty.

Ali
Hey! You're no aunty. Don't ever say that again. You have no idea what aunties are like, and the things they're capable of. Just don't remind me! Just know, though, that you're no aunty. Not by a long shot.

Mona
Awww... You're sweet

Ali
I'm much more than that ;)

Mona
Now you're just being naughty!

Text Messages, June 10

Ali
Told ya we'd have a good time.

Mona
Thank God nobody saw us. I don't ever want to go to such a public place. What if my husband had spotted me????

Ali
You could have said you were waiting for Meera to join us.

Mona
Good idea! But that won't work every time.

Ali
Am I to believe that more meetings are in the pipeline?

Mona
Heh. Maybe.

Ali
You were glowing, though. I liked the effort you seemed to have put into dressing yourself.

Mona
Flattery...

Ali
No way!

–

Text Messages, June 11

Mona
God, this party is so boring. Isn't it?

Ali
Don't ask me. I'm just enjoying watching you.

Mona
Liar! You're backstage. How could you be watching?

236

Ali
Look at the far corner of the stage. To your left.

Mona
Aha! There you are! How do I look?

Ali
You're honestly going to ask me that?

Mona
Humour me...

Ali
You dazzle like the sun has shattered into a million pieces and scattered around you. You look like the moon without its blemishes.

Mona
Oh, I didn't know you were a poet too!

Ali
I love you, you know.

Ali

I want to see you tomorrow. No matter what!

Ali

Hey! Why aren't you replying? Where did you go? I can't see you anymore.

Ali

Mona? Are you there?

12.00 a.m

Ali

Hello?

2.15 a.m.

Ali

I'm not ashamed of what I said. Nobody has made me feel like this. I promise you, Mona, that there is more to our relationship than just secrecy. Just trust me

4.00 a.m

Ali

Hello?

Text Messages, June 12

Ali
Hey, I hope I didn't offend you with my foolishness the other night.

Mona
It's not that. I just don't think we should be meeting anymore.

Ali
But why?

Mona
It feels awkward, Ali. I'm not sure I want a public scandal.

Ali
Is it because I'm not as rich as you are?

Mona
What? Are you crazy? Of course not. It's about principle. As much as I like you, at the end of the day, I have to get back to my husband, and the thought of facing him when I've done all these things embarrasses me.

Ali

You've done nothing.

Mona

That's the thing! I don't like the way I am feeling. The fact is that I want more to happen! I want to do things that I shouldn't even be thinking! Things I didn't even know I could feel.

Ali

Like what?

Mona

Just don't message me again. I may not be able to control myself the next time.

4 a.m

Mona

I need to see you.

-

Text Messages, June 13

Ali

And yet, you still meet me.

Mona

God, I feel horrible. Meeting in secret like this.

Ali

You're the one who insists on secrecy. I'd be happy to tell the world that I'm in love with you.

Mona

Oh, don't say that.

Ali

Why not? I'm in love and proud of it.

Mona

And you really didn't have to buy me those expensive gifts. I told you money doesn't matter to me. It's your company that enchants.

Ali

And yet, you want me to be silent about this. Do you have any idea how you enchant me?

Mona

God! I'm going to go to hell for this!

Ali

You're already there. It's time to come out of it now. You need to live a little… loosen up so to speak. Luckily, I know the exact way to achieve that.

Mona

Haha, don't be so suggestive. People would say it's your profession.

Ali

For you, I'd make this my profession.

Mona

Oh Ali, how you do go on! I'm not sure my heart has beaten this fast in years. I feel like I'm twenty again.

Ali

You certainly look like it.

Mona

Haha! Tomorrow, then…

Ali

Tomorrow.

Chapter Twenty-One

Mona

It was everything she had hoped it would be. She had never dreamed she'd share another man's coffee, let alone his bed, but here she was, going weak at the knees at the thought of their next encounter. If she could, she would have laughed at her reaction to Ali, but there was nothing funny about it. Despite the million rules of society and religion they were breaking, it all seemed right. Sitting now in the midst of so many people, right next to her husband, she couldn't turn her mind away from that first encounter a week ago. She should be terrified, but she wasn't.

She had been breathless by the time she'd reached the hotel. It sat somewhere in the outskirts of Lahore, near Raiwind Road. She wasn't entirely sure that her perfume had managed to overpower the smell of smoke and animal dung that she had absorbed. She didn't drive often, and never such long distances, and definitely not with a heart that seemed like it would burst out of her chest. There had been several enticing U-turns that her failing nerve would veer toward, back to the safety of her home, the monotony of her life, but there was something more urgent that drew her to Ali. She had worn ordinary lawn clothes, a print so dull that it would have blended in with the shirts of half of the middle-class women of Lahore. She had used make-up to hide her blemishes and approaching wrinkles, but nothing too fancy that would catch a man's attention. For good measure, she had covered her hair and half her face with the dupatta. Her eyes were such a common brown that she could have been mistaken for anyone. On her feet, she wore her clunky Chanel court shoes that almost killed her in the heat.

She was certain Ali would have left by the time she arrived – she was that late – but when she knocked on the door on the second floor (thankfully, there wasn't a sign of any cameras in the corridor), she heard a thud and hurried footsteps. She had a brief urge to turn around and run, but the door opened. His hair was tousled as if he had been taking a nap, and his spectacles (he wore spectacles?) were slightly askew as if his face had pressed on them while he'd slept. His shirt also bore unmistakable creases, but his smile was as fresh as ever, his eyes widened in what she thought was disbelief. She found both of them lowering their eyes at the same time. She stepped inside.

After a moment of silence, Ali drew nearer, but instead of making a movement to touch her, he crossed her and closed the door. A muffled click as the 'Do Not Disturb' tag got stuck in the opening. Ali cursed and then laughed. 'I'm all thumbs today.'

Another moment of pained silence. With her eyes closed, she could sense the movement behind her more acutely. She was aware of Ali having taken a few steps in her direction. He was standing right behind her. She could smell the mouthwash on him, the belated sleepiness of his skin, the tang of his aftershave. 'I didn't expect you to come,' he murmured.

Mona opened her eyes. The room tilted before righting itself. Her breath came out in short bursts. She took a deep shuddering breath. 'I got stuck in traffic. Sorry if my lateness put you to sleep.'

His breath caught in his throat. 'It just made me dream of you.' He took a tiny step closer. He was mere centimetres from her. The electricity which sparked when the hairs of Ali's arm brushed Mona's bare wrists caused goosebumps to erupt across her skin. She let out another involuntary shudder and Ali took that opportunity to seize her from behind, his hands reaching across her stomach. He breathed in the scent of her hair, mumbling something incoherent.

Her resolve dissolved completely.

She broke free and ran for the chair near the window before she collapsed on the floor. Her eyes filled with tears, but she blinked them away.

'Should I leave?' His voice sounded distant in between the rushing in her ears. She heard the indecision, the fear in his voice, the terrified possibility of something longed for snaking away from him.

'No.' Her heart had calmed, and her breathing had returned to normal. She let out a short laugh. 'To think I was so intrepid in our text conversations, you must be surprised to find me as dull and fearful as a common deer. God.'

'Please don't say that. Tell me what do you need? Some water?'

'The water here probably comes from the gutter.' Mona slapped a hand over her mouth, but Ali laughed. 'Sorry, I didn't mean that. The hotel is lovely.'

'I love your spontaneity. Luckily, I brought some mineral water with me. Here,' – he unscrewed a water bottle and handed it to her – 'it's not cold I'm afraid. Not in this weather.'

'Count your blessings. At least the AC is working,' Mona remarked and Ali laughed again. After she had sipped some of the lukewarm water, he knelt down with her. His eyes met hers. He took her clammy hands in his own, and rubbed the knuckles with his thumbs.

'If you'd just like to sit and talk, we can do that. There's no hurry. If you simply want friendship, I'm fine with that. I just want to see you smile. I would never dream of pressuring you to do something you didn't want to.'

'Thanks, but it's not that. It's just that I feel I'm about to cross a line. After this, there is no going back. I will live with this forever.'

'We, Mona, we. You're no longer alone.'

Mona's eyes filled with tears. 'Where were you twenty years ago? I would have married you without a moment's hesitation.'

Ali's mouth was still drawn tight. 'I'm serious, Mona. We don't need to rush into anything. We can be friends.'

'Well, I didn't come all this way simply for a friendly chat now, did I?' It felt good to joke; it made everything seem less real, as if poking fun would somehow dull the intensity of what was happening – of what was going to happen.

Ali raised an eyebrow. 'If it isn't a chat you're after, there are other options in my mind that could be well worth our time.' Now he smiled. 'Only if you're up for it.'

There was such earnestness in his eyes – a tenderness she had never once witnessed in Bilal's eyes – that she put her hand over his lips. 'Say no more.'

She had never known a man's lips could be this soft. Bilal's rough lips dug into her skin, his urgent mouth hurting her where she was most sensitive. Ali's lips, his face, his indubitable youth instilled feelings in her that she hadn't known existed, thoughts that she had repressed long ago to some distant corner of her mind since Bilal would never completely acquiesce to her pleasure, so hell-bent he had always been to exact his own. In Ali's eyes, she saw love and passion, a lethal mixture that she stood little chance against. Slowly, she moved her fingers away from his lips, and before another guilty thought could invade her senses, she filled the distance between them, and covered his lips with her own.

If her forward behaviour had shocked her, her energy and passion in what happened later shocked her more.

It was Bilal's voice that interrupted her thoughts. 'I really don't understand.'

Mona blinked her eyes. What had they been talking about? Looking at Shabeena's rigid face, her eyes set on Bilal like a hawk's, she remembered. Religion.

'My dear Shabeena,' Bilal continued. 'Do you honestly believe that fifteen minutes with a stranger, choking him full of lectures on piety will change his beliefs? You honestly believe that?'

'Rome wasn't built in a day, Bilal.' Shabeena's expression was severe. 'We are doing all we can to steer people in the right direction. If there just weren't as many distractions like these silly fashion shows and the morals of our society going downhill in general, this would have been far easier.'

'So you spend your fifteen minutes with them, and assuming they are so affected by your teachings that they see the error of their ways, what do you do when the terrorists swoop in, convoluting everything you've taught them and using it all to their advantage? Because that is how terrorism is born, Shabeena. We need to broaden our minds. We need to become secular or we have no future.'

'Now, really! You speak like a non-Muslim.'

'Shabeena…' her husband said, a weary grey-haired man, covering her hand with his. Shabeena flung it away as if it had scalded her.

'No, you tell me, Bilal. Once and for all. Are you even a Muslim? Or do you laugh at us behind our backs for our beliefs?'

Bilal snorted. 'If I laugh behind your back, it most certainly isn't because of that. There may be other things. If you were more "secular", I'd tell you.'

Shabeena's nostrils flared, and Mona saw a rant coming, but before she could intervene, Alia's husband did.

'Speaking of secular thinking, anyone have a crush on Meera? By God, that woman.' Alia's husband had a habit of looking at everyone with widened eyes as if he were looking at them for the first time.

They were all seated on a round table in Shabeena's dining room, all eight of them. Kulsoom and her husband were eating from the same plate, whispering to each other and sniggering. Mona caught Alia's smirk several times, but didn't acknowledge it. What was wrong with what Kulsoom was doing?

Alia slapped her husband on the arm. 'She's Mona's friend. Have some respect.'

'Well, I'm Mona's husband, and I'll have to agree that Meera is a work of art. I like a woman who knows what to do with herself.'

Mona rolled her eyes. She was surprised to find she didn't care what Bilal said anymore. She was in a land of blissful indifference. She traced circles on her palm, her finger pausing at the place where Ali's hand had met hers, the way he had drawn her hands over her head till they knocked against the headboard. The smell of his musk aftershave still hung in her nostrils.

Suddenly she became aware of the silence around her. Everyone was watching her; Alia's fork paused in mid-air, the piece of shrimp hanging precariously close to her embellished shirt.

'Excuse me?' Mona asked, turning to look at Bilal who seemed to be waiting for an answer from her.

'Well?' he asked.

'Well what?'

'I just remarked that you never told me why you and Meera fell apart. It turns out that none of your friends know anything about it either.'

Now Mona understood the stunned silence.

Something buried deep inside of her squirmed. Mona's stomach clenched. She attempted nonchalance. 'It was so many years ago! I don't even remember.'

'Don't lie, Mona,' Kulsoom chimed in. 'You were just telling us a year ago, before Meera arrived in Lahore, that she had done something that you could never forgive.'

Alia stared daggers at Kulsoom. 'Drop it.'

Kulsoom looked perplexed. 'My fork?'

Shabeena rose to her feet. 'Let me ask the servants to bring in the main course now, shall I? We really should be discussing more pleasant topics. How often do we even get the chance to sit together?'

But Bilal was like a dog with a bone. 'Darling, it was only a simple question. We're curious.' He raised a hand to sweep the hair away from her face. His fingers brushed the earlobe that had been in Ali's possession just a week ago. It seemed like years ago.

'Bilal please...' The thing inside her threatened to rear its head. 'I need to use the washroom.'

Bilal grabbed her dupatta before she could leave. His eyes were narrowed. 'But what could have happened?'

'I said I don't want to talk about it!' she snapped. 'What part of it don't you understand? Let me be.'

Bilal's eyes flashed, and she saw the animal inside him. He let go of her dupatta, and began wolfing down the salad in front of him.

They ended up leaving early, Bilal hardly having touched the main course.

'You should at least have the decency to speak to your husband with respect in company,' Bilal spat at her later in the bedroom.

Mona sat in front of the dressing table, her fingers massaging her temples. 'Let it go, Bilal. I implore you.'

'Let it go? Do you seriously have a death wish, woman? I don't let insults like these slide. You're lucky that I'm not angry enough to beat you, or I would have already.'

'Aww, happy with a new mistress, are we? Is she feisty in bed? Does she let you beat her?'

'Mona...' Bilal warned her. 'What happened between you and Meera? Tell me now, or I will wring the truth out of you.'

Mona slapped her hands on the dressing table and rose to face her husband. 'For God's sake, Bilal. You won't give this a rest, will you? Fine.' She folded her arms. 'I had a crush on someone in college and Meera stole him from me. We – we had made plans to get married, but you know the kind of charm Meera has. She took him from me, and didn't even realise it. After spending a night, she tried to return him to me. As if he were a toy.'

Bilal swallowed her story whole. 'Aha. Young love. Now I know why my wife was less than perfect on her wedding night. Seems like you had your fun back in the day.'

Mona sighed. 'Yes.'

'Did you ever meet him after that? That boy. Did you meet him after you got married?'

'God, no. What do you take me for? A harlot?' The lies stung in her throat. She had already given herself to another man. She took a deep breath. 'Are you happy now? Can we let this rest?'

Bilal slid between the sheets. 'When have I ever not listened to you, my dear? Come to bed now, and let us forget these grievances.'

Mona feigned a headache.

She did everything with painstaking slowness so that Bilal would fall asleep before she slipped into bed. After a few moments, he asked. 'Say, where did you get these beautiful earrings? Did I gift them?'

'No.' The word was out of her mouth before she could stop it. The emerald and gold earrings were from Ali, his gift on the day they had slept together – a very expensive gift. Her hands paused at one of the earrings. She closed her eyes, waiting for the inevitable.

'If I didn't gift these, then who did? Who would give you something so expensive?' Bilal's voice was still playful, but Mona detected the undercurrent of suspicion in it. 'They're definitely not from your friends. Those bitches wouldn't be caught dead gifting you anything.'

Mona hesitated. 'What I meant was that I bought them from my pocket money. You didn't gift these.'

From the mirror, she saw Bilal narrow his eyes. 'Is that so?'

She looked back at him, and gave a false smile. 'You spoil me.'

It seemed to be a day of miracles. Bilal surprised her by neatly swallowing this lie as well. His eyes danced with mirth. 'I do spoil you, all right. Be sure to remember that whenever you feel the urge to talk back to your husband. I went soft on you today, but that won't happen next time.'

Later in bed, he curled his fingers with hers. 'Do you know what I'd have done if I'd discovered the earrings were from someone else?'

Mona went still, but when she spoke her voice was neutral. 'I bought them with money you gave me.'

'I know you did. But if that weren't the case. Let's say, if you were having an affair with someone behind my back.' The pressure on her hand increased. 'Do you know what I'd do to you?'

'I'm not having an affair.'

'I know you're not. But do you know what I'd do if you ever dared?'

When she could trust herself not to react, she turned toward him. 'No.'

He bared his teeth at her. 'I would kill that bastard and make you watch that. And then I'd kill you.'

Chapter Twenty-Two

Ali

Balance: 2.5 million rupees only... *End of Transaction*.

Ali smiled as he read the message, but his happiness couldn't quite assuage the knot of guilt in his stomach. He was building an empire on a pile of dead men. *Ruthless men*, he thought. Men who deserve every bit of the punishment that was meted out to them. Mir Rabiullah had shown him footage and evidence of the atrocities these men had committed, in the name of religion, in the name of morality, for the sake of their sexual desire. Women had been ravaged; poor people had perished, empires had been overturned just to consummate their desires. He forced the surge of triumph to overpower his guilt. He smiled again, wider. He felt like the character in the Oscar Wilde book he was reading.

'What's so funny?' Mona spoke up, her face turned toward him, her body warm against his in bed.

He had Mona. It still sounded unbelievable to his ears. For some miraculous, baffling reason, she was in his life. She loved him back, something he had never thought possible.

'Just work stuff,' he lied.

'Boring you already, am I?' she laughed, climbing on top of him. 'Let's make things interesting.'

He laughed with her, his hands drawing a languid circle around her waist. Behind the Chantilly lace, her skin seemed to tingle. He put the phone and book down. 'You could never bore me. Not in a million years.'

'Think again, Mister. I'm a lot older than you. You might change this opinion in a few years.'

A few years. She was serious about him, he realised.

'And would we still be stealing around like this, meeting briefly?'

She evaded the accusation in his question, and smiled as she leaned in for a kiss. Her eyebrows shot up as she read the title of the book. '*Dorian Gray*? Why Ali, you don't mess around, do you? What kind of crimes have you committed that you need to seek solace in this?'

She held up the book playfully, but Ali felt the familiar knot of guilt inside of him. He quashed it.

Soon.

He would stop what he was doing as soon as he had enough money.

He ran his fingers through her hair, taking care to be gentle. Although she didn't say it, he would feel her flinch whenever he got a bit rough. 'I just realised that I don't really know anything about you.'

Mona's eyes widened in mock consternation. 'Really?' She knotted her fingers in his. 'I think you know me more than anyone. I've never let anyone this close to my heart.'

'It's not that. I – I just don't know what you're like when you're not with me. I want to know you inside out.'

Mona returned to her initial position next to him, with her head resting on his shoulder. 'What is it that you'd like to know then, Ali? Ask away! But remember, this is a two-way street. You're going to have to answer some questions too. Done?'

Ali hesitated, but then agreed.

'What do you wear at home?'

Mona snorted. 'What a funny question. I don't even know how to answer it, but a promise is a promise, I guess.' She took a deep breath, trying not to laugh. 'I wear shalwar kameez, mostly. Sometimes, when I'm going someplace swanky, I wear something Western.'

'I meant what do you wear when you go to bed.'

'Oh.' He could feel her shaking with laughter. 'I don't wear anything.'

'What?'

She laughed out loud. 'Okay fine. Erm, I like to wear nightdresses. From Victoria's Secret. Next question.'

'Do you love your home?'

He could sense her rolling her eyes. 'Everyone likes their home. I feel very relaxed when I'm at home. Next question.' She took his hand in hers. It was so small, it felt like a child's hand as he wrapped his fingers around it.

'Do you still love your husband?'

She stiffened, but other than that, there was no reaction. He heard her laugh again, but this time it was less convincing, less true. He had caught her off guard. 'Sorry,' he said.

She threw her arms across him, and buried her head in his chest. 'No, I don't love him anymore. I thought I did, but now I don't think so. That's as articulate as I can be about this topic. Next question.'

Ali flattened his hands over her shoulder blades. He had been gearing up for this question for a long time. 'Did something happen to you that you felt you had to endure your husband's insults and beatings? Is there a past I should know about?'

255

She was quiet for a long time, her breathing coming out in shallow bursts, and then deepening. He thought she had gone to sleep, but then she spoke, 'That is a question for another day.' Her voice was serious, and it had a tone of finality to it that brokered no argument.

So there was something that had made her so docile. Ali wished she would tell him; he wanted to make things better for her. Surely, whatever it was, it wasn't her fault.

'Last question. Would you like to run away with me?'

'What?' her head snapped up from his chest, and as their eyes met, they both collapsed into fits of laughter.

'My turn,' Mona said, once her breathing levelled.

'That's a question for another day,' Ali mocked her.

She nudged him in the ribs. 'It's just one question.'

She waited for him to nod before rising to get dressed. He watched her slowly put on her things, concealing herself behind a bunch of baggy clothes. She was taking her time. Finally, as she hitched her bag on her shoulder, she said, 'It's not really a question, but I wish you wouldn't get me these expensive gifts. They're lovely, but are you sure you can afford them?'

This is how these rich people probe you, the Mir had said. *Any sign of weakness and they'll disappear like sand in the wind.*

But she wasn't like that. He knew that much. He didn't really get her these things due to an irrational fear of her leaving him; he bought these things because he wanted her to have them. A memento for her in case something happened to him, for he wasn't entirely sure where his relationship with the Mir was headed. He wanted to make the most of his time with Mona. Who knew, maybe someday they could be together for good. But then in the event they couldn't be... He wanted her to have something to remember him by.

'They're not expensive,' was all he said to Mona with a giant smile plastered on his lips. Inside, the knowledge of how far he had fallen for this money grated him.

Mona bent down to kiss him on the lips, a chaste kiss that turned into something else when Ali didn't let go.

'Now really!' Mona panted, pulling back, an embarrassed smile on her lips. 'I need to learn to stay away from you! You're a bad influence.'

She shrieked as he pulled her into bed again.

—

'Focus, Ali!' Meera called to him.

He started. He was standing in the middle of the ramp staring at the blank wall at the end of the hall. 'Sorry,' he mumbled, running his fingers through his matted hair. He had forgotten to take a shower today; the styling gel from last night seemed to have congealed in his hair.

Meera marched toward him crossly, with hands on her waist. 'What do you think you're doing? You're supposed to be setting an example for the newbies, and instead I catch you staring off into space.'

'I'm sorry.'

'Oh for God's sake. Please don't tell me you're in love!'

Ali blinked his eyes. 'Excuse me?'

'I wasn't born yesterday. I know the tell-tale signs when I see them. You forget, I fell in love a hundred times. It's overrated. It's like a climbing a bloody mountain only to find a cliff on the other side.'

'A cliff?'

The models at the back sniggered.

'Shut up!' Meera shouted at them. She rounded at him. 'Yes, a cliff. Jump and you might fly. But ninety-nine per cent of the time, you fall on your ass. Trust me, it's overrated. You're better off on your own. Or maybe with someone rich who loves you.' Her eyes narrowed. 'Unless you have found a rich little Miss "I don't love my husband and my home".'

Ali felt glued to the spot. How did she manage to know everything? 'I don't know what you're talking about.'

Meera cackled. 'Really? Did these Prada shoes fall out of the sky and at your feet? Trust me Ali, there's nothing wrong with it, only as long as you don't let it affect your professional life. Then, it stops being love and becomes a bloody nuisance. Ask me, I know!'

With that she marched away to chastise the models that had sniggered. Ali looked down at his suede shoes. They were a gift from Mona. *Stupid*, he thought. He should have known better than to wear them to a rehearsal. But lately, he hadn't been himself. Ever since that day he had received that ominous text from an unknown number.

> You are needed on Sunday at 3 pm.
> Urgent. Do not forget or get delayed.

Their agreement had been that he would pass sensitive information on someone every month (a guaranteed evil-doer, who had the blood of many people on his hands... according to the Mir anyway). He had lived with that arrangement thus far – it had been over four months – but he had never been called back to the compound. Something about this didn't bode well. The terrorist attacks in the city had dwindled to just one or two every few months. They had been replaced by the much more alarming target killings of elite people in the major cities of Pakistan. Ali could only imagine how many people Mir had to do his bidding. He had grown sick of it. He wanted out. The guilt ravaged him day and night, so much that he couldn't even meet his mother's eyes now.

They were financially secure, but at what cost? The cost of his soul? It had already cost him his job at the bank.

He would get caught into the ramblings of his mind, and forget about the present. He shrugged his jacket into place, and finished the walk.

Sunday... It was just one more day away.

Mona hadn't replied to his texts all day. He pulled out his phone, but there was nothing from her. They hadn't seen each other since last week when she had rushed home to be there in time for her husband's arrival. Her bloody husband. How he hated that man. Apart from his general derision of women, the man was a threat to society with his flagrant disregard for religion. He was like a ticking time bomb when he got drunk. Ali had pressed Mona time and again to leave that man, but for some reason, she just held on, as if she were scared of what might happen if she allowed her world to change.

Change... That is what she claimed she feared, but Ali knew that the reason went deeper than that. There was something about her nature, the vulnerability and silent acceptance of things that seemed to allow Bilal more and more licence to be horrible to her, and yet, when Ali asked her about her past, she would close that door to her world firmly in his face. She never said anything; she was too tactful for that. She simply changed the subject to something mundane. And in spite of that, Ali discovered that he hadn't felt so keenly for anyone in his life. This woman… she had the means to shatter him if she wanted. He put up a brave front, but inside, he was at her mercy.

'So Ali, what are we going to do with you?' Meera had returned. She scrutinised him with narrowed eyes from head to toe. 'You seem in excellent shape as usual. The only thing is,' – she tapped her knuckles on his forehead – 'that I don't know what's going on in that head of yours. You almost look like Mona, you know. She's lost in thought half the time too.'

Ali's ears perked up at Mona's name. He laughed. 'She does like to contemplate things, I guess.'

Meera studied him with a strange look. 'And how would you know?'

Ali attempted nonchalance. 'I've met her quite a bit, Meera. Give me some credit for my observation skills.'

'I suppose you're right. She's happier now than I've ever seen her, but then there is that shadow of doubt that falls over her at times. I wish I could set things right. I wish I could turn back the clock.' Meera wasn't looking at him anymore. She was lost in thought herself. 'I wish it weren't my fault.'

The smart move would have been to let her stew in the past for a few more moments in order to catch her off guard, but Ali's curiosity got the better of him. 'Why, what did you do?' he said, instantly regretting his question as he saw alarm cross her features.

'Who, me? I didn't do anything. What are you talking about? Standing here with you has made me lose myself to distant memories. There must be something in the air. I tell you Ali, I cannot have you so pensive, especially not when I'm about to announce you as the showstopper for my next event.'

'When am I ever not your showstopper?' Ali smirked at her, masking his dismay at the lost opportunity of uncovering Mona's past.

Meera laughed. 'There's the Ali I know. No, it's not a regular show here in Lahore. I'm talking about the big show we're having in Karachi next week.'

'Karachi?'

'Yes, Karachi. It's quite something, right? Sorry it's a bit impromptu, but even I didn't know it was happening until yesterday. In fact, I was just speaking to Bilal's assistant about it. He's the one who requested that I arrange the show. Not that I have any love for that monster, but he is Mona's husband so—'

'Mona?' Ali's body jolted as if he had been electrocuted. 'What does she have to do with Karachi?'

Again, he saw the suspicion cross Meera's eyes as she observed him, her forehead knotting into a frown as if she were trying to decipher a puzzle. 'Bilal is launching a new housing project in Karachi,' she said slowly. 'Somehow he's got it in his head that I should be a part of it. That's where all of my models come in.'

'I see.'

'You've met Mona quite a few times, haven't you? Did she mention anything about Karachi?'

She was fishing. She had no idea what was going on.

'Why would she tell me? I hardly see her,' he replied with a blank look, and what he hoped was an innocent voice.

'They're both in Karachi as we speak.'

'Who?'

'Why, Bilal and Mona, of course. Enjoying the sea air, I presume.'

Ali knew she had thrown this statement to him as a test. He pursed his lips together, and made no comment.

There was a small smile on Meera's lips. 'Mona will be back soon, but I expect Bilal to stay there a while.'

'Excellent. Should we resume rehearsing?'

Chapter Twenty-Three

Mir Rabiullah

Mir Rabiullah paced across the length of his small bedroom. Ten paces to the bathroom door and ten paces back. It was stifling in the room. He itched to get outside and feel the early morning air on his face, but he knew he couldn't. He wasn't prepared; his body thrummed with unease, his temples throbbed. If anyone saw him like this, the entire façade that he had so painstakingly constructed would come tumbling down. And then what would he be? An ordinary human being?

No.

He was being unreasonable. The plan was coming together so well. He had the city trembling in fear; those rich people in their swanky cars and short clothes looked at every bearded man with terror now. But, how he longed for fresh blood to spill, for this city brimmed with it while the people in his area suffered as their homes were blown into smithereens. So many of them had migrated to the cities that many places were now ghost towns.

Cowards.

Playing right into the hands of the Americans.

And these Pakistanis… They were no better. So used to bowing and scraping after the British, they were doing the same for the Americans now. He wanted to see them bow to the Leader like the slaves they were, only so he could land the deathblows on their necks. It had been too long since he had heard the sound of a bomb. There were boys ready to blow themselves up at a moment's notice, but there were no targets. As their organisation grew more advanced, so did the enemy. Everything was harder now; information had become as precious as virgins on a hot night.

If only he could sit and think, but there was no time for it. He needed results. Wasn't that what the Leader had always taught him? His cheeks still singed with his slaps. Even after all these years, Rabiullah quailed at the sight of the Leader, the coarse authority of his voice, his blackened teeth with the tongue poised between them like a pink serpent. One word from that mouth and his fate was sealed. The heavy-lidded eyes that he embellished with black *surma* pierced into the Mir, deep into his soul, threatening to devour all his secrets.

'Not enough,' the Leader had hissed the last time he had seen him in the tribal areas only two days ago. 'You are one of my most trusted men, but you are not doing enough, Rabiullah.'

'Elahi is dead,' the Mir replied. 'Zafar, Chaudhary Ikram and others are also dead. We've almost vanquished them.'

'You fool! Do you honestly believe that the world ends at Elahi? We need to get rid of all of them. We need to plan big.'

'We're making progress.' The Mir pretended not to have been stung by the words.

'And yet, the government continues to rehabilitate the displaced people. Money is still pouring in for the people. The tide is still turning against us. Why?'

Rabiullah had remained calm. That is what he had been taught to do, what he taught others to do. 'I'm doing all I can.'

The Leader held up a revolver against Rabiullah. 'It's not enough. Do you realise how small the pool for potential recruits has become? The Goras will soon have me by the throat if you are not quick in your actions.'

Rabiullah had long since conquered the fear of dying. He was trained for it. His voice remained even. 'We still have hundreds.'

'Uneducated ruffians. They are as good as dead to me. What reply do I give to the others?' The Leader ran his palm across the Mir's forehead and nudged the turban away. Nobody had ever dared to do that in Lahore. For the first time, anger had flared inside Rabiullah. He could lose his life, but he wouldn't lose his respect. 'With the government preparing to launch an offensive and the West supporting them, how do you expect us to survive? Do you want to go back and live in starvation?'

'The one you wish to die will be dead in a week,' he murmured softly.

The Leader laughed, a searing merciless laugh. 'An informant, have you? Someone to infiltrate the ranks?' His tone turned murderous. 'I want him dead. If he dies, the entire rehabilitation programme dies with him.' He stooped down and looked Rabiullah in the eyes. Rabiullah stared back, entranced, at the black irises dancing in the pool of white jelly around them. 'Kill that bastard.'

'We have to be careful, Abuzar,' Mir Rabiullah said calmly. 'My informants have to be well chosen ones. Any hint of suspicion and the intelligence authorities will descend upon our compound like flies. Already, I find it hard to convince the police that I'm running a phil-anthropic mission. I have to bribe them heavily to keep them from sniffing around too much.'

'Kill them all.' The Leader's smile was savage, almost on the verge of madness. 'Kill every last one of them, Rabiullah, or so help me God, I will vanquish the country.'

The Mir shivered now, despite the heat. His austere bedroom held only a single bed and a prayer mat. A lingering smell of faeces hung in the room, a smell that grew more pronounced in the bathroom where the absence of a flush system prevented a complete disposal of waste.

He saw a shape emerge on the bed. His mother, covered in bright blue fabric from head to foot, all except a tiny space for her eyes, sitting on the bed with her legs crossed, deep in prayer, her hands held upward in a silent plea to God. He remembered how her eyes would dance, how she would come alive in the house when she cast away the burqa and came away laughing. She would beckon him to eat the kheer while it was still hot, the sweet milk and rice coagulating before his eyes the longer he left it uneaten. He remembered her kissing his forehead before he would leave for school. 'I will send you to college one day,' she would boast.

He remembered killing her with his bare hands, watching in wonder how the life bled out from her eyes, leaving them still and vacant. He had relished the act.

'Wretched woman, your mother. She should be living a life of chastity and silence after your father's death, but she's been exchanging letters with that postman.'

Abuzar wasn't much of a Leader back in those days, just someone who predicted that fate had promised them greatness.

Mir Rabiullah had never regretted killing his mother. She was a whore whom he had caught red-handed, blushing as the postman took her hand and brought it to his lips in the alley behind their house. But then, why did he still miss her? As if there was a void inside him that ached to be filled. If only he could forget her and live his life in peace, but no, she came back to him every day, and especially when he was at his most vulnerable.

'Leave me alone, Mother,' he murmured. 'It has been sixty years. Leave me in peace.'

She blinked back at him, cocked her head and laughed, covering her mouth with her hand as she did so. Her trademark laugh. She must have been very young when he had killed her, hardly in her mid-twenties, he realised now.

'Kill that bastard.' The Leader's words still rang in his head like sirens as the Mir made his way downstairs to his sitting room.

Ali was already there when he arrived. He rose when the Mir arrived, confusion and misgiving apparent on his face. 'Asalam alaikum, Mir Sahab.'

The Mir returned his greeting, wondering whether the boy was up to the task. He had advised Gul to stay away from him. There was something wrong with her when it came to Ali. She couldn't function properly. Another unsolved mystery of the female sex that he would take to his grave.

He sank into his seat, and gestured for Ali to do the same.

'I can't do this anymore, Mir Sahab,' Ali said, his eyes downcast. 'I will forever be grateful for what you have done for Hussain, but I can't help you any longer. I can't bear to look at myself in the mirror. It feels as if I'm killing my own people, my family.'

Rabiullah's mother's face flashed before him, her bright, evergreen smile that he had so ruthlessly erased. His mother hadn't struggled when he had choked her; she had looked at him as if she understood everything. But then, just before he had panicked and let go of her, her eyes had turned upwards and gone vacant. Forever.

'If you want, I can return the money,' Ali was saying. 'I just want out.'

'Those who you consider family are slaughtering people as we speak. Would you consider them family if I showed you the extent of their cruelty? They kill innocent children and label them as terrorists. They sell our women in the streets of Lahore and Peshawar. They leave them to rot in brothels and then mock them for producing illegitimate children. A cycle of horror and violence that will never end unless we do something about it.'

'But is killing necessary? Surely, if they knew about your true nature, they would stop...'

How could the Mir tell him that his true nature was his thirst for blood, for anarchy? 'My dear boy,' he cried, using the soothing voice he had mastered. 'Do you think wars have been won by kindness? Even if we go on live television to state our kind intentions, they will not relent. They'll just find another way to twist our words into something nefarious.'

'Surely—'

'One more time,' the Mir cut him off. 'I need your help for the last time.' It took all of the Mir's strength to

268

plead like this, to be so robbed of his dignity. He could tell the boy was on the precipice of change, that if he didn't handle him with care, he would lose him. And then, what answer would he have for the Leader? His own death didn't concern him, but the Leader's displeasure did. The ramifications did. He would shame himself, the Leader and ultimately, God. He couldn't have that.

'Just one more time, my boy. Imagine the lives you will be saving, the grief you will be saving many mothers. Already, the enemy bombings in the tribal areas have shrunk to a quarter of the original number. Without these traitors to provide the West with valuable intelligence about potential targets, nobody knows exactly which place to bomb. Even these Goras cannot get away with bombing entire cities if there are no known terrorists hidden there. We might have saved thousands of innocent lives already. If not for yourself, think of the world you will be building for the children to come. Do you want them to be born in a country of violence? Because violence begets more violence. This country is on the precipice of civil war. Do you want to be the instrument that triggers it? Do you?'

'But, Mir Sahab, this is violence too.'

Mir Rabiullah closed his eyes once and then opened them. *Stay calm*, he warned himself. His fingers itched to grasp the dagger sheathed around his waist. He yearned to behead this man, to sit on his chest, and bring his dagger down on his throat again and again until he felt the delicate tendons of the neck slicing, and finally the clunky sound of the vertebrae snapping. 'We have nothing against the Government,' he lied. 'We only want to display a show of strength, a sense of resilience against their unfair attitude toward us. As soon as we manage to finish off the dangerous influence of these men on the government, these men who are so heavily involved with the sinister force of the West, we will enter negotiations for a progressive and peaceful Pakistan. We might not even need to kill anyone. All we need is some intel.'

Ali sighed, and Rabiullah saw the indecision cross his features. 'I don't know. I feel trapped.'

The Mir leapt in once more, before Ali could change his mind. 'I need you, Ali. Just like you needed my help that day for your brother. Today, I need it. Do the honourable thing.'

'Mir Sahab—'

'Pass us information on one more person. That's all you need to do.'

Ali met his gaze. Mir Rabiullah saw the misgiving in his eyes. Mir's fingers curled around the dagger. If Ali refused him once more, God be his witness, he would slice his throat, come what may.

'Who's the person?' Ali asked quietly.

Mir Rabiullah smiled his most magnanimous smile yet, but inside his heart leapt. 'The most heinous of them all, the most evil. His name is Bilal Ahmed.'

Chapter Twenty-Four

Mona

Mona woke up gasping for air. She felt as if someone was squeezing her throat. Her breath rattled out of her mouth as she clawed at her neck. She groped for the lamp on the bedside table. It was just a nightmare, her mind assured her, but her body seemed to have lapsed into a catatonic state.

A glass of water was pressed to her lips, and she realised that Bilal had woken up too. 'Drink this,' he said gently, holding the glass with one hand while with the other he raised her head.

She was too riled up to drink any of the water; her stomach threatened to churn out the rice and yellow lentils she had eaten. She desperately wished to be able to talk to Ali, but all she could see was the water sloshing around the glass. She parted her lips to allow some of it inside her mouth. The coolness of the water stung her throat. Her eyes darted at her husband fearing he could read her mind, but he was staring at her with concern, his hair standing on end. He seemed genuinely worried about her.

Gradually, her terror dissipated. When her breathing had finally steadied, he withdrew his hand. 'What was that? I have never seen you like this before? A bad dream?'

'A nightmare,' she muttered, unsure of whether she could trust her tongue.

Already, she could feel Bilal withdrawing from her, his classic reaction after the end of a crisis. She needed to be held, but Bilal let out a gigantic yawn, and collapsed back onto his pillow. 'You had me worried for a second. Don't do that again.'

'I can't control my nightmares, Bilal,' she said, her voice shaking. She drew the covers back over her trembling body. 'Bilal?'

'I have an early meeting tomorrow, Mona. If you're in no further danger, might I be allowed to go back to sleep?'

'What are these meetings that have become so important for you?'

'I'm involved in something big, Mona. Something that has ramifications for the entire country.'

'Ah, Bilal Sahab, the future Prime Minister of Pakistan.'

'Don't be dramatic.'

'Won't you even ask what the nightmare was about?'

Bilal snorted. 'Let me guess. It was something to do with diamonds, or lack thereof.'

Mona sighed, but did not reply. Bilal's back rose and fell with his breathing, but she knew he was awake.

'Would you like me to hold your hand?' Bilal asked her finally, turning around to look at her. She saw the mirth in his eyes, the underlying taunt at her weakness. 'I can do that, and much more,' he added with a wink.

'You've done enough Bilal.'

'Hey, I was just trying to cheer you up! Don't I get any credit for waking up in the middle of the night for you?'

She threw off the covers, and marched to the adjacent guest room carrying her mobile with her, her finger hovering over Ali's number.

'Don't be late for tonight's flight,' Bilal called after her. She heard his head sink back into the pillows. 'Whatever happened to those romantic nights we had in Karachi?'

'There were no romantic nights,' she shot back, before opening the door to the guest room. 'You hardly ever came to the hotel.'

'Classified stuff,' Bilal replied, his voice already heavy with sleep. He was snoring by the time Mona closed the door of the guest room.

She didn't immediately call Ali. She locked herself into the bathroom and began rummaging inside the cabinets. She knew she had bought more than one of those things. Her fingers riffled through a box of sleeping pills and painkillers when finally they touched something more concrete. She held up the stick to the light and slid out of her nightdress before sitting on the commode.

She tried not to think while the stick soaked up her urine, her mind too afraid to venture back to that time all those years ago when she had sat just like this, her thin body shaking at the possibility of what she would find. What was the use of dredging up empty memories, things she had long ago buried deep in her heart. But had she ever forgotten them? She had been nineteen years old, old enough to understand the potential outcomes of her behaviour. But how was she to know it would come to this? How was she to have known anything?

—

Meera's shrill, excited voice rang in her head as she scampered across the dark, menacing lawns of the college, one hand clasped firmly in Mona's. 'Come along now, Mona, or the matron will find out. And this surprise simply cannot wait.'

They stamped on the dewy winter grass, Mona's feet already soaked and frozen inside her thin bedroom slippers. Her heart fluttered as she ran after Meera, barely able to see her form in the darkness. The candle-lit rooms of the girls' hostel had disappeared from view as they ran deeper into the lawns, through the clutch of shadowy trees. If it hadn't been for Meera's hand, Mona would have been lost. She had never ventured into this part of the campus. It scared her. There had been an unscheduled power outage and the whole campus was plunged into darkness.

Meera seemed to know the way, though.

After they had put some distance between the girls' hostel and themselves, Meera slowed their pace. In the cold, moonless night, the sense of foreboding was heightened, and after Mona screamed twice at the thorns that stuck to her kameez, Meera flicked on a torch. 'Stop the screaming. That will most probably give us away before this torch does.' Arriving in the shadow of a large building, she shone it over the steel plaque affixed on a large wall.

It was the boys' hostel.

Mona looked around. Except for some dim lights in one of the windows, the place seemed dark. Deserted, most probably.

'There's nobody here, Meera.' Mona said, her heart sinking at the sight of the large, imposing building. 'Let's get out of here before we get caught and expelled. I don't want to risk it.'

Meera scoffed as she produced a key from a chain she hung around her neck, and punched it inside the keyhole. 'Everyone's probably asleep in their rooms.'

The door unlocked, swinging open of its own accord with a loud creak.

'Oops,' Meera whispered. 'Let's hurry before the warden finds us. Third floor it is.'

'But why are we going into a boys' hostel in the dead of the night?' Mona whispered.

'It's a double date, silly. Your birthday present. Remember I told you I'd give you the gift of a lifetime? Well, listen to this, my boyfriend lives on the third floor. He's promised to introduce you to a friend of his. A real gentleman.'

'You have a boyfriend?' Mona's shock was absolute.

Meera giggled. 'I'm twenty, for crying out loud. If not now, then when? When I'm an old hag? You're just so prudish. No wonder I never told you about this secret part of my life. Hee. Now promise me you won't balk and embarrass me. Just say hello, have a drink – fine, you can have a Coke for God's sake,' she added hastily when Mona clapped her hands to her mouth and shook her head. 'We'll be out of there in no time. I just want to show you that there is another world that waits for us other than this constant studying. A world full of titillating possibilities.' She grinned.

'But, I don't want to meet any boys,' Mona cried, her feet dragging against the flagstones as she resisted Meera's tugging. 'What if my parents find out? I'm going back.'

'Oh, don't be a baby. Iftikhar is a really good fellow. You can trust him to have invited one of his finest friends.'

'You're going out with Iftikhar? That hairy fellow?' Mona was horrified. Iftikhar was younger than them and a downright sleazeball.

Meera tutted. 'Just trust me, okay? You don't need to do anything with him. Not yet. Just talk to him, okay?'

The power outage had extended all the way to the upper floors of the hostel. Mona had the haunting sense of being watched. 'Meera, this doesn't even look like a hostel. It's so creepy... I really don't think—'

'Thirty-one, thirty-two, thirty-three, here we are.'

Without warning, Meera turned the brass doorknob, and thrust the door open.

They were glued to the doorway, too stunned to move.

'Meera.' Mona's voice shook badly. 'What is this?'

Ten burly men of indeterminate age stared back at them with Iftikhar sitting in the middle, grinning like a jackass. 'Welcome, ladies.'

'Oh shit,' Meera said. 'Mona, RUN! Iftikhar, no!'

—

'Iftikhar,' Mona said now with a lisp, her tongue so unused to the way it clicked against her soft palate to produce the sound of his name, a name she hadn't dared utter in many years. She had no way of knowing that Iftikhar was the father of the child that was never born, but something inside her knew that it had been him. His uneven, jagged teeth that had grazed against her neck, the viciousness of his bites, the curiosity of his hands that went everywhere, sweaty and eager in their groping. For years, she had held an irrational fear of people with sweaty hands. She would reel back at their touch, her mind immediately conjuring up Iftikhar. She had had nightmares for years, even after she had been married to Bilal who knew absolutely nothing about her past, and to his credit, hadn't said a word back when he'd found that she was clearly no virgin. No questions about the past – that had been their motto, something Bilal had adhered to for many years. What had happened to sour them away from each other like this, she wondered. Had she become too distant, damaged beyond repair as she was, too afraid to even hold her own babies when they were born? Passing them off to the waiting nanny, she would ignore their cries in the middle of the night as the nannies tried to calm them, terrified that the darkness in her would leech onto them if she spent too much time with them. She had been astonished when she had given birth, so unconvinced was she that her womb would ever produce something so beautiful.

If she listened closely, she could still hear Bilal snore, oblivious to the turmoil that was splashing over his wife's life. Mona screwed her eyes shut as she allowed her lungs to expand with air, holding up the stick in front of her so that when her eyes opened, the first thing she would see would be the result.

Chapter Twenty-Five

Ali

'Iftikhar,' she mumbled into her pillow. She was fast asleep on her stomach, arms and limbs splayed out, kind of like how a child would sleep. He had never seen her sleep with such abandon, and yet there was something that was unsettling her. A series of lines had broken out across her forehead as she was deep in contemplation while dreaming. Ali wondered if it was possible to think while dreaming.

He lay next to her, listening to her soft intakes of breath, one arm thrown behind his head to cushion it against the hard headboard. His other hand trembled, his fingers itching to hold a cigarette. How he longed for a drink, but he couldn't. He knew that if he relented, he'd sink right back into that dark hole, and this time there would be no escape for him.

After the gentle cajoling a few days ago, the Mir had called him again, this time from an unknown number. 'I hope things have been going well,' were his words. After the tedious process of exchanging greetings and pleasantries, the Mir proceeded to business, the business of killing people. It was from a distance, away from that arresting face of his, those hypnotic eyes that Ali was able to discern the indifference in his voice for the people he killed. The Mir tried hard to infuse vengeance into his voice, to produce feelings of patriotism and sacrifice in Ali, but it all sounded flat to him. 'So, have you managed to secure information for our little project?' he asked him. His voice had been as sweet as honey, but there was that breathlessness to it, the avid curiosity.

When Ali expressed his uncertainty, the Mir went silent. After a long time, he said, 'Of course, I understand Ali. I wouldn't dream of pressuring you to do something you're not comfortable with. I was planning to visit your dear mother and that wonderful boy Hussain soon, just to see how he was getting along. Ah, family. What a blessing from God, for after all, where would we be without our loved ones?' His voice had possessed the same sweetness as ever, but the words were poison. Ali knew that now.

No matter how much he tried to evade the inevitable, he would have to bend to the Mir's will, but if he passed information, what then? Would this dreadful cycle ever stop? Could money ever make up for what he lost of himself when he did this despicable act? Wouldn't it be easier to just kill himself and end it all?

He looked down at Mona sleeping, her face now smooth from all worries. Her mouth was slightly open. Could he ever forgive himself for doing that to her? No matter how badly he wanted to be with her, could he really be the instrument that killed her husband and changed her life? Would she ever forgive him?

But how could he live with the knowledge that the Mir might kill his family and still do nothing? Was he a self-sacrificing hero?

Mona's forehead creased again, and he laid a hand gently against it, smoothing out the skin with his thumb.

She opened her eyes. After those first moments of confusion after awakening, her eyes found his. He knew she would smile and she did – a smile that lit up her entire face. 'You need to stop watching me sleep. I probably snore.'

'I enjoy it,' he replied, his hand still on her forehead.

She blinked her eyes several times as if banishing a bad memory.

'Bad dream?' he asked.

'Not really.' She didn't quite meet his eyes as she rolled over and threw her legs across the side of the bed. She bunched up her hair into a ponytail. 'Is that the time? Shit, I need to catch a flight.' She turned to him. 'You're supposed to be there too, remember? What a silly idea to launch a housing society with a modelling and awards show. I swear Bilal's going senile. Did you know he'll be staying at Alia's deserted Karachi home for one day, and then to some other friend's place in Defence for the next day and so on. He's making me stay in a hotel, but for him it's going to be a nomad's life. Says he can't take any chances with his security.' She laughed as she sat down in front of the dresser and opened her handbag. 'As if he's the Prime Minister or something. I'm telling you, he's going senile.'

Ali wished he could have covered his ears. He didn't want to be burdened with the knowledge of Bilal's whereabouts. He didn't trust himself in the Mir's presence, especially not when he began making those veiled threats. He didn't know what he was going to do, but he most certainly wasn't going to wilfully allow a man to die, no matter how much he was threatened. He knew that now. He couldn't do that to Mona, and he couldn't do that to himself.

'Who is Iftikhar?' he asked, in order to change the topic.

He asked it casually, but Mona froze, the hand holding a hairbrush hanging over her head, her face suddenly white as a sheet. 'Where did you hear this name?'

Ali sat up. 'I – well you were mumbling it in your sleep. I didn't think – I thought he was a friend you knew or some—'

The rest of his sentence was drowned in the sudden commotion as Mona dropped the hairbrush she had been holding, and pressing both hands to her mouth, she ran toward the bathroom. Inside, he could hear her retching.

Ali banged on the door. 'Mona, what is it? What's happened?'

'Stomach bug,' she called out feebly. 'Don't worry, I'll be out in a moment.'

'Let me in,' he insisted.

'I'll be out in a moment.'

It was fifteen minutes before she emerged from the bathroom, pale but looking better than before. Her face and hair were dripping with water. She muttered 'thanks' as she accepted the towel Ali offered her.

Once she was settled in front of the dressing table, Ali broke into a flurry of apologies and questions.

'I'm sorry, I didn't know you weren't feeling well. Who is Iftikhar? Did you feel ill because of him? Why didn't you tell me you weren't feeling well?'

Mona waved all of his questions away. 'It's just something I ate yesterday,' she explained. 'A wretched kebab by the looks of it.' She sighed as she picked up a bright red lipstick. 'Anyway, it's all out of my system now, and I feel much better. No wonder I slept like the dead. I was exhausted all day.' She examined the effect of the lipstick in the mirror. 'Kind of look like Dracula, don't I? Pale face and a red mouth. I should lather on some more face powder and foundation. It will give Bilal a right fright.'

Ali wasn't amused. He kept watching how her hand travelled to her belly from time to time as she massaged it. She was trying to make light of the situation, but her hands were shaking badly. She could hardly hold the eyeliner stick in place.

'You should leave him,' he said before he could stop himself. 'Leave Bilal. Come with me. We'll go somewhere. Some place far away from here. We'll all go. My family and us.'

She didn't laugh at him, but neither did she say anything. Ali sat rooted to the spot, the sounds of make-up pots being screwed open and lips being smacked filling the air.

'What has brought this on?' she asked him.

'Do you still love your husband?' he blurted out. 'Do you love me? Because if you do, what am I doing here in this room while you live with your husband in that fancy mansion?' His breathing came out in pants.

He caught her reflection in the mirror. She was staring at him. 'No, I don't love Bilal anymore, Ali. And no, I cannot run away with you. Do I love you? Yes, I do. But do I think that running away is an option? No, I do not.'

'I hate it when you drag pragmatism into our relationship. It's as if you don't care.'

She put down the eyeliner. 'I don't care? If only you knew, Ali. Please don't act childish.'

Ali aimed a kick at one of his shoes, hitting it against a wall.

Mona resumed applying a fresh layer of lipstick on her already rouge lips. 'I don't think you understand the gravity of the situation, Ali. If we are to be together, it has to be handled delicately. One step at a time. If I spring the knowledge on Bilal that I'm seeing someone, he might very well kill me. And you.'

'I'd like to see him try,' Ali growled.

'Be that as it may, Ali. For now, we can only meet in secret. I will leave Bilal for you — yes, I've said it. And I mean it. But it will be a gradual process. I have kids to think of, my social standing.'

'So you consider your social standing more important than me?'

'Don't be a child.'

'Oh yes, I am the child, aren't I? I'm not penniless, you know. I have enough money to maintain your social standing. You won't have to work and grovel if you're with me.'

Mona rolled her eyes, her hands still shook and she kept running her hand across her belly. 'I'm not feeling too well, Ali. There is still dinner with Bilal to get through. Can we talk about this later?'

'Yes, let's put Ali on the backburner. That's what he's good for.'

Mona closed her eyes. 'Please don't be like this.'

Ali stepped toward her. 'Why won't you tell me what's going on with you? Why do you insist on shutting everyone out? Why do you hesitate to love, Mona?' He spread out his arms. 'This is love. This is us. It's time to face it. You need to forget about your husband.'

'It's not like you tell me everything.' Her voice was quiet. 'Have I ever questioned you about your involvement in that horrible incident? Elahi's murder? No, I did not. I never even brought up that topic because I know you. And I trust you.' Her eyes were filling with tears.

283

'So I ask you to just trust me, to give me time and if you cannot do that, I don't know what to say.'

Ali paused on his way to her. He was going to throw his arms around her, to wrap her close to him, but her words held him back. They tore through him, her unassailing belief in him. He felt sick.

'I'm leaving, Mona. I'll see you in Karachi.'

He closed the door quietly on his way out, leaving her sitting there with that stark white face and awful red lipstick.

Chapter Twenty-Six

Mona

She heard a loud police siren and winced. Even loud noises gave her a headache these days, and Karachi seemed to be rife with them. Hardly two minutes would pass before a wailing siren rattled by, causing her nerves to grind together. The thought of eating food at the event almost made her vomit again. She leant against the ornate wallpaper of the hotel room to steady herself, and took deep breaths.

She hadn't told anybody about it. She couldn't tell anybody, she realised. Shabeena, Alia and Kulsoom were out of the question, and even Meera, her best friend, might accidentally give away her secret, such was the style with which she spoke and the fearlessness with which she lived. No, she couldn't tell anyone. Not even Ali. Not yet, anyway. She hadn't spoken to him in a week. The way he had closed the door in her face, leaving her sitting at the dressing table, she didn't think she'd ever want to see him again. And yet, she did. She yearned for it. She spent hours deleting his messages and missed calls from her mobile each day only to find them built up the next day. Maybe it was the pregnancy hormones, but her mood swings had so far held her back from responding. One moment, she wanted to wrap her arms around him, to inhale the fresh scent of him, and the next moment, she wanted to hit him with something. She realised she was being unreasonable, but something in Ali's eyes that night had reminded her of Bilal. That same cruelty… it smelled of Bilal. And that is why she couldn't forgive him yet.

Her hand ventured toward her belly. She hadn't decided whether she was going to keep it. She figured she was about two months along, but she was too afraid to go to see a doctor in Lahore. The risk of word getting out was too great. She would get herself checked somewhere here in Karachi, but so far, Bilal hadn't let her out of his sight. Terror threats, he said.

And even if she did end up at a hospital, then what? Would she end it all? She caressed her belly like she had been doing so often the past few weeks. She had to stop that. If Bilal noticed, there would be no end to his questions. She had seen the curiosity in Ali's eyes when they'd briefly met at one of Meera's dinners to celebrate the event in Karachi. Their argument stood like a wall between them. She had noticed him watching her as she ran her hand across her belly – more than twice. And yet, she couldn't stop doing that. Something about the gesture calmed her. There was no hint of the baby as yet; her stomach was still flat. If anything, she seemed to have lost weight, since she could hardly keep anything down.

She checked her appearance in the mirror. Tonight was the night she would have to face Ali again, to have the chance of gazing up into that troubled face she had come to love so much. A baby… a living thing they had created together. She had been pregnant thrice in her life, but never had she felt the experience so acutely as she did now.

The red lipstick looked awful on her pale complexion, and it reminded her of that time she argued with Ali, but there was nothing to be done about it. She was too exhausted anyway.

Pulling on a patterned silk kaftan over her thin body, she cinched the belt tight to emphasise her slender waist, and slipped on a pair of flat-heeled shoes. *A dead giveaway*, she thought, choosing a pair of towering platforms instead.

Before she could leave the room, Bilal pushed inside with the phone pressed to his ear.

He was early.

'Yes Minister Saheb, I understand what you're trying to say, but I can't backtrack now. That would be suicidal for my investment,' he said.

'Bilal, what—' Mona began, but he motioned for her to keep silent.

'I really wish you could have come for tonight's show. My wife was so looking forward to meeting the lovely Shireen. She could hardly wait.'

Mona rolled her eyes, and sank into the bed with a sigh. The platforms were already beginning to bother her, so she knocked them off, and reclined in bed.

She tuned out Bilal's pleading with the Minister, and focused on dozing off. It was curious how pregnancy made one oblivious to everything except one's own comfort.

Just when she was losing herself to sleep, she felt something land in her lap. She awoke with a yelp. It was Bilal's mobile phone.

'Goddammit. I am not letting this guy get in the way of my event.'

'I was sleeping, Bilal.' Mona massaged her neck. She had heard a worrying ping from her vertebrae when the shock of the mobile phone had woken her up, but thankfully, everything seemed to be in order. She did feel annoyed, though. 'Did you hear what I said?'

No answer.

She knew she was playing with fire, but at this point, she didn't care. 'I said I was sleeping.'

'Go to hell, woman. It is the night of the show. You should already have left for the event. Imagine my irritation when the driver tells me that you're still "resting" at the hotel. What's the point of my staying elsewhere if I have to come to the hotel? It makes me a target, Mona. The world is falling apart, and all you're worried about is your precious beauty sleep.' He snatched up his suit jacket that lay on the sofa. 'Get real for once, would you? I beg you. You've kept yourself shrouded in indifference for so long, I feel as if I don't know you anymore.'

'Oh, please. It's not as if you're the epitome of kindness. When was the last time you even spoke to me as if I meant something to you?'

'Oh God, not again. Please, don't.'

He began tapping the wooden sole of his shoe on the floor. She closed her eyes, hoping he'd stop, but he didn't.

Finally when she couldn't take it anymore, she opened her eyes. With a supreme effort she composed herself and smoothed the bed covers over her lap. 'The Minister won't be coming, then?'

There. She was the first one to extend the olive branch. Like always.

Bilal had his fingers in his hair. 'No. This Minister is as intrepid as a mouse. He's trying to dissuade me from going to the show. He says there is a great terror threat there.'

Mona forgot about their little tiff. 'But why? We're not in politics or anything. Why would terrorists give a damn about us?'

'He meant it in general,' Bilal replied. 'Honestly, Mona, don't you ever tune into the news?'

Mona's eyes widened. 'Why would I?' And then she froze. 'What happened now? Please tell me it isn't another bomb blast.'

'A bomb. Right in the heart of Lahore. Dozens dead. Scores injured. The list goes on and on.' He shook his head. 'Tonight, many families will have the misfortune of burying their loved ones. It's a dark day.'

'Oh God.' Mona bit into her knuckles to stop herself from being sick in front of Bilal. She could feel the bile rising up her throat, but with Herculean effort, she managed to swallow it down. It left a bitter taste in her mouth.

Her other hand ventured to her belly. She wasn't sure whether it was her maternal instinct kicking in, but she felt like caressing it, protecting it from this evil world. 'Oh those poor mothers.' She met her husband's gaze and withdrew the hand from her belly. 'Why are you looking at me like that?'

Bilal had his head tilted, his eyes searching hers. 'This might be a stupid thing to say, but all of a sudden I get this impression that you've never looked more beautiful in years. Your face… there is an unmistakable glow to it.'

Mona felt the heat rising to her cheeks. 'One minute, I'm a stone-hearted woman, and the next the most beautiful you've ever seen in years. I suggest you make up your mind, Bilal. And, you're right. This is a very silly thing to say, especially during this moment when the world has imploded for so many people.' She scooted off the bed and picked up the TV remote. 'I need to watch the news.'

To her surprise, Bilal rose and took her into his arms. 'I'm sorry. It's just these blasts. These bloody terrorists. I'll show them. I'd be damned before I let them ruin my event in Karachi.'

She broke away from the embrace, feeling strangely vulnerable to Bilal's words. He sounded so sincere. 'I'm not sure how you can do anything to stop these blasts.' She searched his face. 'Oh my God, Bilal. Are those tears in your eyes?'

Mona watched open-mouthed as her husband explained his involvement in the movement against terrorism, how he was building homes in the Northwestern Areas of Pakistan for the refugees – for money yes, but also to stop those people from turning to the terrorists for help.

'As long as they know that someone from the government will always be there to protect and help them, they will never entertain the terrorists. After all, nobody likes blowing themselves up, I think. Of course, these boys have made a sport out of this. Who will blow himself up first and earn a place in heaven?'

He laughed, but Mona heard the emptiness in it, the pain in Bilal's eyes. 'Bilal,' she whispered. 'I had no idea.'

'That your husband is a human? Believe me, Mona, the guilt of how I've treated you kills me. I promise I'll be a better husband.'

He took her in his arms again. They stood like that for a long time, Bilal's hands wrapped around her waist while hers pressed against his chest in a bid to shield her non-existent belly.

'Mona?'

She attempted to break free to look into his face, but he wouldn't let her.

'You won't leave me, will you? Ever?'

Mona froze. Did he know? Surely, he couldn't.

'Bilal, I—'

'I might be a bastard most of the time, but I love you very much. You are the mother of my children. The love of my life.'

'You have a funny way of showing it, Bilal.'

'Here,' he said, releasing her from his grip and rummaging inside his pockets. He pulled out a small velvet-lined box. Inside was a diamond ring.

'Five carats,' Bilal explained. 'Just a small token of my love.'

Mona tried not to let the disappointment show on her face. Here was her husband, trying his best to be a good man, and yet she wished he'd stop weighing his love in diamonds. She had been with him for more than two decades, and he still hadn't been able to judge her feelings. When she loved, she loved with abandon, with an utter completeness. Like the way she loved Ali. Like the way she had once loved him. She was proud of the man he was in the world, but she didn't love him anymore. She respected him, at times even liked him, but she knew with certainty that she didn't love him anymore. And watching the earnestness in his eyes, she knew without a doubt that she'd leave him. She'd leave him for Ali in a blink of an eye.

She took the small box containing the ring, and without thanking her husband, she locked it in the safe and proceeded toward the door.

'Coming?' she asked him.

Chapter Twenty-Seven

Ali

For the twentieth time in the space of an hour, he saw Meera's name blink on his screen, but he ignored it.

Mir Rabiullah's eyes flicked toward the blinking screen, but like Ali, he ignored it as well. They sat on either side of a narrow, rickety desk, in a small room somewhere deep within the bowels of a building in Lyari. The smell of faeces and garbage was nauseating. From the smell and the sound, he judged there was an open drain nearby.

The Mir looked around at the grim surroundings and smiled. 'What a cheerful little place. Oh, I've missed my dear old Lyari.' His gaze locked into Ali's. 'Do you like this place?'

Ali swallowed. His mouth was dry. 'Yes,' he managed to say with effort. 'It's nice.'

'You like lying, don't you?'

Ali remained silent, but the way the Mir's eyes flashed scared him. 'You like lying so much that you're willing to die for it. Is that it? Have you learned nothing from us?'

He wasn't afraid of dying. All he was afraid of was losing his family, and missing the chance of ever seeing Mona's face again. So much had remained unspoken between them. How could he ever tell her about everything he felt for her? For he knew that he had been brought in here to be killed.

'Did you think we wouldn't find out?' the Mir whispered. 'That you have been passing us false information? Sending us sniffing in places where there was no hint of Bilal. Did you get a kick out of wasting our time? I hope you did, because what is about to happen to you is so bad that I'd advise you to cling to that happy memory.'

'I'm not afraid of dying.' Ali's teeth ground together so hard that he thought his words were incomprehensible, but he saw the Mir's nostrils flare and knew that he'd heard.

'My brave, fearless boy. Oh my dear Ali, how I wish I could have turned you into one of us. You had such promise. You could have one day been where I am today, maybe even further. You could have replaced the Leader.' He joined his hands together on the desk. 'Now, I guess we'll never know.'

'Kill me if you want, but I will have no further part in your madness. You've exploited me enough.'

'Dying is not the worst that can happen to a person.' Mir Rabiullah shook his head with a sadness that seemed real to Ali. His eyes when he looked up were deep pools of despair. 'What would we achieve by killing you here? Just the satisfaction of throwing your body into the *nullah* for the dogs to fetch and enjoy? No, that is a very small compensation for the trouble you have caused us, and being one of the closest people in my inner circle, you have to pay the ultimate price for disappointing me, for I don't like being disappointed.'

Ali struggled against the steel shackles that bound him, but they were too tight. He was glued to the chair. 'Kill me,' he said. 'I will die happy in the knowledge that I managed to foil at least one of your evil plots.'

'Gul was right about you. You have that spark of resistance in you. You could have done very well, indeed. At least that girl was good for something. Too bad she died such a stupid death.'

A roaring filled his ears. 'You killed her?'

The Mir smiled, and this time with the light of the single, dangling bulb shining on his face, he looked like a man possessed. 'The same fate awaits you, my boy, for deserting us. Are you sure you're ready to die? I wouldn't be if I were you, especially after I've received word just now that your dear mother and brother have kindly joined us in one of our centres in Lahore. Hussain and Jamila, if I'm not mistaken. I remember paying for your brother's prosthetic leg. I should learn to know a bad investment when I see one. What a waste of a good prosthetic leg.'

Ali felt the fight leave his body, the blood drain from his extremities. He felt numb. 'You're lying,' he stuttered. 'You're bluffing. There is no way you could know where they are.'

The Mir's eyes gleamed. 'We're not called one of the world's deadliest terrorist organisations for nothing, Ali. Do you think it was hard to track your family, especially when they spent half the day basking in the sun outside your friend Majeed's home? A boy with an expensive prosthetic leg in Gulshan-e-Ravi. Tell me, Ali, how many boys in prosthetics would you find in an area like Gulshan-e-Ravi, an area where people struggle to make ends meet?' The Mir made a show of waiting, before shaking his head, his mouth still broken in a mad smile. 'No? Well, allow me. The answer to the question is none. You won't find one boy in Gulshan e Ravi with a prosthetic leg so expensive. So imagine our surprise when we heard reports of a lively little boy hopping around the streets of Gulshan e Ravi, closely watched over by a beautiful lady with blue eyes. Just imagine our surprise, Ali.'

Ali closed his eyes. How many times had he stressed the fact that the need for secrecy was paramount? He had lost count of the number of times he had made his family sit around the dining table to listen to the security threats they faced. From his mother's pinched face, he had thought she understood. It turned out she hadn't.

'Let them go,' Ali whispered.

'You forgot the magic word.'

'Please,' Ali pleaded. 'I'll do anything.'

'Anything?' the Mir echoed.

'Yes, anything!'

'Well, then why didn't you say so before? As it happens, I have the perfect task for you, my boy. The perfect task.'

–

The breeze outside did nothing to calm him. He walked like a man dead to the world, and yet one who carried the weight of it on his shoulders. In the sweltering Karachi heat, the shawl and jacket made breathing almost impossible. How he longed to tear both away, flinging them somewhere in the sea, but he pressed on, careful not to make any sudden movements. He even sat in the car like a pregnant woman, cautious with one hand laid protectively over his belly.

Hussain looked like he hadn't eaten in days; he was so skinny. And his mother, his beautiful mother who had only just begun to reclaim the light that had vanished from her eyes; how sunken her eyes had looked. As if he were staring into the dark pit of an empty well. Dim and lifeless. If it hadn't been for the fierceness with which she clung to Hussain, Ali would have thought her long dead. Peculiar as it was, they had had nothing to say during the video conference. Hussain was too shocked to speak, and his mother had said a single word, his name 'Ali', before sealing her lips. The bearded man next to her nudged her to cry for help, but she sat there, stoic and unyielding. When nudging didn't work, the guard resorted to grabbing her by the shoulders and shaking her, so hard that he saw the whites of her eyes as they rolled back in her head.

'Do it and their misery ends,' Mir Rabiullah had said quietly, one large hand caressing his shoulder like a father trying to knock sense into an errant son. 'Bring glory to your country, my boy, to your family. Agree to this, and I will personally make sure that your family wants for nothing. I'll send Hussain abroad for studies, anywhere his heart desires. Your mother will live like the queen she was always meant to be. Wouldn't you like to see her eyes light up again? Are you so heartless to deny your family these comforts when they are within your grasp? Are you so selfish?'

The Mir's words had rung in his head like a million gongs, each harder than the last and he watched transfixed and mute as the guard shook his mother over and over again, her mouth beginning to spout bubbling white foam, his brother trying and failing to stop the guard.

'Do it!' shouted the Mir.

That was when he had capitulated. Bound to the chair, he had lifted himself up, bent over with the chair dragging along, and rushed to break the TV screen, anything to vanquish the image of that torture. He could do anything for his family. All it took was one nod at the Mir and the torture ceased. Ordering his immediate release from the chains, the Mir embraced him like a son. Even though he knew the Mir's true intentions, he couldn't help breaking into tears at the first sign of affection, no matter how staged.

He wiped away the tears with the end of his shawl, his eyes gazing unseeing at the sights of Karachi. Seeing him sweating, the driver cranked up the air conditioner, but all it did was awaken some old muscular pain in his shoulder. He couldn't even think of Mona. How complete his betrayal of her was. He was going to kill – no – blow her husband into smithereens. In a single night, she would lose both the men in her life. He loved her more than life itself, and yet when it came to choosing between her and his family, he had chosen his family. For he knew it the moment the Mir had shown him the video of his family that he'd do anything for them. Kill or get killed. He didn't care.

He wished Mona hadn't told him the whereabouts of Bilal, the places he would be staying in, but sooner or later the Mir would have tracked him down, and one couldn't really outrun a merciless organisation like the Mir's, so bent on killing and destruction. He almost felt a grudging respect for Bilal for having stirred the terrorists to the point where they were willing to resort to any measures to have him killed. He'd hoped for a better life with Mona, a life away from the madness of the city, somewhere calm and secluded. But that was never going to happen. They were going to part today, forever.

Why did he have to fight with her when he knew how vulnerable she was to criticism? What had got into him that night?

They were crossing Frere Hall, but Ali closed his eyes. It hurt to see the world moving on, oblivious to the approaching destruction he wore on himself.

'The Mir will kill your family if you chicken out, you piece of shit,' one of the men in the front spat out. 'Remember, you get as close as you can to Bilal before you press the button. And don't you dare blow yourself up on the lawns. We want destruction. We want buildings to come down. We want terror to reign over Karachi tonight.'

'Inshallah,' murmured the driver. 'We will have this city by force if she won't come to us willingly.'

'Oh the Leader has grand plans for this city,' the other man said. 'This den of vulgarity and perversity will suffer the blow it has always deserved. The hand of the Leader will come crashing down on these pampered rich kittens, so lost in sex and alcohol, they can't recognise their sister from their wife.'

The driver laughed. 'Is that really so, Ameer Bhai?'

Ameer sniggered. 'The Mir doesn't need to know, but after the bomb goes off, the place will be ripe for our picking. We can pick up a few of those unsuspecting rich sluts, and none would be any wiser.' He looked back at Ali and bared his teeth. 'This little pimp won't be telling our secrets to anyone once he's pressed that button.'

'Are you sure the Mir hasn't bugged the car, boys?' Ali asked them, surprising even himself by his spontaneity. That earned him a few minutes of silence.

'Don't try to be smart with us, pretty boy,' Ameer whispered, evidently still worried about the bug. 'Just get on with what you're supposed to do or the woman and kid die.'

'How do I know they won't be killed anyway?'

'The Leader always keeps his word. We are not like you people. We have principles. Your family will get all that the Mir and Leader have promised you.'

'That really reassures me,' Ali replied as bitterly as he could.

'Shut up!' the driver said. 'We're here.'

Ali's heart sank. 'Where have you brought me? This isn't the guesthouse I told you about.'

Ameer's eyes shone. 'Not so clever now, are you? We told you that the Leader was planning something big for tonight. It can't get any bigger than this.'

Ali's first thought was of Mona as his eyes scanned the massive tented area, Meera's vans parked everywhere, models he knew and worked with spilling out to rush to the back entrance. Somewhere in the distance where the lights shone the brightest was the main entrance. Mona might be here. The knowledge chilled him to the bone.

'Please,' he murmured, not caring how weak he sounded. 'I can't do this. Our deal was to blow up Bilal.'

'Shut up,' the driver said again.

Ameer smacked his lips. 'The Leader was right. The glory this would bring our cause. You were born to do this, Ali. I finally understand the Mir's interest in you. You're like a diamond in the mud. Worth billions. For who else could get past security without a pat down other than one of their own?'

'They'll search me,' Ali enthused. 'Your plan will come to nothing. They will search me and arrest me, and you won't get anything. The best thing would be to head to the guesthouse this man is staying in and wait for him there.'

Ameer got out of the car, stepped round the bonnet and opened Ali's door.

'Do I look like an idiot to you?' He dug his fingers into Ali's bicep. 'Get out of the car this instant or your family will pay.' He threw a mobile phone at him. 'And remember to pick this up when we call. We will wait for an hour. Another car is waiting at the front entrance. If you warn the crowd about the bomb and they rush out, your family dies. If this place doesn't blow up in one hour, your family dies. Get it? Now get out.'

Ali gingerly stepped out of the car, careful not to put any sort of pressure on his jacket. It was heavy and warm, and coupled with the thick shawl wrapped across his shoulders, he was drenched in sweat by the time he reached the back entrance. These entrances were hardly ever used by anyone but the staff members. Ali recognised the bored-looking guards from Meera's home back in Lahore. They welcomed him like an old friend and ushered him inside, not even giving the policemen time to pat him down. 'You are late as it is,' one of the senior guards said, pushing him in the direction of the make-up rooms. 'And you look like shit. Go wash your face, take a shower or whatever, or there will be hell to pay later.'

A policeman stepped forward to stop him, but Meera's guard waved him away. 'He's one of our own. He's the last person you should be searching. Make yourself useful at the main entrance.'

Ali lifted the flap and entered the tent, blood roaring in his ears, his mind racing back to how he could have done everything differently. Would things have been different if Mona hadn't come into his life, if he'd never met Gul, if the bomb blast hadn't taken Hussain's leg? He walked down the narrow corridor leading toward the backrooms, his feet trudging up sand. For a brief moment, he wondered why the event was being held in such a deserted place before he realised that the whole purpose of it was to provide security and offer guests a chance to view the area they were supposed to be investing in.

No, he would not have done anything differently. His choices had brought Mona into his life. Knowing her, even for such a brief time, was worth a life lived well. He wouldn't change it for anything. Even if he were to die today, at least he'd die content in the knowledge that he'd found love. For there was no other way he could describe the feeling.

The bomb weighed heavy on him, the weight of the lives he might take much more than the weight of the actual jacket. Was he brave enough to press the button with Mona present? Could he take the life of the person he loved?

The make-up rooms were empty. Even the assistants were absent. *How strange*, he thought, gazing at the rows of empty chairs with the bulbs dotting the mirrors left lit. There was an eeriness to the place, as if it expected a sinister intent. There was the dulled sound of a massive crowd mingling somewhere beyond, the cacophony of a thousand excited people. *A thousand people*, Ali thought, suddenly aghast. He sank into one of the make-up chairs. A thousand souls and the click of a single button. And then, the booming voice of Meera suddenly filled the tent. 'Ladies and gentlemen. The investors are here, the sponsors are here, the glittering Karachi society is here and the models are here. Let the show celebrating the Karachi Marine Housing Scheme begin!'

Thunderous applause filled the tent, but Ali jumped at the sudden tremor in his pocket.

It was the mobile phone.

He put his face in his hands and wept for the first time that evening.

Chapter Twenty-Eight

Mona

There was something wrong. She was sweating too much. It wasn't even hot in the tent with the makeshift air conditioners blasting cold air in her face. Something was wrong with the baby, she was sure of it. Nausea sliced through her, threatening to bring up the food she had nibbled at during dinner. She leaned against a wooden pole supporting the tent and took deep breaths.

'What is it?'

It was Meera, having arrived from the stage.

Mona turned away from her. 'Shouldn't you be focusing on the show? I'm fine.'

'It's not much of a show,' Meera said. She ran her hand over Mona's back in circular motions. The gesture calmed Mona. 'The models are only here for decoration. I don't know why Bilal insisted on them. They look like losers standing there, clapping at the images of those disgusting houses on screen. Are you sure you're all right? You're sweating.'

Another wave of nausea hit her, and Mona retched, but she only brought up saliva.

'Oh God, what is wrong with you, Mona? You look like a ghost. You are white as chalk.'

Meera's eyes were round with concern.

'I'm fine,' Mona laughed, but then another spell of retching assailed her. 'Just some shrimps I ate,' she lied. 'Please don't let Bilal see.'

'Everyone is busy watching the models and the advertisements.' She took Mona by the arm. 'Come with me. I'm taking you somewhere you can rest. And you need to tell me why you're hiding your pregnancy.'

Mona stared at her friend in horror. 'How did you know?'

Meera arched an eyebrow. 'You forget that I've seen you pregnant before. That bastard Iftikhar.'

'Oh Meera, that is ancient history now, and totally irrelevant.'

'It was relevant enough for you to not speak to me for twenty years.'

'Please don't dredge up the past,' Mona whispered. 'Not now. And,' – she squeezed her friend's hand – 'yes, it is irrelevant now. It was stupid for me to let that get between us.'

'Always the late bloomer, Mona,' Meera laughed. 'Now, I can't wait to hear about everything you've been up to. You might be able to hide it from the world, but not from me.' She tapped a finger on her chin. 'Let me guess. Ali, right?'

'Oh God. You know everything.'

'Of course.' They reached the area leading to the make-up rooms. Meera turned to her before turning the knob. 'I wasn't there for you before, Mona, but now, no matter how serious the problem is, you can always count on me.'

Before Mona could reply, Meera turned the doorknob and ushered them inside.

Mona had to blink twice to register what she was looking at. Ali sat on one of the chairs, wrapped in a thick woollen shawl, weeping like no man she had ever seen.

Her nausea evaporated. 'Ali,' she breathed.

Beside her, she saw Meera turn toward her. 'What's the matter with him?'

But Mona had eyes only for Ali. He looked terrified with his arms wrapped around his knees, his face shiny with tears. 'Oh Ali, what happened to you?'

In a flash, she was with him, ready to embrace him, feel his heart beating against hers. But he shrank from her touch.

'Don't,' he said, moving away from her.

'But Ali, I'm sorry. I didn't mean to be angry for so long.' Mona didn't care if Meera heard. At this moment, all she cared about was taking Ali into her arms. They had been apart for too long. 'I was acting foolishly, and I'm sorry for that. I promise I will never again do this, but please don't turn away from me. Not now, Ali, when I have something so life-changing to tell you.'

'Mona, please don't touch me.'

'Why are you being like this? Look at me, I'm here. I'm here for you now.'

'I'll give you two some privacy,' Meera muttered, retreating.

'I need you to run away from this place as fast as you can, Mona. As fast as you can.'

'I'm not going anywhere until you tell me what's happening with you. Are you going to let a small argument come between us?'

Ali let out a groan. 'You don't understand. We are not meant to be together. Just go away. Leave. Run.'

'I'm pregnant,' Mona declared at the same time as Ali said, 'I am wearing a bomb.'

They both stared at each other, lost for words.

'A bomb?' Mona whispered.

'Pregnant? With my baby?' Ali asked her weakly, his face draining of colour. 'Oh.'

Chapter Twenty-Nine

Ali

He watched her expression change from concern to disbelief. He saw her run an instinctive hand over her belly. She was pregnant. With his child. He could see the truth of it in her eyes, the knowledge of what he had told her fighting over her own news for precedence.

'Why?' she said softly, as if it was the most logical question in the world. 'Why are you wearing a bomb?'

Before he could think of what to say, he told her everything, his tongue working of its own accord. He told her of Mir and Gul, of his unknowing involvement in the plot to kill Elahi, of his deliberate involvement in another plot, and then of his crushing guilt, the never-ending regrets of how he could have avoided it. He told her of his love for her, how he wanted to lay the world at her feet. Finally, he told her of the bomb he was carrying, the impossibility of the situation. And then, he apologised to her. He apologised for everything.

He spoke for more than ten minutes, the words gushing out of his mouth like hot lava, scalding his tongue. All through his monologue, she didn't utter a single word, her eyes blank, one hand over her belly, the other hanging uselessly at her side.

A tense silence stretched between them after he was finished.

'Say something,' Ali whispered. 'Anything.'

Mona rose from the seat she had taken and walked across the room as if in a trance. 'Wearing a suicide vest,' she murmured to herself. 'A suicide bomber.' She paused before a mirror, the bulbs bathing her face in a yellow glow. 'Did you ever love me, Ali?' she asked, not looking at him.

'Of course I did, Mona. I still do. With my entire being.' And he meant it. Seeing her like this made him want to throw his arms around her and never let go, to protect her from everything, and yet, here he had brought the greatest danger imaginable right to her doorstep. 'But you need to go. Now.' His voice broke. 'We need to say goodbye.'

'Goodbye?' Her eyes assumed the same blankness again. She rolled a strand of hair over her index finger. 'But what about the baby? Our baby.'

'Mona, I – I'm wearing a bomb and there is no way I can defuse it even if I wanted to. This is the end of the line for me, but you still have your whole life ahead of you. Stay alive for me, for our child. Go.'

'You speak like a martyr, but you're not one,' she said. 'You're a heartless liar who took the easy way life showed him.'

Ali's heart squeezed at her words. 'I did it for you. For us. I wanted us to have money.'

For the first time since entering the tent, a sharpness entered Mona's voice. 'Do you think I want money? I've been running away from it my entire life, and yet you bring its destructive influence back to my doorstep yet again. If you thought I needed money, then you have never understood me. And here I am, pregnant with your child at the age of forty-two and you tell me you did it all for me. That you expect me to raise a fatherless child. The child of a terrorist.'

'I'm not a terrorist.'

'You're as good as.' Tears leaked from Mona's eyes. 'Oh Ali, why couldn't you have let life take its own course? Why the greed?'

'For you. For us,' he repeated. 'Go now, Mona and take Meera with you. She doesn't deserve this death. Nobody does. Take as many as you can.'

'And leave the rest? Would you really be able to blow up a thousand people?' She crossed her arms over her chest. 'I am not going anywhere until you make some decisions. Will you give in to the terrorists or do the right thing and report this?'

In spite of himself, he laughed. 'There is no reporting this. They can't defuse this bomb, and nor do I want them to. If a thousand lives is what it takes to save my family, then so be it.'

'Look at yourself, Ali.' She crouched before him and grabbed his knees. 'Your knees are shaking,' she murmured. 'You're terrified. Don't do this, Ali.'

'I don't have a choice,' he whispered. 'I wish I did.'

'There is always a choice.'

Ali let her grasp his hand. It was warm in his cold one. 'I don't have a choice. I wished that I'd get a chance to say goodbye to you, and now I have. Go, Mona. You've put up with a failure like myself for long enough. It's time for you to be free.'

But she didn't move. Instead, she laid her head on his knee. 'But don't you see? My freedom was always with you. If you won't be there, then what's the use of anything?

Our fates are bound together, Ali, whether you like it or not. If you die, then I die. Our baby dies.'

His eyes filled with tears. He brought her hand to his lips. 'I love you,' he said. 'Please go.'

She looked up at him, her own face tear-stained. 'Do you?'

Before he could answer, the sound of rustling filled the room, and Bilal rushed in with Meera close behind him. 'I'm sorry,' Meera said. 'I tried but he wouldn't listen.'

To Ali's utter surprise, Mona didn't move. She kept resting her head on his knee, silent, her hand still clasped in his.

'Well,' Bilal said, his voice tight as if it was coming from far away. 'Well well well...' His face was ashen, but Ali noticed the wounded pride in his eyes, the gathering storm of anger. 'So, what I suspected is true.'

'You didn't suspect anything, Bilal,' Mona replied, her eyes downcast. 'To suspect anything, you'd need to have an interest in that person.'

'She seems to have developed a tongue too.' He turned to Meera. 'Congratulations. You've turned her into yourself. You must be so proud.'

'This is not the time to be pointing fingers, Bilal,' Meera replied. 'We have a live show running and I cannot have you falling to pieces.'

'What do you take me for, woman? A blubbering teenage girl? If there's someone who's falling to pieces in this room, it's my dear wife and her lover whom I'd prefer to cut to pieces myself.' His gaze locked with Ali's. 'You bastard.'

'He has a bomb.' Mona said.

'Shut up, Mona. I'm going to deal with you in a moment,' Bilal shot back before turning to Ali again, but

Ali saw that Meera had understood. He saw her clap her hands on her mouth.

'You filthy bastard,' Bilal began.

'He is wearing a suicide vest, Bilal!' Mona shouted.

A shudder passed through Bilal. 'What?' he asked his wife. 'Who's wearing a what?'

Ali saw Mona's eyelashes rise. She must be looking at Bilal. 'My lover, as you put it, is wearing a suicide vest. And, I'm pregnant.'

Chapter Thirty

Mona

Her secret was out. The secret that she had kept hidden for months, tortured herself over, the one thing she had thought would kill her if it came out, had been revealed to the one person she feared above all else, and she felt nothing. Not an ounce of fear.

She felt liberated.

She saw her husband advance on her, the terror and anger mixed into an unrecognisable expression on his face. 'What did you just say?' he sputtered. 'What did you just say?'

'I'm pregnant,' she said, rising from her place on Ali's knee.

'Oh Mona, not now,' Meera moaned.

'With his child,' Mona continued, reaching down to hold Ali's hand. Ali stood up too, the shawl wrapped tightly around him. She noticed now how bulky he seemed around the waist. For the first time that evening, she felt pure fear slice through her. Could he really blow himself up? Wouldn't she do the same for her kids? The thought terrified her.

Bilal had stopped in his tracks. She saw pain take the place of incomprehension. His eyes bulged, his full lips quivering so much that he seemed like he would go into convulsions at any moment. She looked at her husband and the decades played out in front of her eyes. She saw how she had been reduced from a human, a wife to just a decoration in his home. His reaction today had surprised her though; she didn't think he was capable of feeling like a human. The pain and hurt on his face seemed as if he actually cared for her.

'Mona,' he wheezed. 'Why? And with a terrorist?'

'He's not a terrorist,' she said in a level voice. 'He might be many things, but he is not a terrorist. I love him. I love him as I've never loved anyone in my life, and for him, I will leave you Bilal. I will leave you forever and nothing would give me greater pleasure.'

Bilal lunged for the nearest piece of equipment on the desk and knocked it against the mirror with a roar. 'You bitch!'

The stream of conversation outside ceased for a few seconds before resuming.

'I don't know how you guys can even have this conversation right now. We can discuss this later.' Meera's voice was trembling. 'Right now, we have a bigger problem to deal with. The bomb.'

'I don't care about the bomb.' Bilal's breathing came in heavy bursts. 'You can blast me to your heart's fill, boy.' He spread out his arms. 'See if I care.'

'Don't be melodramatic, Bilal,' Mona replied. 'Ali is not blowing anyone up.'

'You're right, Mona, I'm not.'

Mona closed her eyes in relief. 'Oh thank God.'

She saw Ali grab the nearest table for balance. 'I wish we could have had a life together. I wish I could have seen the birth of our child. I wish I could have married you, Mona. I wish so many things.'

Mona put her hands on either side of his face. 'And we can have all that. I promise you, Ali.'

Bilal collapsed into a chair, his head in his hands. He was clawing his hair out. A sliver of pity made its way into her heart for him. True to form, he had smashed things, but surprisingly, he had also acted like a man in pain. From the way his body shuddered, she knew he was crying, and for a moment she let her mind absorb the fact. She didn't think she'd ever seen him weep. Not in twenty-two years.

'No we can't, Mona,' Ali said, and she knew he had seen her watching Bilal. She could tell from the smile on his lips. 'You can't marry a terrorist. And I cannot let you ruin your life. I won't allow it. So, I've made a decision.'

He stepped back from her.

Her hands dropped from his face.

'You will find happiness again, Mona. I can see it in your eyes. But sadly, I won't be a part of it.'

Mona stepped forward. 'Don't do this.'

'I love you Mona, but I also love them, my family. And I can't see them die.'

'Somebody stop him,' Meera screamed, running toward the exit. 'Is somebody there? Help.'

But in a flash of black, Ali was gone.

Mona fell to her knees.

It wasn't until Meera started shaking her that she noticed the blood pooling on the floor.

The baby...

Chapter Thirty-One

Ali

His heart began to pound in his chest from fear and exertion, but his mind was clear. He finally knew what he had to do. For once in his life, he knew what he needed to do. For if he didn't do this, he wouldn't be able to live with himself. And what was the point of living a life knowing he could have saved his family and he didn't?

His feet dug into softness of the wet sand, but he pressed forward. He was panting. It had started to rain and within moments, he was drenched. The mobile phone beeped an incessant tone before starting to ring. It rang and rang. He didn't care. He couldn't let anything deter him from his purpose.

He kicked off his shoes and sighed as he felt the cool sand on his feet. He ran faster now, as fast as he could. It wasn't far. Images of Mona's face flashed before him, the disbelief as he left her, the anguish that she must have felt knowing she'd have their baby alone.

His baby would never know its father.

The night he discovered he was to be a father was to be the same night he'd make the biggest decision of his life.

He pressed ahead, the weight of the jacket pulling him down, his breath coming out in frantic pants. But he didn't allow himself to stop. He had to do this or they would catch him. And he didn't know what he'd do if they caught him.

Worse, he might lose his nerve.

The distant ringing of sirens hit his ears. Meera had tipped them off, he was sure.

A yard or two more, and the water sloshed over his feet. The sound of sirens died off amidst the crashing of the waves. He stood facing the angry Arabian Sea, the full moon straight ahead of him.

He looked down at himself. He was still wearing the shawl.

He tore it off and watched the wind carry it back to the rocks where the police vans were congregating. The policemen were filing out now. In the midst of dozens of officers, he thought he saw the swirl of chiffon, a woman in a kaftan getting out of the police car.

He wanted her face to be the last thing he saw, but he couldn't let them get too close.

He had let others dictate the terms of his life for too long. He should at least have a say in how he died. And he wanted to die alone, not with a thousand innocent people. He wanted his baby to see the light of the world, the wonders of life.

His mother and Hussain might already have arrived where he was heading. Maybe they'd be there to greet him.

He looked at the flashing lights once again and saw the figure in the kaftan standing still, her face too far to make out, her hair billowing in the wind. She had come to watch his final moments. Someday she might even forgive him.

He smiled as his thumb came down on the button.

Chapter Thirty-Two

Bilal: 2 months later

She was unaware of being watched. Her maroon dupatta caught in the wind, tugging at her neck where she had carelessly draped it. Her whole outfit was peculiar, a motley collection of multi-coloured garments that she seemed to have thrown on in a hurry.

But hurry for what? These days, she did little more than nibble at her food, sleep and watch television. However, Bilal could tell she was into none of those activities. Hunched up on the couch in their bedroom, she would gaze at the television screen with a vacant expression, her eyes hollow and red-rimmed as she would lift a finger to scratch her neck. The skin on her neck bore angry pink gashes from the relentless scratching, and far from treating them with alcohol or even cologne, Mona seemed not to notice them at all. All she lived for was the daily trip to the graveyard. At 4 p.m. Like clockwork.

She even avoided the kids. Aimen tried everything to gain her mother's attention. She brought her the latest movies, sidling herself on the couch with her, flicking on the television as she narrated the premise of the movie. Mona's favourite designer bags found their way into her room; their son came armed with her favourite pecan

317

nut ice cream. However, all they got from Mona was an uncertain shake of her head.

When Bilal talked to her, her eyes would be on him, but she would be miles away, perhaps in the arms of that bastard. His name still caused Bilal's blood to boil. Hearing the name 'Ali' uttered from her lips drove him mad; the anger seeped into every pore of his body, bloating him. He wanted to hit her with the flat of his hand, land a blow on her face so hard that it would knock some sense into her, but then, no matter how terrible his fury, how could he beat such a pathetic creature? 'What is wrong with you, woman?' he was only capable of shouting. 'Why can't you see me, your husband, standing here trying to talk to you?'

His despair at the extent of her betrayal was colossal; he felt as if his rage would kill him. But before that, he wanted to kill Mona, squeeze the life out of her with his bare hands. When it was evident that she had been sleeping with this man behind his back, at first he wanted to laugh at the sheer irony of it. For years, he'd been doing the same to her, not once caring what she might feel. He had thought she was incapable of emotion, that their relationship at this point was a façade erected for the benefit of society. But the knowledge that she had been unfaithful to him – he wouldn't wish that pain on anyone. He felt naked, stripped of his dignity. Was he never able to physically satisfy her? The question would ring in his mind for months to come. Was he such a bad husband?

It was when he'd moved to strike her that he'd noticed Meera shaking her by the shoulders and the blood seeping out of Mona's dress, staining the beige carpet.

So much blood. He'd panicked then; his first instinct was to save her, protect her from harm. They rushed her to the hospital, but she forced them to take her to the beach. Somehow, she knew where Ali was headed. She even mustered the strength to get out of the car. And watch.

They never really discovered what the reason for her haemorrhage was. And he dared not ask the doctor.

'It was shock,' Meera told her. 'It happens.'

He had never felt more humiliated in his life. He wanted to kill her, and then himself.

And yet, here he was, watching his wife pay tribute to her dead lover. His father would turn in his grave if he could see how weak his son had become.

Bilal was surprised himself about the depth of his love for his wife. If only she could have understood him. One sharp word from him, a casual rebuff, a brief argument, and she would retreat into that shell of hers, refusing to talk to him for days on end, and when she did talk, it was only to reprimand him, to remind him of his cruelty. How could he restrain his hand then?

Did she not see how he tossed and turned in bed for hours, suffering over the outburst, struggling to find a way to mend fences? *Did you see nothing, Mona*, he thought now as he watched her bend over that bastard's grave, placing a garland of big red roses on the mound of packed earth.

She had been coming here for weeks, arguably the only physical activity she undertook all day. She'd come into the lounge casually, grab the car keys and head out. He thought she was getting better, glad that she was taking initiative. Until he had followed her. For more than four weeks now he had been following her, parking his car in a shaded alcove with towering trees that afforded him a good view of the graveyard without being seen.

He had long ago ceased feeling guilty over his spying; rather, he believed it to be his right. He would ogle at her for whole minutes without blinking, his eyes taking in her every movement, every gesture, and comparing it with her behaviour back home.

It was unvaried. She was as dead here as she was at home. But then, what compulsion drove her here every day? Did she feel guilty? Did she still love that guy?

In the hours she spent bunched up next to his grave, tendrils of perfumed smoke from the *agarbati* wafting around her, Bilal reflected back on their life. In the shade of the shisham trees, a picture of their life together began to form.

They had spent more than twenty years as husband and wife, and it surprised him how little he knew her. Her approach toward life, her likes and dislikes... he knew nothing. When was the last time they had had a proper husband-wife discussion. Even about trivial matters?

It had been years.

He would watch couples making small gestures, a wife reaching forward to rub a smear of sauce on her husband's upper lip, a husband wrapping his arm around his wife, the flat of his hand resting where the waist ended, and the hips began, a wife clapping her husband on the back while sharing a joke. Intimacy... it meant so much more than just primal desire. It dawned on him how much he missed those small gestures. Theirs had ended when he started having affairs. Maybe he was to blame for the way things were today.

He missed his wife. Even with her present in the same room as him, he missed her. He wanted the old Mona back.

Had he forgiven her for what she did? Could he ever forgive himself?

He didn't know. All he had come to realise was that he could not kill her, no matter the extent of her transgressions.

For years he had snubbed her, avoided her, insulted her to her face; it scared him how much he had come to rely on her, how much he needed to see her face before he left home. Even when she slept in another room, he always opened the door a crack to see her before leaving for work. Sleeping beneath the covers, her heart-shaped face looked so beautiful, tranquil. The sight filled his heart, but as always, his pride came between them. Sometimes as he would peep inside, she would be awake, watching him, perhaps willing him to make a move. Instead of stepping in and taking her in his arms like he wanted to, he would close the door with a firm snap, and depart. He now realised that he had tried to possess her and own her thoughts. In his own perverse way he had loved her. He wondered if she ever knew, if he would ever get the chance to tell her.

Without warning, Mona rose from the damp earth, brushing down bits of leaves and dirt. Bilal ducked, raising a hand to cover his face.

Watching from the space between his fingers, he saw her stand still for a few moments as if lost. She was leaving early today, after a mere thirty minutes as opposed to the usual two hours. He surveyed her as she picked her way through the plethora of graves, holding on to marble pillars of the ostentatious graves several times as she walked toward the gate. She was so weak.

Bilal watched her, transfixed.

Stepping out of the decrepit black gate, Mona paused at the edge of the road, glancing first left, and then right. She turned her gaze left again, staring straight into the alcove where he sat with his car's engine idling.

For a moment, Bilal's heart stopped. He peered at her, unsure of whether she had seen him or not.

She began to walk in his direction, her face an emotionless mask. With mounting suspense, he saw her approach the alcove, and the absurdity of spying on his own wife struck him like a whiplash. Immediately, his pride took over. It shook him: *Are you scared of a woman?* But he was. At that moment, his heart was pounding.

When it was obvious she was headed toward his car, and his heartbeat had reached a crescendo, Bilal unlocked the doors. Mona opened the front passenger door, and slid in.

For the first time in months, she looked at him. Really looked at him. He could tell he had her complete attention. Behind the hollowness of her eyes, there was a flicker of life.

He turned over his open palm in her direction.

After a moment's hesitation, she took his hand in hers. 'Let's go home,' she said.

A letter from Awais

I am so excited that Hera Books have published *In the Company of Strangers*. It is my debut novel and I'm sure most people would know just how close authors are to their debut novels. This book is the result of years upon years of struggle and perseverance.

I first began writing this novel in 2012 when I took the Faber Academy 6 month Online Novel Writing Course. At the time, I had no idea if I would be able to finish this book, let alone see it published one day. There is a certain image of Pakistan portrayed by media in the west. It is generally considered to be a volatile country where you can't step outside from fear of getting blown to pieces. I wanted to change that narrative. I wanted to delve into the secrets and lives of Pakistan's elite class, a very elusive part of Pakistani society that is seldom written about. I wanted to normalize the image of Pakistan and show that people here are not always thinking about the next bomb blast, but the fact that things like family and relationships exist here as well… people like to mingle, live a little, possibly fall in love. I wanted to show that no matter how forbidden that love might be, it still tends to happen.

In the Company of Strangers is centred around Mona, a rich housewife in her forties who is bored out of her mind with her decadent lifestyle and yearns for change. When she meets Ali, a male model years younger than her, sparks fly and they embark on a journey – a relationship – that is not only treacherous, but also forbidden. Set against the overall backdrop of crime and terrorism as it existed in the country then, *In the Company of Strangers* offers an honest, if at times painful and horrifying, look into life in Pakistan's elite circles.

I always love to hear from my readers and can be found very widely on social media:

Facebook: @awaiskhanauthor
Instagram: @awaiskhanauthor
Twitter: @AwaisKhanAuthor

I hope you enjoy reading this book and I can't wait to hear your thoughts. I am once again very thankful to Hera Books for publishing it.

Best Wishes,
Awais Khan

Acknowledgements

I would like to thank my parents and my entire family for their wonderful support. *In the Company of Strangers* is my debut novel and although it took a lot of my sweat, blood and tears to get it out in the world, there are countless people who helped me along the way, and for that, I shall always be grateful:

My agent, Annette Crossland, for taking me on without a moment's hesitation in 2017. She plucked me out of her slush pile and helped me launch my writing career. She promised me that we would achieve great things together during our first meeting in London, and she has lived up to that promise.

Keshini Naidoo and the entire team at Hera Books for giving *In the Company of Strangers* a new life. Keshini is a thorough professional, a seasoned publisher and when she told me that ITCOS had made her cry, I knew I'd written something worth reading. I am so delighted and honoured to be published by such a great publishing house.

Hazel Orme, who has always been my first editor and constant support. She was the first person to take me under her umbrella back in 2014 and I haven't looked back since. Whatever I write has to go through Hazel first.

Alex Chaudhuri, for being the best supporter and friend one could ask for and for always standing by me as I weathered the highs and lows of publishing. Her support means the world.

Alan Gorevan, for being a best friend and constant source of wisdom, friendship, humour and support. Thanks for urging me to believe in my talent and in myself.

Faiqa Mansab, for being a great friend who has always offered me the best critical feedback and sage advice. Without her help, it would have been impossible to navigate these waters.

Paula Robinson, for her generosity and friendship. For me, she has been a light in the darkness.

Sabine Edwards, PR maven and the kindest person on earth. I can't thank her enough for deftly handling all the PR stuff and for organizing the launch event of a lifetime. A true friend.

Kirstie Long, for bringing her expertise and professional flair to A for Authors and for being so incredibly generous.

Sayantan Ghosh, Editorial Director at Simon & Schuster India, for publishing *In the Company of Strangers* in South Asia during a very turbulent time. He is now a friend I know I can always turn to for advice and support.

Kirsten Arcadio, for being my first true supporter and for standing by me for almost a decade now.

Sarah Faichney, for being a fabulous friend, critic and an all round amazing person.

Damien & Amber Hine, for being true friends and staunch supporters.

Liam Chennells, for being a huge source of inspiration.

Helen Edwards, for loving my work enough to take it on.

Zaeem Siddiqui and Shireen Quraishi, for always being there for me.

Shirin Amani Azari, Anita Chaudhuri and Amna Boheim for showing me kindness when I least expected it.

For their love and support over the years: Ayo Onatade, Rob Barrow Carla Webb, Alex Morrall, Milly Burton, Kairen Cullen, Paul Waters, Naima Rashid, Jacky Collins, Danielle Price, Roy Leadholm, Kiren Parmar, Avkirat Dyal, Rob Parker, Eve Smith, Tony Frobisher, Brad Grant, Mehr F Husain, Mina Malik Hussain, Helen Francis and Abhay Singh.

Heleen Kist, for being an honest critic and friend.

The Book Guild, for taking a chance on a newbie author.

Sirah Haq, for always being there.

And last but certainly not the least, my wonderful students at The Writing Institute.